Plague Sally

Paul McDermott

Whimsical Publications, LLC

Florida

To purchase the authorized electronic edition of *Plague Sally*, visit www.whimsicalpublications.com

Cover art by Janet Durbin
Editing by Brieanna Robertson

Published in the United States by
Whimsical Publications, LLC
Florida

ISBN-13: 978-1-936167-92-0

She picked up her travel bag and prepared to move off.

Suddenly, Tom froze and stared hard at a clump of bushes about twenty paces downhill from the cave. Sally was puzzled. Fending for herself for so many years had made her sensitive to any sound or movement that might suggest danger, or at least something not quite right. She hadn't seen or heard anything out of the ordinary, but as she glanced once again at Tom, she was convinced his nostrils were quivering. Could he have *smelled* danger?

"Back away, slowly! Return to the cave, and don't turn your back."

"What have you seen? What's wrong?" Sally crabbed toward the cave entrance, switching her gaze from Tom to the bushes and back.

"Rats! And plenty of them, too—scores, if not hundreds! They run in packs, cowards that they are. Out here on open ground we have no chance against so many!" Suddenly, he sprang from his semi-crouched, defensive position and aimed a boot at the remains of the fire, scattering embers and coals into the bushes. High-pitched squeals and a thrashing of branches confirmed that most of the salvo had found a mark. Tom snatched one of the remaining logs from the fire pit and joined Sally at the entrance to the cavern. "Help me secure these screens against the bushes. We need a solid wall between us and them, even if it's only reeds and grass. When they attack, we have to slow them down any way we can to have a chance of driving them off!"

"They also feed on anything they find!" Sally cried. "Dead and rotting flesh, animals that have died of an illness, spoiled fodder no other creature would touch. They spread disease with their sharp fangs. I have treated many who have been bitten by them, and not all have survived, even with my most powerful medicines!"

The screens were grimy on one side and shiny on the other. Sally guessed Tom had used them as sleds to drag cut turf back to his temporary shelter. The barrier was quickly in place, and there were no sounds to indicate the return of the rats.

"Now we make as many torches as we can. In order to

fight our way out of here, we need to be able to *see* the enemy when they arrive!"

Long, dry grasses, probably intended as sleeping mattresses, were swiftly bound to tree branches with thin strips Tom cut from his stock of animal pelts. He hefted one and gave a satisfied nod. He turned and stood close to the wall of screens with a murderous-looking tree root in the other hand.

Sally tightened one final knot, lit the torch, and jammed it into a crack on the wall. She picked up one of the smaller torches and hesitated a second, torn between the knife she was familiar with and the somewhat clumsy alternative of using a club.

Tom seemed to sense her thoughts. He grinned. "Take the tree branch! A knife is better for close-range combat, but you want to keep a safe distance if you possibly can. They're too small and too fast for you to be sure of stabbing them."

As he spoke, a few leaves rustled close to his feet. His club blurred through a short, vicious arc, and three small bloodstains appeared on the cavern floor. Startled, Sally spotted movement at the very edge of her field of vision, but she was slow to react. Her club came down on nothing, but the intruder retreated rather than run into the cave.

Tom inspected the business end of his club, shrugged, and tossed it onto the fire.

"I hit that one a bit harder than I meant to," he growled. "But at least we've plenty of branches to use." He chose a replacement and gave it a couple of swings.

"Wait, Tom! Let me look at that weapon." Sally took it and examined it more closely. It still had a few small, half-curled leaves on it. "As I thought, this is from a yew tree."

"Yes. Strong, and still slightly green. It will last a bit longer than the first couple of blows."

"I've got another use for it. You've given me an idea!"

Acknowledgements

For anyone who ever combined compassion for others with a careful observation of what Nature can offer in treating illnesses.

Chapter One

Finally, the first bubble formed on the surface of the infusion Sally had been preparing all morning. The liquid in the small pot had reached a temperature at which the herbs and leaves would at long last release their healing powers. The telltale bubble bobbed uncertainly, jigged left, then right, and eventually burst. A second formed to take its place, then a third. A stray raindrop found its way down from the smoke hole above the meager fire and plopped in the pan. Occasional hisses recorded raindrops landing in the fire itself, cooling the embers, prolonging the cooking time.

Skeins of color started to percolate from the lumpen mass in the base of the pot, predominantly the beautiful—yet potentially deadly—feathery greens and bold purples of carefully measured, fine-chopped root of azalea. The natural medicines were bled from her selection of plants and into the slowly strengthening tea water. Sally stirred it with a cautious, none-too-clean finger, more to test the temperature than an attempt to speed up the blending process. To be effective, the concoction had to reach a reasonable temperature, but it must not boil. That would have been unlikely with such a paltry fire anyway, but quite apart from nullifying the medicinal benefits of the concoction, it would also have made the drink too hot for comfort. She could feel herself fading rapidly. She was becoming weaker by the minute. She needed the remedy, needed it desperately.

More bubbles appeared on the surface, and the hovel in which Sally sat was suddenly filled with a powerful aroma suggesting health and healing, an ozone-heavy, oxygen-rich alternative to the stench of damp, rot, spoiled food and worse, which had pervaded the room until the moment the pot and its contents began to take effect.

An icy wind whistled through each of the many cracks between the bothy's sods of turf, despite Sally's attempts to block them with rags and whatever else came to hand. Sally knew that she should be feeling this, but her gaunt frame told her that she was burning, burning from the inside out. She grubbed around, chose a knife that seemed relatively clean, and used it to stir the pot, releasing more of the plant juices she so desperately needed.

Unable to wait longer, she took the pot from the dying ember bed, judging that the residual heat of the fire was unlikely to warm the broth any further. She glanced around, hoping to find a container to decant it into. Her hands shook, and she was perilously close to dropping it untasted. Her need escalated, becoming a full-blown craving. She raised the pot and held it an inch from her nose, inhaling the vapors until her lungs could hold no more. Her mind cleared for the first time in days, and she remembered to purse her lips and clench her teeth to strain the liquid from the semi-solid dregs of plant residue at the bottom of the pot.

She wiped the inevitable acrid fibers from her mouth with the back of her hand and placed the pot on one of the two pieces of furniture she possessed, a rough wooden table. She could feel the healing powers of the draught she had painstakingly concocted beginning to take effect. She had only a short time left before the euphoric rush of the healing process took control of her mind and her actions.

She knew she was about to become oblivious to her surroundings for an indeterminable period, quite possibly several days. To the world around her, she would almost certainly appear dead. To avoid any possibility of misunderstandings, she had withdrawn completely from all contact with village society, actively discouraging visitors. There was no point in curing herself of this malady only to wake up and discover that she had been buried alive...

The fire—if it still deserved the title—glowed a last gleam of defiance before extinguishing itself with the tiniest wisp of smoke. There was no danger of an unattended spark cremating her body while she lay defenseless in the induced coma that she hoped would lead to healing. She felt prickling from nerve endings that had been numb for several days. Her rough clothing scratched unbearably on every square inch of her supersensitive, overheated skin, and the sweat on her brow was enough to blur her vision. It was time for her to stagger to her bed, where she barely managed to collect every spare rag of clothing she possessed to retain every available scrap of bodily warmth while the medicines took effect.

"Ah mischla, ah cushla..." she breathed as she lay flat on her back and desperately tried to recall the traditional wording of any of the most common prayers approved by the Church for use over the sick and the dying, but her memory was failing along with her control over her bodily functions. A high-pitched whine grew painfully loud in her ears. She strove to relax and concentrate on establishing a deep, regular breathing rhythm as she felt the muscles tighten across her chest, warning her that her auto functions were preparing for total shutdown. For better or worse, she had committed herself to a treatment that was her only chance of a cure.

The last of her senses to shut down was the first she had experienced as a new-born, her sight. As she lay and fought to keep her eyelids from closing, she sensed the shadows growing from the dark corners of her minimal shelter from the elements, closing to a tiny dot close to the smokehole in the roof before winking out of existence as her eyes finally closed.

Chapter Two

Hungry!

An instinctive reaction for anyone waking from a night's sleep. Even more understandable—and to be expected—when the sleeper has been in a drug-enhanced comatose state for considerably more than a typical eight-hour sleep period.

Sally's diet in the days leading up to her total fasting had been sporadic at best, and certainly not balanced. She had been able to forage for plants and herbs to eat, but poverty and a lack of opportunity to hunt or trap animals meant that she was denied the basic proteins from meat or fish. With no significant reserves of body fat, she had been significantly underweight to start with. Having not eaten for a lengthy period, her weight had dipped still further, and she was also suffering the ravages of dehydration from not being able to replace the body fluids she had lost.

Her larynx felt as if it was coated in coarse, gritty sand. Even if she'd had a cat or some other familiar, any attempt at speech would have been doomed to failure. Sally fought to force blood to flow through her veins and arteries, flushing through her vital organs, reawakening their allotted functions. Nerve endings tingled, and the savage stabbing pain of the pins and needles throughout her body as sensation returned was almost unbearable.

As her circulation stabilized, the agonizing pinpricks eased. Still there, but under control. She forced herself to breathe deeply, evenly, following the mantra: *In through the nose, out through the mouth...*

She had to be in full control before attempting the next

stage of her recovery. She could sense that her body was responding to her first instinctive commands. Now she needed to know just how well the healing process had worked.

Her breathing eased another notch and she felt renewed, rejuvenated as the blood continued to flow more freely. She made a conscious effort to unclench her fingers, which had been knotted together on her motionless chest for several days. They refused to cooperate, and she had to dig deeper into her mental resources.

Still no reaction. What could be wrong? How long had she been lying immobile? Had her scrawny, gaunt frame suffered irreparable dehydration, become mummified? Before anything else, she had to inspect her body for possible damage.

Opening her eyes should have been even easier than unclenching her fists, but mild panic set in when she discovered that this simple action was just as difficult to perform. Her eyelids refused to part.

You must stay calm! she scolded herself, and reiterated the breathing mantra until she regained control of her emotions and could think logically. There had to be a reason, and within seconds, she had identified the problem.

Your lids are sealed with salt from the tears that have dried on your face while your body lay and battled against the malady with which it was threatened. To unseal them, you need but raise a hand and rub at them with finger or sleeve, unless you can raise a tear or two to dissolve the salt cakes.

Sally still felt as weak as a newborn kitten, helpless and blind, with the added disadvantage of not having an attentive mother to lick at her eyes with a rough tongue until they unclogged. She sensed the cramped muscles in her fingers beginning to relax, but try as she might, she was unable to unlock the major muscles between shoulder and wrist that she would need to use if she was going to rub at her encrusted eyelids. This involved a certain amount of pain, and with it a minimal trace of moisture behind her eyelids. She felt—or imagined she felt—the dried salt cake soften as the salty tears burned their way across the sensitive surface of her eyeballs and leaked away at the outer edges then cascaded down her cheeks, running into her hairline just behind her ears as they obeyed the immutable laws of gravity. This was all the incentive she needed, and with a soft cry of frustration mixed with relief, she made one more supreme effort to raise a hand to her eyes and scrub furiously at the offending crud. It was essential she was able to inspect both her healed body and her immediate surroundings.

Even the slight effort this required was enough to start a pounding in her ears, deafeningly loud as her blood pressure spiked. Through her tears she could just about recognize the branches woven together to form the framework of the roof less than three feet above her head. With a supreme effort that set her heart racing once more, she rolled onto one elbow and used her free arm to remove the excess tears blurring her vision. Another, more careful inspection of the roof appeared to confirm that her vision at least was still as sharp as ever it had been. That *had* to be a good start.

By straightening her elbow, she managed to force herself into an upright seated position amongst the inadequate pile of furs and clothing that had somehow prevented her from freezing to death. Her recovery was quicker this time, her breathing almost unchanged, though she still panted a bit. At twenty-eight she no longer thought of herself as a "young" woman. Several of the friends she had grown up with were already dead.

There could be no further delays or excuses. She had to find out how effective her self-administered healing remedies had been. It was time to inspect her body from head to toe, or at least as much of it as she could see, looking for any blemish or hint of discoloration to suggest that the Black Death was still there, patient, awaiting its chance to strike again.

Against all odds, it seemed as if she had put together an effective medicine that had cured her as she lay in her crude bothy, touched by lengthening shadows from the Pennine Hills as the weak winter sun sank in the waters of the Atlantic Ocean.

Her gastric juices roiled again as her bodily functions took control and reminded her forcibly of her immediate needs. She stood slowly, fighting off another brief bout of dizziness, and shrugged off the rags she wore to inspect as much of her skin surface as she could. Still no telltale marks or blemishes. She leaned heavily on her staff and gave thanks for her good fortune to all the gods—whether recognized by the Established Church or not. She was not prepared to take unnecessary chances.

She re-dressed and picked up a gather sack and a small pot. After a few days standing, any water she might have had would have been stagnant and therefore undrinkable anyway, and she wasn't in the habit of keeping any food in the hut. This would have been a waste of time, as she would have to guard and defend it against a small army of rodents and other animals, and probably finish up sharing it with them anyway. Water at least was available from a small, clear stream yards from the clearing she called home. Slaking her thirst was just as important as easing her hunger, and the easy option before scavenging further afield in the search for more solid sustenance.

As she stooped to fill the pot, there was a blur of movement in the corner of her eye, a shadow just beneath the surface of the stream. Automatically, without taking conscious aim, she thrust her staff unerringly and impaled a fat, juicy carp against a flat stone on the streambed. This was an unplanned bonus. She could now break her fast in style. Perhaps it was a sign of some sort, having her first meal supplied in such a fortuitous manner.

All the same, she'd have to scurry if she was going to prepare and cook the meal. It was too late in the day for her to hope to use the lens she kept to enhance the sun's rays and start a fire quickly. She would have to resort to the time-consuming, tiring older method of creating a glow from the friction of spinning a twig in a hole.

The fish was still twitching at the bottom of her gatherbag as she returned to her shelter, collecting firewood as she went. She filleted it swiftly while the light was still good, before building a small firebase on the hearth and setting the fire stick into its charred hollow. She concentrated on directing all her energy into spinning the stick as fast as she could, and was rewarded almost immediately by the first encouraging wisps of smoke as the kindling responded. Within minutes, the flames from her cooking fire became the main source of illumination as the last of the day's natural light faded completely from the sky. The fish was spitted above the flames so that its juices dripped onto the embers with an angry hiss. Inevitably, her gastric acids were threatening to etch holes in her stomach lining long before the cooking process was complete.

"Patience," she muttered to herself time and again as the temptation to pluck the meal from the spit and risk illness from gorging the half-cooked flesh became almost irresistible. Past experience combined with her learning and lore regarding basic health and hygiene persuaded her not to give in for the sake of a few more minutes. By the time her pot of water had warmed sufficiently to infuse a blend of herbs and produce something drinkable, the fish was done to perfection.

Before the light from her cook fire had completely died, she was careful to hang the fish skeleton to dry in the gentle residual heat. She would carefully wrap the bones in a scrap of cloth and include them in her travel bag when she left at sunrise. There were a number of uses she could find for them once dried—repair needles for cloth and small injuries, for example. The bones could also be ground and used in powder form, both as medicine and also as glue. The spine might possibly be useful as a small but lethal hand-held weapon. Lashed onto a reasonably straight ash staff, it would be a deadly accurate spear. Other bones could be shaped and decorated to become useful trading tokens, ornaments valued by males wanting to impress young girls in the community.

She paused as she came to this final use for the inedible parts of her catch. It had indeed been a very long time since any male in her community had approached her with such a token, and in one respect, her conscious decision to alienate her closest neighbors before attempting her self-healing had proved a final, irrevocable step. She was now regarded with suspicion, even hatred. On the short journey back from the stream, she had noticed tokens that had not been there when she had entered her recent state of suspended animation. These tokens were traditional charms that many believed effective against a witch—the jawbone of a horse, the fried skin of a toad, and a miniature besom or broom. Horses were reputed to be able to see ghosts, and were often thought to be able to identify a witch.

She glanced around. There wasn't a lot to choose from, and even less she cared for enough to pack on the off chance that it might prove useful on a journey, one from which she had no intention of ever returning. There was nothing to persuade her to remain another day here in the Yorkshire dales, under the ominous, looming shadows of the Pennines.

The smallest of her pots, a pair of knives, a clam shell she used as a grinding bowl, a pestle to go with it, a drink horn, and a spoon all found a place in her gatherbag. What clothing she could not comfortably wear would be abandoned, and would probably rot apart before long anyway.

There was little or no wind that evening, and her hovel, for once, was tolerably warm. She banked the last embers of the fire and lay down to enjoy the deep, relaxing sleep of the pure at heart.

Chapter Three

Sally woke from the first full night of natural sleep she'd had in some considerable time, roused by an errant beam caressing her eyelids as the sun showed itself above the eastern tree line and pierced one of her flimsy shelter's many cracks. She felt fully rested and ready to face what the day might bring.

There was, as usual, nothing edible to hand, and her water pot was already packed. In other words, there was nothing to hold her back, no reason to postpone her planned journey. In reality, "planned" was something of an overstatement, as it could be summed up in one word—westward.

She stopped only to fill and seal her water carrier. A random thought occurred to her as she laid the jar on its side and waited for the stream to fill it. *Nobody I know has ever traveled more than a day's journey from this dale,* she thought. This should have terrified her, but she felt strangely calm.

The only reason you haven't heard *tales of someone traveling further than visiting a distant relative is probably because they found something better,* she decided as she rammed the tight lid into the neck of the bottle and sealed it by looping a strip of cloth around it to form a sling she could carry over her shoulder. Sally was a typical product of her time. She knew nothing of national or world events, and the only "news" that might hold her attention for more than a few minutes at a time was of a practical nature—what weather might be expected, and how this could affect the crops or local food production, local marriages, reports of raiders and those "outside the pale," the lawless, the land-less, the disenfranchised bands of strong-armed brigands who preferred to roam the countryside stealing whatever they could rather than settle in one place and till the land.

The mean, niggling voice inside her head suddenly became more waspish, more severe. *That's what you've decided to do just yourself. You've no right to judge them at all!*

This was so unlike any conscious thought Sally had ever had she stiffened and blinked, caught unawares by its alien nature.

It didn't even sound *like my voice!*

Sally had lived alone for the best part of two decades, ever since she'd been old enough to fend for herself. Her mother, she'd been told, had died bringing her into the world. Her father had disappeared soon afterwards, and she had been brought up by a couple claiming to be her only relatives, an aunt and uncle. All she could remember of the first half dozen or so years of her life was being treated as a virtual slave by two people who were as fair as she was dark and showed her no affection whatsoever. She strongly suspected that they were in no way related to her, but they were both ancient history now, and she felt charitable enough not to wish ill on the dead. That was another strange thought that had crept into her mind, or so it seemed. She was starting to make a habit of this.

Or was someone, somehow, attempting to *control* her and her manner of thinking? Making a basic gesture to ward against most general evils, she froze at the edge of the stream before taking the first irrevocable step of her journey into the unknown. Slowly, with perfect balance, she paced out the intricate steps that accompanied a powerful incantation she had learned, one which she had been assured was sufficient to protect her against any imaginable evil.

The grass beneath her feet rippled and flattened, forming a perfect circle around her. The myriad of early dawn sounds of nature, bird song and leaf rustle receded to insignificance and Sally held her breath, straining to catch the least possible whisper of any possible presence.

Nothing, or at least, she corrected herself, nothing she was aware of. That didn't mean there was nothing to be afraid of, however. All it really meant was that she didn't have the experience she needed to deal with a problem she sensed was close at hand, but had not yet been identified. Still, if the danger was indeed "close at hand," it made her intention to leave immediately and not return her safest course of action.

With no further thought or delay, she settled the water container more securely in its shoulder sling and stepped out of the still-flattened circle of grass with her eyes on the range of mountains that she had to find a way past. They resembled nothing more than the spine of a gigantic creature sleeping on a comfortable ledge that separated the eastern and western halves of the country, and it had to be the first task facing her on her journey into the unknown. Without so much as a backward glance, or the least suggestion of regret about leaving behind everything she possessed, Sally took the first steps of her long trek into the unknown. As she wound her way through the woods and around a bend, the flattened circle of grass formed during the casting of her protective charm spell turned to a deep, dark shade of dead brown, suggesting that no known plant, tree, bush, or even weed was ever likely to grow there.

Sally had time on her hands as she made her way through the woods. She started by breaking her fast, scavenging a wide variety of ripe fruits from bushes on both sides of the path, which, for the moment, at least, took her more or less in the right direction. It was an ideal time of year to travel— blueberries, blackberries, raspberries, and other high sugar fruits were all perfect for picking, and she barely broke stride as she ate all she wanted, and filled a couple of pouches and folds in her robe with more solid fare that would not crush, such as apples and pears. Once she had eaten her fill of fruits, she chanced to find one of her favorite fungi, which she munched with great pleasure as she cleansed her palate of residual sweetness.

She was still in the process of assessing her improved state of health, and this was the first opportunity she had since reawakening to subject her body to a real endurance test. She had to pace herself, of course; it would be asking for trouble to stretch herself past sensible limits, but there was no fixed timetable for her journey, and she could rest whenever she felt the need. At this time of year, there was plenty of food freely available in the fields and bushes along the way for someone with her skills and knowledge.

She glanced at the sun, trying to estimate how much of

the day remained. It was still some distance from its zenith, which gave her many hours of daylight in which to travel. The track she was following was distinct, but faint. It was almost certainly an animal trail rather than a path beaten by regular human use as the shortest distance between two villages or townships. For some reason, this thought pleased her. She had never felt comfortable in the company of others, even in the small village community she had been obliged to interact and trade with for essentials such as dairy products, or the occasional tool to replace something that had reached the limit of its usefulness. Her skills with herbs and medicines were something she had developed by trial and error, working alone, using her own body for all her testing. She'd only been seriously ill once or twice as a result of unwise choices, so her success rate with medicines had been steady, dependable if not spectacular, and her reputation as a healer had spread through the closest half dozen villages by word of mouth.

"I wonder, how long will it be before someone comes to look for me, asking for some medicine or a charm," she mused, then started. She'd caught herself speaking the words aloud, even though she knew she was alone. She shrugged and grinned. Why worry? She had nobody else to please but herself. Why shouldn't she talk, laugh, sing as the mood took her? Close by but unseen, a bird she couldn't identify trilled out a phrase of song, and she responded by attempting to copy it. It wasn't a very good imitation as it was the first time she'd ever attempted it, but no more than a few seconds passed and what she imagined was the same bird called out again, slightly louder, as if responding to a challenge. She smiled, concentrated on the musical phrase, and made a conscious effort to repeat it more accurately.

Still unseen, but sounding just as close as before, the same thread of melody was repeated. Her competitor seemed to be keeping pace with her through the woods, and for some reason, this amused her. She continued the impromptu duel of wits and warblings as she strolled and skipped between the trees, following the track as it meandered in roughly the direction she wished to travel. Soon she could hear that her renderings of the simple phrase were improving, and she even began to think of words the phrase suggested.

"Little bit of bread and noooo cheee-eeese!"

Eight notes—four quick, like running steps, then two

somewhat longer, like getting ready to take off, finishing with two long notes, taking flight. Yes, she decided, that was just the way certain birds she'd observed wound themselves up with a short run to gain the speed they needed to soar off into the sky.

What would it be like if I could fly like them? she found herself wondering. This time, she was sure her random thought had remained unspoken. It was such an impossible concept, that a person could ever learn to fly.

The forest petered out, giving way to open heathland with stunted bushes dotted haphazardly here and there. She was slightly disappointed to discover that her unseen adversary had opted to remain hidden in the woodland rather than expose his or herself so she could catch a glimpse of the plumage and put a picture to the voice for future reference. She knew the names of many of the common birds, and had a feeling she'd heard the distinctive "no cheese" melody before, but couldn't be certain which bird it might have been. She turned briefly back to face the woods and dropped her most elegant curtsey as thanks and acknowledgement to her rival in the unequal singing contest, which she conceded she had never had a chance of winning. As she turned to continue her journey, she heard a final cadence, the two long notes she thought of as *"no-oo chee-eese!"*

She looked at the sun again, which was by now directly overhead. There was barely a cloud in the sky, and this was the hottest part of the day. It made sense, therefore, to take a break here in the shade at the edge of the forest before venturing out across the open heathland, where there was minimal shelter to be found. The same track she'd been following until now could just about be seen when she was ready to carry on, so she sat down on a convenient log and poured a small amount from her water gourd into the drinking horn. It seemed like a reward for her decision when she discovered a large crop of her favorite chantrelle mushrooms next to it. They were just as delicious raw as cooked, and she wolfed them unashamedly, dipping each one into her drinking horn to rinse the soil from the roots.

For dessert she took out two plump pears and ate every scrap right down to the core, savoring every mouthful and making efficient use of her tongue to remove every trace of the juices when she discovered that the fruits were so mature the juice was beginning to turn alcoholic. As thanks for the food she had eaten, she scraped away an inch or two of soil at the very edge of the forest and planted the half dozen seeds she scooped from the pears, giving them plenty of space to grow into bushes for the sustenance of a future traveler.

Without the close confines of the trees, she could now make a more realistic judgement of the distance she still had to travel to reach the mountains, the first landmark she'd set for herself. She still had no clear purpose or final destination, and she'd already traveled further from home than she'd ever been before. There was no way she could reach the foothills of the mountains in one day, that much was now clear, but she didn't think she'd have to spend more than the one night in a temporary bothie on the heath. With the bracken that grew everywhere, she needed little more than a couple of sturdy twigs to build a shelter for the night.

For the moment, the only thing that mattered was making progress, and that meant carrying on across the open landscape. Having a clear view of the mountain range was encouraging. She developed a healthy rhythm on the open, level ground. She caught herself humming a wordless melody, and increased her pace to fit the tempo of the music. The memory of her one-sided contest with the bird in the woods returned briefly, and she smiled, then frowned as a second thought popped into her mind.

Is it possible to add words to any piece of music? Is that how songs are made? Can anyone do it?

She turned the idea in her mind, imagining herself holding it up to the light to inspect it for flaws or weaknesses. She found none, and decided that putting words to music was something she might enjoy doing as long as she could find a way of remembering them in order to sing them for others. She knew about the skills of reading and writing, but at the same time, these were privileges that were only possible for the wealthiest in any community. Even the traveling priest who came to the village as often as he could didn't actually read from a book. On the few occasions Sally had attended a service, she'd noticed that the leather-bound book of scripture readings had remained firmly closed on the altar, and he had recited the prayers entirely from memory.

She made good progress the rest of the afternoon, with

one melody after another floating through her head. Many of them were popular airs, frequently songs with words that everybody knew. Occasionally, a melody occurred to her, which, as far as she knew, didn't have words set to it. When this happened, she tried to fit some simple words to the natural rhythm of the notes. It didn't always work, but she did manage to string together a few lines for some of them, and felt an almost childish delight with her efforts.

Sally glanced at the horizon and, to her amazement, discovered that the mountains that had seemed so distant were visibly far closer than she would have thought possible. The music and the mental exercise of setting words to melodies had kept her walking tempo rhythmic and steady while her conscious mind was elsewhere, and she had actually reached the foothills.

The track she had followed from the woods across the heath had petered out and reappeared several times during the day, proof in itself that it had been carved in the dust by wild animals rather than regular travelers. Now she paused at the top of a slight rise and looked in all directions before continuing. She appeared to have covered well more than half the expanse of the dale; the forest seemed considerably further away than the mountains themselves, the tops of which were shrouded in low cloud.

She was reluctant to eat from her carefully gathered stock of apples and pears without knowing when she might be able to replace them, and she checked her pace so that she could scavenge trail food as she walked. The sun was now beginning to cast longer shadows as it raced behind the clouds that concealed the highest of the mountain peaks. Soon she would have to decide where and how she would spend the night.

At the top of another, slightly higher rise, she paused once more. Prolonged use of the muscles in her legs was beginning to take its toll, and every hill now seemed just that much steeper and harder to climb than the one before.

It took her a moment to identify the unexpected aroma that came to her nostrils, carried on the first suggestion of a breeze. She hadn't noticed it until she reached the top of the hill, which meant that it probably originated from somewhere to the west.

Faint but distinctive, and unmistakeable—she could smell

smoke! And since she was reasonably certain that there had been no lightning strikes throughout the whole cloudless afternoon, the smoke must originate from a fire. A fire meant there had to be someone to light and tend it. Perhaps she wouldn't need to build a shelter for the night. Anyone who chose to build a fire out here in the middle of what seemed like nowhere in particular was here for a purpose. If they'd built a fire, they were planning to stay close to it rather than leave and travel to a village or other small community this late in the afternoon. Surely she could barter something in exchange for an overnight place close to the fire, or if she was really lucky, a share of the fire builder's night shelter.

It took several slow passes and a degree of luck before she spotted the faintest suggestion of an all but smoke free heat haze some fifty paces west from the hilltop and slightly to her left. Whoever had built the fire wasn't actually trying to conceal their presence, but was almost certainly a seasoned traveler who didn't make the basic mistake of using damp or sappy wood, which tended to give off more smoke than heat, as any village hunter/trapper would know.

She frowned. This didn't seem quite right. Why would someone hunting and trapping to provide food for even a small community be plying his trade in the middle of an open heath, far from any hint of a village of any size or consequence? Yet, try as she might, she couldn't think of a good reason for anyone to be out on open ground and apparently planning to remain there overnight. A split second later, the logical half of her brain reminded her that, by the same token, her own presence on the heath was no easier to explain.

She checked once more to get an accurate a fix on the hummock where she'd spotted the heat haze. It was still where she expected to find it, and without shortening her gaze, she let her feet find a safe place to tread without the guidance and benefit of sight. She made no attempt to approach undetected or in secret, and when a figure rose from somewhere off to her right at the edge of her field of vision, her first reaction was one of relief and pleasure. Her instincts had once more proved to be correct.

On the other hand, as soon as she took in the details of the apparition rising silently—and for all she knew by magic—from a position in the short, stunted growth of heather, other emotions—none of them hopeful, or even positive—crowded into her brain.

It was human—or at least, humanoid—in shape, and although she was far from the tallest in her own faraway community, she was definitely taller than...than *him*, she decided. He carried a weapon, and was bare-chested. Only men were allowed to carry weapons, and she was also certain that she would have been able to detect any suggestion of breasts if the blue figure had been female.

But blue...*blue?* What sort of man had blue skin? She thought of the folk tales and other stories she had learned as a child in the all too brief period when she'd been allowed some instruction, before her step parents had begun treating her as worse than a house slave. Traditional paintings showed the Romans who left their mark on England were much darker in skin tone than any of the native tribes of her homeland with an oily complexion, swarthy. The Vikings, who were the next wave of foreign invaders to arrive, tended by contrast to be extremely pale, their hair so blonde it was almost white. She'd also seen pictures of men, possibly Roman slaves, whose skin was jet black, and secretly wondered if this could possibly be true. Blue skin, though; this was something totally unnatural, and because of that, it also frightened her.

Sound broke through the curtain of blind panic that was threatening to overwhelm her. To her genuine amazement, Sally realized that she understood what was being said. While it was true that the person addressing her had a strong accent, the words he used to greet her were without question those of someone born and raised in England.

"Ho, lady! Whither from, an' where hence? For I'm thinking, ye'll find no shelter 'twixt my poor fire and the mountains, you!"

He shook his short, cruel-looking spear at the granite range filling the horizon as he named it, almost as if he were uttering a curse directed at a personal enemy.

Sally stood and gaped. She was momentarily lost for words, and knew it was rude of her to stare, but she was unable to look away from his unnatural blue skin.

"Where are you from?" she stammered. "I am a traveler not from this region, yet we speak the same language, even if your manner of speech is...not like mine," she concluded lamely.

The stranger tipped his head to one side and made a peculiar noise, which startled Sally. It took her a few seconds to realize that he was actually laughing.

"My people have always lived in this area" he said proudly. "We were here before the dark-skinned fighting men in metal skirts came from the south with their war chariots. We kept out of their way, for the most part, and 'tis said they learnt little of our presence. They thought us to be spirits, and it suited us to let them live in their ignorance, as we were too few to confront them in battle. 'Twas easier to frighten them into leaving us alone. Many years later when they left to return home, they carried no stories of the Brigantii with them! For all their fine armor, they were afraid of us with our poor weapons and our woad."

"Woad?" Sally had heard the word, but struggled to recall where and in what context.

"Woad—the pigment we use to cover our bodies when it suits our purpose. Sometimes we use it to scare an enemy, but most often because it is convenient and gives protection against the rain, the wind, and the weather. Neither does it rip or tear as clothing would every time it snags on a thorn bush."

During the whole of this speech, he had danced about on a hillock scant paces from her and of similar height. He spun and caught his spear constantly without dropping it once, seeming to know exactly where it was at all times. It was almost as if it had a life of its own with him partnering it in an intricate dance.

"And does your Brigantes tribe have a name ceremony? Do you have a name yourself?" This was where Sally had to be careful. Some of the communities she had dealt with and advised on medicines and healing over the years had proved to be extremely wary about names. Some thought that by offering your name to a stranger, you were leaving yourself open to misuse, even a curse or attack from a malicious spirit or a vengeful caster of spells.

The small, bright blue figure brought his capers to an abrupt halt and tipped his head, this time in the opposite direction. He looked at her once again, this time more thoughtfully, with a look in his eye that verged on solemn respect.

"We are not as superstitious as some tribes, but you are wise to show caution when asking a stranger. To me, you appear to be a genuine, polite person, and for that reason, if no other, I have no problem with revealing my name to you. 'Tis in truth a common name—plain old Tom. Tom of the Brigantii, and your servant, my lady!"

His eyes sparked with laughter, and he added in a teasing tone, "Now you have the advantage of me. I trust you will return the honor?"

Sally felt a flush of embarrassment at Tom's semi-formal manner of speech, which she sensed was intended to set her at her ease. Quickly, she gathered her wits and sought to make a fitting reply in similar fashion. "My people live close to that forest in the distance," she said, with a broad sweeping motion of her arm. "They settled in the area many generations ago. The tribe called themselves the Parisii, but intermarriage with others over the years has meant that the name is no longer in use. I have spent many years learning to serve my community as medicine woman and healer, and I am known as Sally."

"You have indeed chosen a noble calling, and this poor turf-cutter is indeed your servant for a second time. Your skill is surely one held in high esteem by your community, and I wonder that they allow you to leave them without your services while you are away from home traveling?"

Sally felt trapped by the apparently casual question, and hesitated before replying. She was incapable of hiding behind a lie, and even avoiding telling the full truth was something she found distasteful, though it had occasionally been necessary with seriously ill patients.

She had to respond immediately. If she didn't, Tom would surely sense that she was being less than completely honest. She shook her curls into place and tried to appear more dignified by straightening her robes and squaring off her shoulders, standing as tall as she possibly could.

"In truth, Tom, I have spent most of my days alone, in the peace and solitude of my workshop, preparing all the potions and medicines that are most often asked for by our little community. Everyone knows where to go for medicines, and there are others in the village experienced in medicines who can find and administer the correct doses for those who need them."

This much was true, but Sally was painfully aware of the fact that she had not given Tom the complete picture. None of the medicines prepared and stored, for example, had any form of identification on them, as Sally had never learned her letters. The same could be said for the vast majority of the other inhabitants of the village. Tom appeared to take this at face value, and nodded his acceptance of her assurances.

"The hour is late, Sally. Will you honor me by accepting a warm meal and lodging for the night?"

"Thank you, Tom! That will certainly save me building a shelter of my own. But where is your...?"

"I don't have time to travel back to my village every night when I am working. When I come out on the heath to cut turfs, I sleep close to my work until I have enough, then move camp and begin again."

"Forgive me, Tom. You've mentioned your work a number of times now, but I don't know the term itself. What *is* this 'turf' you cut? What is it used for once you have cut it?"

Tom blinked comically, then collapsed onto his backside, hugged his knees, and brayed with laughter, genuine and unrestrained mirth.

"Forgive me!" he spluttered eventually as he picked himself up again. "Forgive me, please! We may speak the same language, or nearly, but turf is so central to the lives of everyone in our community that I hadn't considered there might be other villages where the turf-cutter and his skills are unknown or unneeded." He beckoned Sally to follow, and led her by the hand down the furthest flank of the hillock he'd been standing on and across two or three others similar in size and close together. "I cut turf from the heath, which we use for different purposes" Tom said. "The turf itself is the grass growing on the heath, and the first few inches of soil underneath. I cut it into squares of a size that is convenient to carry and stack them to dry. Once they have dried out, they can be carried back to the village. They can be used in building houses and shelters, but for the most part, they are used for fuel. They burn longer than wood, and are all but smokeless. I can hardly believe your people do not burn turf!"

Sally looked around her, then dropped on one knee to give the soil itself a thorough inspection. She took a handful of loose dirt and crumbled it slowly between her fingers. As she did this, a faint aroma reached her sensitive nostrils. She thought how important the scent of a new combination of ingredients had been in helping her decide if a particular medicine was likely to be effective, or even, on occasion, too dangerous to use.

The sample of soil and plant roots in the palm of her hand gave off a distinctive scent, one she was certain she had never come across before.

"The soil is not like this where I live, and the plant growing in it is not the sort of grass I have seen...in and around our village." Why was she consciously avoiding any sentence that involved the word "home", she wondered? Firmly, she pushed the distracting thought from her mind. She had something here that she sensed was important, and needed her specialist knowledge of plants, herbs and medicines.

She held a sample directly under her nose and inhaled deeply, then wet a fingertip and—very cautiously—tasted it with the tip of her tongue. It wasn't an unpleasant taste, but it was unexpectedly sharp, acidic. She lifted a smaller sample and examined the root network of the plant that was not a grass. It reminded her of a miniature version of tree roots, much more durable than ordinary plant roots.

"I have always used dried grasses to help with starting fires quickly," she explained to Tom. "But they burn quickly. The dense roots of this plant suggest to me that it will burn much longer. I can understand why you would use it as fuel instead of burning wood. I suppose that is why you stack it and let it dry before you use it?"

Tom nodded, grinned, and danced enthusiastically.

"Exactly! Also, once it has dried, it's not as heavy to carry. Come, come!"

He scampered off over the nearest hillock, turning to make sure Sally was following. On the other side of the mound was an area where the top layer of turf had been neatly stripped off and stacked in regular square blocks. Each block was about three hands across, she estimated, and there were about ten or a dozen in each stack. A swift glance told her that he must have been working on this particular field for many days. There had to be fifty or sixty stacks drying in the wind.

"How long have you been working here?" Sally swept her arm out across the worked area.

"About thirteen, fourteen days," Tom replied after some checking, which seemed to require the use of most of his fingers.

"Half a moon cycle," Sally murmured. Her method of counting the passage of time was clearly not the same as Tom's, but it came to the same thing. She continued,

"And how long must this...these...your turf stand to dry before you can take it away and use it?"

Tom shrugged. "If the weather is kind, perhaps a full moon cycle—yes, I noted that you count the days in a different manner—but of course it can take longer. When I leave here, I will head for a stack of turf I built some three cycles ago, perhaps a day's journey from here and much closer to the village where I live. They've had the whole of the past summer to dry out, and I'm sure they'll be ready for use by now. Come, sit and rest while I prepare us something to eat."

On the lea side of one of the humps, presumably opposite the direction of the prevailing wind, a section of the hillside had been carved away to form a shallow cavity. Most of it was clearly intended as a sheltered sleeping area, indicated by a fair sized pile of furs. A few tools and a log to sit upon were the only other evidence of Tom's temporary tenancy. The area immediately around the mini-excavation was grass free and well-trodden, confirming that Tom had been working hard in the immediate vicinity for some time.

Tom wandered to a small circle of stones close to his hand-wrought lodge but not under the overhang. He took a stick and prodded at a dark mass within the circle, which immediately released small wisps of smoke. He bent low and blew gently on the bed of embers beneath the cut turf until they turned into small, dancing flames. Pleased with the results of his exertions, he sat back on his heels and beamed at Sally.

"One of the best things with turf is, it will smolder slowly, untended, for a long time before it burns out and needs to be re-lit. I built this fire as soon as I arrived here, and I haven't needed to re-light it yet, not even when the weather was so wet I had to stop cutting for a few days."

As the flames broke through and fastened into the covering turf, Tom took a fresh slab and placed it carefully on top.

"When that takes a firm hold, I'll have a pot ready to place over the fire and I'll cook us a warm meal."

"In that case, you must allow me to offer the last of the

fresh fruit I have carried with me; they may spoil by tomor-row," Sally insisted, ignoring Tom's none-too-serious pro-tests.

By the time they had eaten, the last light of the day had gone. Replete, and with the unaccustomed luxury of hot, sol-id food in her belly, Sally could barely keep her eyes open long enough to drag a few of Tom's furs off the pile and col-lapse in one corner of the shelter. She was vaguely aware of Tom sliding down close to her, wrapped in his own furs. Just before losing consciousness, she stretched out her arms in an instinctive plea for the benefit of shared body warmth, barely registering Tom's reaction as he placed one arm around her shoulders.

Chapter Four

It took Sally a few seconds to work out why she was so pleasantly warm when she woke the next morning. The wanton luxury of the loaned furs jogged her memory a split second before she felt Tom's companionable arm draped casually around her shoulder. From his deep, rhythmic breathing—not quite a snore—she guessed he was still asleep.

If he was cutting and digging turfs all day yesterday, she thought, *he must be exhausted.*

It was pleasant to feel so warm under so many furs, and particularly considering that they'd spent the night in what amounted to no more than a windbreak in the middle of an open heath. The shared body warmth was a welcome bonus, of course; she couldn't recall how long it had been since the last time she'd shared a bed with anyone, but it was too long. Following the path of a medicine woman had been her choice. Nobody had forced her into doing it, but if she had chosen *not* to develop her natural skills as a healer, many in her village would have died from petty ailments.

The role of a medicine woman was often shrouded in superstition, and was almost always a lonely existence. Once she had escaped the drudgery imposed upon her by her abusive adoptive parents, she was almost a full grown woman of about sixteen summers, as close as she could judge. There were no records of her birth, of course, though someone had once told her that she had been baptized, and her details had been recorded in the local church. Without the skill of reading, she'd had to take this on trust.

After living as a virtual house-slave for so many years,

and with only limited opportunities to get outside and meet other people of her own age, making friends was also a difficult thing for her to do, mainly because she felt there was nobody she dared trust. This may have become one thing that persuaded her to embrace and accept the solitary existence of a healer.

The temptation to remain under the mountain of warm, comfortable furs was almost irresistible, but Sally steeled herself and slid carefully out of the nest without disturbing her generous host's hard-earned slumbers. Having observed how he had resurrected the embers of the fire the previous evening, she decided to take this opportunity to return his favor by preparing an infusion of dried leaves from her store, one which would not only warm them and refresh their energy levels, but the particular brew she had in mind also tasted good—one of her favorites.

She'd made a note of where Tom stored his tools and supplies, and measured out enough fresh water for what she had in mind. Not knowing how far away the nearest supply might be, she was reluctant to use more than absolutely necessary. A swift glance confirmed that Tom was still asleep, and with a nod of satisfaction, she turned her attention to the fire bed.

Imitating Tom's sequence of actions, which she had studied carefully, she soon had a cheerful blaze licking around the sod, and she placed the pot carefully upon it. Perhaps due to the combination of small crackling noises and the aroma of the smoke, which Sally's first attempts at fire building could not completely avoid, Tom half-rolled and showed signs of life, but by the time he had roused himself sufficiently to be aware of his immediate surroundings, Sally had blended the ingredients of her own special brew, and the water in the pot had heated it to an ideal temperature. The one thing Sally hadn't found was a second drinking vessel, but as Tom sat up and showed his appreciation by wrinkling his nose at the aroma rising from the pot, she decanted just less than half the liquid into her own drinking horn and carried it to where Tom sat.

"Taste, and see what you think. It's one of my own favorite blends."

Tom took the drinking horn, but to Sally it seemed that he was more interested in the cup rather than its contents.

"It tastes best while it's still hot!"

Sally was slightly cross at the thought that Tom might not fully appreciate the drink she had prepared so carefully if he let it cool too much. There must have been some hint of this in her tone of voice because Tom tore himself away from examining the drinking horn and looked Sally square in the eye.

"Your kind thoughts, and this cup of morning cheer, are both very welcome, Sally, and the smell of the infusion intrigues me! Hot drinks are something I can only hope for when I am home between journeys. I never learned the difference between herb and weed, and would not trust myself to gather the right sort of plants for making drinks. I'd most likely poison mese'n!" he ended with a grin. "But, if you say it tastes best hot, why don't we share this draught while it's still warm, and I'll find another vessel after we finish it?"

Sally could see the logic behind Tom's suggestion, and half suspected that he had made it sound like a sensible solution.

She watched carefully as he raised it to his lips, still keeping rock steady eye contact. He paused once more before drinking and inhaled deeply to taste the wisps of steam rising from the surface. He spoke around and above the rim of the drinking horn.

"I'm no herbalist, so I wouldn't know any names for what you've used in this drink, but I recognize a number of aromas I have smelled before and know that they are none of them unpleasant or of a dark nature intended to harm the unwary! You honor me once more by allowing me to drink first. It will be my greatest pleasure to share this with you, and any other distillation or infusion you may care to make under our travels together."

He lifted the horn in a deliberate, formal gesture of salutation, and drank. When he swallowed the liquid and passed the horn immediately, Sally saw that he had judged it nicely. She estimated he had left her just over half the tea to enjoy, and she wasted no time drinking her share. It was still surprisingly hot, hotter than she would have expected it to be after all their light chatter and semi-formal toasting.

When next she glanced at Tom, he had what was evidently a drink vessel of some sort in his hand, though she was certain he'd not moved from that spot, nor had he had the opportunity to conjure it from thin air. It was an odd shape, about four inches across the top, neither round nor heart-shaped, but something in between. A short, flat blade protruded from the lip, presumably to avoid scalding finger-tips while holding a hot liquid.

Tom noticed Sally's interest straight away.

"Those of my people who consider such things important call this a *Kosa,*" he said "Though I know not why, or if the word has any meaning. If it ever did, that knowledge is now long forgotten, but the name remains *Kosa!*"

He stretched out his free hand, silently suggesting that Sally should fill both drinking vessels from the pot, which had been left at the fire's edge to keep the contents warm. She obliged, then glanced at the bottom of the pot and carefully poured away the dregs of liquid and the now-cooked plant mass amongst the cooling coals on the downwind side of the fire. There followed a few startled hisses and then, after a few seconds, a very pleasant aroma drifted up from the fire and settled around them.

She turned to Tom and smiled when she saw the puzzled expression on his face. "Does that seem strange to you? Don't be afraid to admit it, nor think to spare my feelings by hiding behind an untruth! I can tell you this, you would not be the first person to ask me for an explanation or a reason why I do this."

The final wisps of fragrant smoke curled between them and evaporated away as Sally spoke. She inhaled as deeply as her chest muscles would allow, luxuriating in the untaint-ed air that scoured and cleansed her body deeply from with-in. She felt as if her eyesight was sharper, her sense of smell more acute.

"My people have a tradition of sharing teas, especially with visitors. One of them is when we share a drink with new friends, we should remember to include the hearth gods— who made it possible to prepare the drink—in our thanks. We do this by offering a portion from the lees remaining in the empty pot."

Tom nodded his acceptance of this information, but Sally could see that his attention was fixed on the drinking horn she still had in her hand.

"May I have a closer look at that?" he asked.

Slightly puzzled at the unexpected question, Sally passed it to him. He emptied the remaining dregs onto the fire base, creating a second small puff of scented steam, and concentrated his attention on the decorative markings etched on the outer surface.

"You named your people Parisii, I think?" he murmured, glancing at Sally for confirmation. She nodded, and he continued. "It seems that my tribe and yours may have a common ancestry somewhere. Many of the symbols you have used to decorate your drinking horn are identical with mine, and our tales of the Brigantes include many stories in which a horn of this type is often mentioned."

He passed his *kosa* to her. Immediately, she saw the similarity in the decorative markings carved into it.

"We don't have the same tradition of offering a portion to the hearth gods each time we drink, but it's a courteous gesture, and one I may suggest to our elders in council that they might want to introduce," he added. "Come, now. I had been thinking of moving on from this site anyway. Allow me to prepare some solid food for us while the fire is still burning, and I will guide you on your journey. My home village lies to the west, so our paths are entwined for a while, wherever you may be headed, and you may be glad of some company getting through the mountain passes at this time of the year."

Tom cooked up some sort of stew, which Sally could see was mostly vegetable, but she was too polite to ask what sort of animal he had caught and diced into small, anonymous lumps. It was tender enough to be chewed and swallowed, and the protein it gave would be useful in the days ahead. The trail food they would be relying on while they traveled usually consisted of whatever could be scavenged in passing from the landscape, and was almost invariably some form of plant food that did not require stopping, building fires, or cooking.

"Won't we need some of your furs?"

Tom had collected a few of his tools and a water bag, but seemed prepared to leave everything else in his shelter. Sally's question provoked another rill of genuine laughter from him. Sally had already noticed that this seemed to be his instinctive reaction to just about anything that happened.

"No, Sally, we're within comfortable distance of another of my many home-from-homes, and I keep all of them well stocked with the essentials—furs, pots, some tools. The furs are too heavy to make it worthwhile carrying them any distance, though I may decide to take a couple with us when we attempt the mountain passes. The weather can be treacherous at this time of the year!"

"Attempt the mountain passes? What do you mean by that? Is it dangerous?" Sally demanded

"The mountains can be dangerous at any time of year," Tom said, with a who-cares shrug of his shoulders. "But in the coldest months, a single slip can mean a broken bone, and almost certainly you'd freeze to death. Then there's the wildlife to consider. The wolves will have been hungry for some time, and there are even reports of bears roaming the hills!"

"Bears? Surely not!" Sally protested. Of course, she'd heard as a child all the tales told by village elders, intended to scare children into staying safely indoors, but as far as she knew, bears had been hunted to extinction.

Tom shrugged. "The mountains are not the friendliest of places, and when full winter arrives, they will be impassable. There are many who believe that there is some malevolent creature that inhabits the mountains, and preys on unwary travelers. Whether we name them bears, ogres, or another evil legend, we are well advised to show caution when we are in the mountains themselves. 'Tis best if we are close enough to start the climb itself at first light, and attempt to force our way across to the other side before nightfall. Spending a night in the mountain passes is not a good idea."

"You have a...travel base, or whatever you call them, closer to the mountain range?"

"I do, and with enough furs to equip ourselves for our passage west."

"In that case, we should be on our way as soon as possible."

They stopped at a clear, shallow stream to refill their water containers, and turned toward the next stage of the journey. Sally's skills in identifying edible plants and finding ripe fruits came into play, and they were able to keep up a steady pace throughout the day, grazing a variety of foods that grew close to the route they followed. There was no longer a visible track, but they were able to take the most direct line, and reached the first rocky outcrops of the mountains late in the afternoon. The clouds had settled lower down the flanks, suggesting rain on the way.

The foothills became steadily steeper and the bushes petered out. They were replaced by granite boulders, which soon
came to dominate the landscape and slowed their progress.
By mid-afternoon, they were scrambling, using their hands as
often as their feet, and panting hard from the unaccustomed
exercise. They were now high enough to be climbing through
the clouds, and Sally felt her clothing clinging to her, clammy
and damp. She turned to Tom, who was scrambling over a
couple of rocks.

"We should get a fire started straight away before everything gets damp," Sally said.

"Tonight, at least, we have more protection than last
night's bothy gave us," Tom replied, guiding Sally round one
last corner on the trail. He dragged aside a stunted bush to
reveal a small cave; there was just enough light left in the
sky to confirm that the supplies Tom had stashed on his previous visit were undisturbed.

"We can even build our fire in the entrance. The smoke
will drift out of the cave, but most of the heat will remain inside to keep us warm."

Sally glanced around the barren ground in the immediate
vicinity. "I regret my foraging skills will not feed us this evening." She sighed.

Tom chuckled, bouncing on the spot as he did so. "I was
here a few weeks ago, to check on my stores. I knew I would
be staying here at least for one night once I was finished cutting where you met me. That was always going to be my last
trip of the year; it's pointless trying to cut turf when the
ground is frozen during the winter months. I stored some food
here, which should still be good to eat. I knew I would be
needing plenty of food before chancing the mountain passes,
where the most I can hope for is fresh water from melted
snow. There will be no food, and nowhere safe to stay if we
are caught in the open at night."

"What have you stored? And how have you preserved it?"

Sally knew that to stand a chance of surviving a winter
journey of any length, they needed solid, nourishing food,
the sort that would stick to their ribs and sustain them if they
were forced to skip a couple of meals and keep moving in
order to survive adverse conditions. Her usual diet of pulses,
nuts, and plants would not be appropriate, nor would it be a
useful preparation for the journey on hand. What they need-

ed was a carnivore's diet, protein-rich fish or meat.

Tom ceased his capering and hopping about, but lost none of his boisterous humor. He paused, perched on one foot, and grinned up at Sally with an almost serious look in his eyes. "What I left here against my return includes none of your pale vegetables or bitter herbs, that I can promise you! It was all good travel food—some fish, fresh caught nearby, which I salted and then dried in the sun, and a brace of small rabbit besides."

He crouched once more and loped into the shadows toward the rear of the cave. Sally heard the sound of stones being tossed to one side, and Tom returned a few seconds later with a carp in one hand and a pair of rabbit in the other. He laid the rabbit carcasses on one side and handed Sally the fish.

"This need to be soaked in fresh water before it is cooked. If you'll mount the rabbit on spikes, I will build a fire and we can roast them while the fish softens."

Sally squatted close to one side of the cave and poured a grudging minimum amount of water over the fish, conscious of the fact that every mouthful used would have to be replaced for the following day's journey. She was acutely conscious of Tom's movements just out of her field of vision; every tiny noise was amplified and echoed, bouncing off the hard, cold surfaces of the cave walls until they sounded like a whole army of Toms scurrying hither and yon.

As Sally sat close to the fire bed, the moisture from her rain-drenched clothing began to evaporate. The fine mist lingered in the cave, gathering under the low ceiling. She was conscious of the acrid smell of stale sweat, which seemed to cling to the steam, spreading throughout the confines of the cave. Tom squatted close by in companionable silence. She stirred, and drew the smallest of breaths. At once, Tom's head snapped round to give her his full attention

"You have another advantage over me now, my friend. My clothing is soaked through, and I cannot decide whether they or my body is in most urgent need of cleansing. Does your woad wash off you when it gets wet?"

Tom almost fell off the rock he was seated on, seized by the fiercest explosion of laughter yet. "I told you we use woad as a covering for convenience and for comfort, as well as a means of scaring foes. It's pretty hard wearing, but we tend to paint fresh layers on from time to time. It can be scrubbed off if you really *need* to, but I have a bath every Yule, whether I need it or not, and that's about the only time I'm reasonably woad-free."

His eyes twinkled as he spoke, and Sally wasn't sure whether she ought to believe him or not.

He saw the doubt in her eye and smiled. "If you wish to bathe after we've eaten, there are plenty of pots to heat water, and plenty of dry furs you're welcome to use while you wash your travel garb. Sadly, I cannot offer you any of the things that I know women in our village use to clean clothes. I don't even know what the plants are called!"

"I have some soapwort in my gather bag, which is gentler than wood-ash and lye," Sally replied. "Though I would not normally use it to wash myself. And the use of warm water instead of a cold mountain stream also has its attractions, but can we spare the water? Is there a source close at hand for what we will need to carry?"

"There is, and if you wish to bathe in private, I will refill our gourds now and remain at the mouth of the cave until you are finished," he said, simply and sincerely. He paused, then with a grin he added, "You shouldn't believe everything people tell you straight away. There are those who would take advantage of you for trusting them too much, though I'm not one of them. And most of what I've told you about woad is true, except for the part about keeping me warm. I need the furs for that, just like everyone else."

Sally was grateful for his thoughtfulness, and rummaged through the furs and pelts to find some dry clothing to wear, tossing her travel-stained clothes in a heap to be laundered after their evening meal. As her eyes grew accustomed to the reduced level of light, she was pleased to discover that there was a natural ledge about knee-high running along the cave wall. She turned to sit on it while she skewered the rabbits on two sharpened sticks, grateful to take the pressure off the soles of her aching feet. She was not accustomed to trekking non-stop for so many hours in a single day. The sun was now low in the sky, and for a few minutes, at least, it would be at an ideal angle to show her some details of the cave.

She took in as many of the features as she could absorb in the short time available before the sun withdrew completely for the night, leaving her dependent on Tom's fire-tending skills for light as well as heat. There had been no nasty surprises waiting for them in the cave, no dangerous beasts disputing ownership, or poisonous snakes to be evicted. Sally thought this was most likely due to Tom's thoughtfulness in blocking the entrance of the cave with the sturdy bush she'd seen him rip away.

Her super-sensitized ears told her that Tom had stopped moving round collecting things, and was now doing something else. He appeared to be mumbling something; she couldn't make out the words he was using, which were being distorted by being bounced off the confining walls, but there was a definite rhythm to them. Was he singing, perhaps? She listened more carefully, and realized that there was another regular sound, faint but distinct, just below the melody of Tom's voice. It sounded as if he was striking something hard against another object, in time with the song he was singing. She saw odd flashes of light appearing between Tom's hands every time the unfamiliar scraping noise was heard. As she watched, one of the flashes developed, not fading like the previous ones. Tom immediately stopped what he was doing and leaned forward. He appeared to be blowing gently in the direction of the firebase.

Suddenly, the smallest imaginable yellow flame appeared. It licked hungrily at the kindling and spread rapidly. After the all too brief interlude when the sun's last rays had penetrated the cavern's gloom, the shadows had seemed even more profound. Now, as the kindling caught firmly in the small twigs and spread to the slabs of turf on top, the shadows retreated completely and Sally could take in every detail of the cave. Tom had stocked it well. Neat piles of dry turf lined both side walls, fuel enough for many days and nights, and where the cave tapered was a collection of clay pots containing a variety of dried foods. From the roof above them hung the skinned carcasses of a number of animals. Many of the pelts had been carefully cured and laid in neat piles, warm furs of different sizes for sleeping and for outdoor protection.

She took the rabbits to Tom, who hung them above the smokeless flames that had erupted through the turf. As he began to turn the meat so it cooked evenly on all sides, she caught his eye and picked up a pot, signing silently her intention to prepare a warm drink. Tom nodded his approval and turned the rabbits another notch.

By the time they had eaten, the drinks were ready. Tom sniffed cautiously, and nodded. "This is not the same mixture as last time, but it smells...interesting."

Sally smiled. "I'm glad you noticed the difference. I use different ingredients sometimes, particularly if I'm trying to cure someone of a malady of some sort—not that either of us are ill at the moment, though. That was just..."

"An example?" Tom suggested.

Sally realized she was speaking far too quickly. She paused and then nodded. "That's right! On this occasion, I added some chamomile, which will help us sleep through the night."

"That was thoughtful." Tom beamed. "We should be warm enough tonight. I'll replace the bush at the entrance to keep the drafts out, and we can easily lay some extra turf to burn through the night."

"And with the furs, and some body heat, we..." Sally stopped suddenly. Her face reddened with embarrassment as she realized that she might have given the wrong impression. What if Tom thought she was wanton, deliberately inviting him to share her bed for a purpose other than sleeping?

He gazed into her eyes with an understanding smile. "Peace, Sally. I am not one to take advantage of a young lady whose tired tongue flaps too easily. You're safe with me—as safe as you wish to be, that is—until or unless you decide to *invite* me to something more...intimate."

Tom's soft words took Sally by surprise. A wealth of emotion flooded her and she felt moisture in parts of her body that had been inactive for all the years she had opted to live the reclusive life of a healing spinster. Her breath quickened, keeping pace with her hammering heart as her blood circulated more eagerly. Her skin was suddenly sensitive as every nerve tingled. Even the softness of the cured pelts she had put on just a few minutes ago seemed too warm, too constricting to wear a moment longer, an intolerable itch against her fevered skin. She simply *had* to be free of them.

Without quite knowing how, she was aware that she stood naked, towering a head above her travel companion, running her fingers through the stiff blue curls plastered to his skull by woad as he kissed her breasts. One of his hands was clenched firmly around her buttocks; the other was doing indescribable but wonderful things in and around her womanhood, where the moistness she had not felt in many years was rapidly becoming a flood of liquid pleasure.

She tugged slightly at a lock of Tom's hair, distracting him from her left breast, which happened to be the object of his attention at that exquisite moment. She was far from displeased when he failed to respond immediately, but when he eventually—and reluctantly—did, she turned his face upwards with a gentle finger under his chin and kissed his lips passionately. By now the fire was warming the cave efficiently, but it was not the main cause of the light sheen of sweat, which caused Sally's body to glisten in the ever changing pattern of light and shadow.

She eased her head back far enough to gaze calmly into his eyes, and with her free hand, disengaged his from her loins, where he was continuing to pleasure her with a soft, gentle, rhythmic massage she had never experienced before. Without a word being spoken, she led him by the hand to the pile of furs in the corner that were intended as their bed for whatever remained of the night once they had sated each other's needs.

By now Sally was panting with desire, and acutely aware that Tom had said little so far other than to suggest that he would not take her by force. Did he expect her to start every move during their lovemaking? Did he think of her as an older woman, more experienced in these matters than he was? Looking at him again, Sally didn't think he could be any younger than she was, despite his lack of inches. There was something about him that told her he had a wealth of life experience that can only be acquired with the passing of years. In fact, she thought he might even be older than her.

At the edge of the pile of furs, she turned and took both Tom's hands in her own. Slowly, she sank to her knees, deliberately conceding the advantage of her height, allowing him to stand in a superior position from which he could for once look down into her submissive eyes.

Neither had spoken a word thus far. In the circumstances, this seemed perfectly natural. Still in silence, Sally unbound the single knot in the loincloth that was Tom's only attempt at clothing. More than once, Sally had thought it was simply for a convenient place to lodge his dagger when he wasn't using it. Freeing his loins of the single wrap of cloth, she was unable to suppress a tiny cry of pleasure and anticipation when she discovered what lay concealed. Tom's race might not be as tall as hers, but the same didn't seem to apply to other body parts.

"Does this woad of yours *taste* of anything?" she growled, running her fingers several times along the full length of his shaft as it glistened in the reflected firelight.

"I've no idea, Sally. Why don't you find out, and you can tell me later?"

Chapter Five

Sally woke with a slight headache and a vague feeling of panic. There was a scent in the air, faint but unmistakeable, which she associated with danger.

Still half asleep, she rolled onto one elbow and struggled to free herself from the furs, her heart hammering wildly.

The greatest fear of all who lived as she did in dwellings built almost entirely from wood was the pungent smoke of a fire, trapping her in her shelter, transforming it into her tomb.

She was on her feet in an instant, frantically looking to all sides for the source. The cold stone of the cavern floor penetrated the soles of her bare feet, and memories of the events of the past twenty-four hours came flooding back to her as her confused mind caught up with reality. The faint trace of smoke was from the fire that had continued to smolder through the night, keeping the cavern tolerably warm. It posed no threat to her immediate surroundings, and she allowed herself to relax.

Her abrupt explosion from the furs had roused Tom, who appeared fully alert, balanced easily on the balls of his feet. Perhaps he'd caught a whiff of her fear and reacted instinctively in his own male fashion; she was convinced his frantic glances in every direction were an attempt to locate a weapon. They looked at each other across the fire pit, two totally vulnerable and defenseless mortals, naked, without weapons, but ready to fight for survival by any means possible. There was no danger, no threat, no assailant or enemy to challenge them. The ludicrous situation set them both off laughing uncontrollably and they collapsed into each other's arms for support. Sally felt secure with Tom's protective arms around her and didn't want the moment to end, but after a few seconds, Tom kissed her bare shoulder and pulled his head back to a focusing distance. He licked his lips with a mischievous glint in his eye.

"You taste as good as you smell!" he teased her. "If that's what soapwort does when you use it, I'll wash myself every night."

Once she had recovered from the exhilarating natural high of spontaneous lovemaking, the practical side of Sally's nature had insisted that she should wash her clothing, as planned. For her, it made sense to wash herself at the same time, sluicing away the unpleasant odors of stale sweat along with the travel grime.

"You'll find this fresher to wear, too." She laughed, tossing him the deeply woaded loincloth she'd automatically included in the impromptu laundry session. She turned her back and dressed swiftly. When she turned around, Tom still stood naked, sniffing at the cloth cautiously, running his fingers along its length.

"Is something wrong?" Suddenly, she was fearful she might have offended him, broken some tribal taboo she had not been aware of.

Tom smiled. Once more, she was aware of how even the smallest thing seemed to amuse her new companion.

"No," he replied. "Far from it! But apart from rinsing off the occasional bloodstain, I've never washed this before. I didn't realize how much softer and more comfortable it would feel." In a matter of seconds, he'd wrapped it around his hips and secured the ends, using a complicated knot that his hands achieved with the ease of daily habit. "Your clothes are definitely paler to my eye, but I doubt a single wash will have made much difference to the woad stain in mine." He grinned as he turned to glance at the cavern's mouth. "I think we should make an early start. We're going to need a full day to get clear of these mountains, and the weather can change swiftly at this time of the year. Do you have a secret herb you can infuse that will help us to fly off this hill?"

Sally smiled. "None of my teas are magical, I fear," she said in response to his upbeat fey mood. "So we'll have to remain earthbound. But I can certainly find something to ensure we do not tire easily as we travel."

The tea blend Sally prepared included the dried berries and leaves from a blackberry plant, sweetened after pouring with a few drops of wild honey.

Tom had watched her compose the blend while he arranged the leftover cold rabbit and fish from their evening meal on two platters. "Very good," was his verdict. After one cautious sip, he'd upended his *kosa* and poured the rest of the tea, which Sally thought was still too hot to enjoy, down his throat with no apparent discomfort. "Any more left?" He held out the *kosa* hopefully, and Sally drained off the last of the pot, reserving only the customary lees to offer the hearth gods.

"Does everything make you laugh, Tom?"

After breaking their fast, there were very few practical matters that needed attending to. Tom made sure the cavern was as secure as he could make it against wild animals or other uninvited intruders. They added to what they had worn so far with suitably sized furs for the next stage of their journey. The only task remaining was to make sure there were no embers left in the cooking fire.

Tom plucked a fur from the pile and twisted it into a head protector before he replied, "Some time ago—more than two summers ago, it must have been—my tribe was visited by a traveler. He was not born on these shores, but in a place much further north where he claimed they have winters with no sun, and at the height of their summer, there is no night. He spoke little of our language when he arrived, but he stayed three months with us for the best trading against his goods, and by the time he left, we could carry out a simple conversation. He called what we were doing...last night..." Tom seemed just a fraction tongue-tied. He tried again. "He said his people had a special name for it. They called it 'laughing together,' and that it was the one thing that kept many from going completely insane during the long, dreary months when the sun failed to rise above the horizon."

"Clever, pretty words!" Sally exclaimed. She was listening carefully and paying attention to what he was saying, but at the same time, she was examining her skin thoroughly, with a medicine woman's eye, for bruising or other telltale signs of a possible return of her sickness.

Tom looked at her curiously. "I thought I'd told you that the woad won't rub off."

Sally reddened. Of course, this was but one of many things she hadn't yet explained for Tom. It wasn't because she'd avoided the subject, but because there were far more interesting things to talk about than an illness she'd managed to cure by relying on her own medical knowledge and skills. Now, she realized, she had to be honest with him. There was always the possibility that she might suffer a relapse, and she was also wise enough to know that she might still pass the sickness on to him. Better safe than sorry, she decided, and signed for Tom to sit next to her by the fire pit. In a few words, she told him of the serious illness that had cost so many lives in her little community, and how she'd needed to isolate herself in order to administer the potent draught that had cured her.

"From what I saw of the sick people I treated, the discolored lumps and bumps were a common sign in everyone, and that is why I feel it's necessary to check my skin every day. Unfortunately, I can't see any way of checking you for lumps and bruises. They'd all be hidden by the color of the woad!"

"You seem to have a drink for any occasion, and every illness," Tom said, his eyes dancing with humor.

"I've had many years to learn how to combine plants and herbs, mostly for medicine and healing, it's true, but there are also blends that are used purely for the pleasant taste."

Tom nodded, and looked over her shoulder toward the cave mouth. Seemingly reluctant, he rose to his feet. "We're going to need every possible minute of the day's light to reach the safety of the lower hills in the west," he said. "We should make a start."

Ten minutes later, Tom carefully replanted the bush he used to conceal the cave entrance. The sky was brightening to the east; they had timed their departure well. Tom paused and faced the point on the eastern horizon where the still-unseen sun was due to show itself and bowed three times in silence. Puzzled, Sally caught his eye, then slipped her hand into his and repeated the formal obeisance, realizing that it must be some sort of ceremony that held an important meaning for him.

"Is that some sort of...prayer, greeting, something of that

nature?" she asked as they turned their faces westward and began the day's trek. "My people have no such traditions, but I understand that all tribes are different."

"We've heard the stories told by traveling monks, tales of a holy man in a faraway land who wants everybody to follow him, though the monk I spoke to couldn't tell me *where* the holy man was going."

"For the moment, I'll pray to any and all of the gods out there to look kindly on me—your pardon, milady, on *us*—as we start a difficult and dangerous part of our journey."

Sally nodded. The Christian religion was well established in Yorkshire, but in isolated communities such as hers, it was still regarded as a skin-deep, cosmetic cloak, or a convenient gloss disguising older beliefs held sacred for countless generations and rooted in an understanding of and respect for natural forces and the elements.

She picked up her travel bag and prepared to move off. Suddenly, Tom froze and stared hard at a clump of bushes about twenty paces downhill from the cave. Sally was puzzled. Fending for herself for so many years had made her sensitive to any sound or movement that might suggest danger, or at least something not quite right. She hadn't seen or heard anything out of the ordinary, but as she glanced once again at Tom, she was convinced his nostrils were quivering. Could he have *smelled* danger?

"Back away, slowly! Return to the cave, and don't turn your back."

"What have you seen? What's wrong?" Sally crabbed toward the cave entrance, switching her gaze from Tom to the bushes and back.

"Rats! And plenty of them, too—scores, if not hundreds! They run in packs, cowards that they are. Out here on open ground we have no chance against so many!" Suddenly, he sprang from his semi-crouched, defensive position and aimed a boot at the remains of the fire, scattering embers and coals into the bushes. High-pitched squeals and a thrashing of branches confirmed that most of the salvo had found a mark. Tom snatched one of the remaining logs from the fire pit and joined Sally at the entrance to the cavern. "Help me secure these screens against the bushes. We need a solid wall between us and them, even if it's only reeds and grass. When they attack, we have to slow them down any way we can to have a chance of driving them off!"

"They also feed on anything they find!" Sally cried. "Dead and rotting flesh, animals that have died of an illness, spoiled fodder no other creature would touch. They spread disease with their sharp fangs. I have treated many who have been bitten by them, and not all have survived, even with my most powerful medicines!"

The screens were grimy on one side and shiny on the other. Sally guessed Tom had used them as sleds to drag cut turf back to his temporary shelter. The barrier was quickly in place, and there were no sounds to indicate the return of the rats.

"Now we make as many torches as we can. In order to fight our way out of here, we need to be able to *see* the enemy when they arrive!"

Long, dry grasses, probably intended as sleeping mattresses, were swiftly bound to tree branches with thin strips Tom cut from his stock of animal pelts. He hefted one and gave a satisfied nod. He turned and stood close to the wall of screens with a murderous-looking tree root in the other hand.

Sally tightened one final knot, lit the torch, and jammed it into a crack on the wall. She picked up one of the smaller torches and hesitated a second, torn between the knife she was familiar with and the somewhat clumsy alternative of using a club.

Tom seemed to sense her thoughts. He grinned. "Take the tree branch! A knife is better for close-range combat, but you want to keep a safe distance if you possibly can. They're too small and too fast for you to be sure of stabbing them."

As he spoke, a few leaves rustled close to his feet. His club blurred through a short, vicious arc, and three small bloodstains appeared on the cavern floor. Startled, Sally spotted movement at the very edge of her field of vision, but she was slow to react. Her club came down on nothing, but the intruder retreated rather than run into the cave.

Tom inspected the business end of his club, shrugged, and tossed it onto the fire.

"I hit that one a bit harder than I meant to," he growled. "But at least we've plenty of branches to use." He chose a replacement and gave it a couple of swings.

"Wait, Tom! Let me look at that weapon." Sally took it and examined it more closely. It still had a few small, half-curled leaves on it. "As I thought, this is from a yew tree."

"Yes. Strong, and still slightly green. It will last a bit longer than the first couple of blows."

"I've got another use for it. You've given me an idea!" She turned and added more fuel to the fire as she continued. "Not everything Mother Nature provides can be used safely. The sap from the yew tree can be used as a deadly poison, and I have in my bag a further two plants that are even more deadly. I can blend them into a real 'witch brew' and coat the base of the screens with it. When they feel it on their fur, the rats will lick it off."

"And poison themselves." Tom finished her sentence for her, then frowned. "But surely it's going to take at least a few minutes before it works?"

"It will slow them down, and they'll also rub against other rats as they try to wash themselves. I can even pour a pool of the potion on the cavern floor in front of the screens."

"Will it take long to prepare? How strong can you make it?"

"I told you I have charms in my pack far more potent than the sap of the yew tree. The dried powder of belladonna dissolves at once in warm water, and if I add paste from the oleander flower, it will stick to the screens and the rats themselves. It will kill a human swiftly; make sure you don't step in it, especially barefoot! I've never tried to feed it to rats, but I cannot imagine such a small animal lasting more than a half dozen breaths after licking its own fur."

As she spoke, she was unpacking her bag. Wisps of steam began to roil on the surface of the pan of water. She stripped the bark from the yew branch, tossing it into the pan in small slivers, then used the wand to stir in the powders she took from the pouch. The water immediately turned jet black. Tom took a backwards step, expecting a foul stench to cloy the cavern, but Sally reassured him.

"The power remains in the potion. You needn't worry about poisoning yourself by breathing."

She twisted the wand in a paste and added it to the pot. The liquid became noticeably thicker at once, and she hastened across the cavern floor to pour it at the foot of the screen before it congealed. There was still no sound of squeak or rustle to indicate a second foray from the rats, but Sally knew she'd been working flat out to prepare the lethal cocktail, and she didn't think it had taken her too long once the water had become hot enough to dissolve the ingredients.

"Is there another way out of this cave? Have you explored it on an earlier visit?"

"There are a number of passages that end in rock fall, and others I have noted but not ventured into. I cut the smoke hole myself; the earth's crust was thin at that point, and I suppose I could widen it so we can slip out that way, if we must." Tom didn't seem too pleased with this idea, and continued, "I have noticed faint currents of air in some passages. It must be coming from outside, somehow."

"All we can do is wait, and see if Ratty dares make a second assault."

They didn't have to wait very long. Surreptitious rustles and muffled squeaks suggested a certain degree of intelligence, and even the capacity to plan, was found in the brains of their rodent foes. The sounds of preparation, if it could be called that, ceased abruptly, replaced by a silence that took on a menacing aspect as it stretched...thirty heartbeats, forty...forty-eight, forty-nine...

Suddenly, the screen was alive and bucking across its full twenty paces, the width of the cavern entrance from one slate wall to the other. Chitter-chatter screams of fury at being defeated by the close weft and warp of the screens, and the discomfort of the sticky, oily substance clogging their fur, rose in pitch and volume as the vanguard tried to turn back and were unable to force their way past the second wave of rats following hard on their heels. A few paws, tails, and snouts pushed clear of the screen. As soon as they touched the obsidian black puddle that lay like a defensive moat hard against the reeds, there was a serpent hiss as the body part melted and dissolved, leaving behind a stench that churned Sally's stomach. She doused a scarf in water and tied it rapidly around her mouth and nose, tossing a second scarf to Tom. He lost no time copying her, then turned once more to face the screen with a fresh club in his fist.

"Be careful, Tom! Don't let a drop of this liquid splash back on you!"

Tom crouched lower and stared intently at the gelatinous pool at the foot of the screen, the width of a hand from one cavern wall to the other. "You called this a 'witch brew.' That seems a good description, Sally. Look! It's carving a channel in the floor of the cavern!"

It was true. The floor of the cave wasn't stone, but tight-packed earth. Tom took his turf-cutting knife from his belt and dipped it carefully into the liquid. When he withdrew it a few seconds later, the tip was sparkling clean, as if new-forged. The rest of the blade was stained with the grime of years of use in all weathers. Somehow, it even *looked* dull and blunt by comparison.

"I don't think we should be trying to push our way past the bushes to use the main entrance," Tom said, looking in awed wonder at his knife.

"The mixture is far stronger than I thought possible! And have you noticed? We haven't heard a sound from beyond the screens for some time now. I doubt the rats have all perished, but perhaps the survivors have retreated to lick their wounds?"

"And kill themselves in the process." Tom grunted, with a malicious grin. "Come, bring your travel bag. We'll not be leaving this way. That passage behind you is one that I think may lead to an exit. See how the smoke from my torch is drawn into it? The draft has to be caused by a hole or a crack of some sort."

The passage narrowed to little more than a crack, barely wide enough for them to wriggle through, but the air current became noticeably stronger. Soon, Sally could feel it on her cheeks, and the smoke from their torches led them onwards.

"We may not need to dig our way out," Tom said. "It must be a fair-sized hole to create such a strong draft."

The passage had continued to hem in around them as they slipped and scrambled around half-seen obstacles, and they were now crawling on all fours. The smoke continued to flow freely. The exit point they sought had to be close at hand. Another tumble of fallen rock halted their progress. Tom rose to his feet and inspected it.

"I should be grateful we of the Brigantes are small in stat-ure." He grinned. "For once, it's an advantage to be able to crawl into smaller spaces." He hoisted himself up on the pile of rocks blocking their path and reached just beyond the height of Sally's head. "I can see daylight not far ahead!" Tom's words were slightly muffled, but clear enough for Sally to hear. "It might be a tight fit for a longshanks like you, but we'll have to use our hands to clear the way. You can leave the torch, but push your magic potions in front of you. It looks too tight for you to get through with the bag on your shoulder."

Negotiating the last section of the passageway was every bit as difficult as Tom had guessed. Several times, Sally cursed and swore, regretting the fact that even among her own tribe she was considered taller than average. Being young and reasonably supple went some way toward redressing this, however, and with the help of some unnatural contortionist body shapes combined with a stubborn refusal to admit defeat, she managed to squeeze her shoulders through the narrowest of gaps and took what felt to her like the first double-lungful of clean air she'd tasted in...how long?

She automatically glanced upward to check on the position of the sun. It was approaching or just beyond its zenith; almost half the day had passed while they'd been underground. One day only, she decided. She wasn't tired, as she would inevitably have been if they'd been trapped for more than a day without sleeping, especially considering the energy they'd used climbing out of the cavern system. No, there was no question about it. It *had* to be the same day. They couldn't possibly have been longer than that in the cave.

Sally felt slightly disoriented, but then this was completely unknown territory to her. They'd emerged close to the crest of a hill. By the time she'd brushed some loose soil from her clothes and checked the contents of her travel bag, Tom had bounded to the top of the hill and was looking around in every direction. Without so much as a glance at the sun, he stretched out his arm and pointed.

"That's the way we must travel."

"Is it? How can you be sure—" *That we're both going the same way* was the question she almost asked, but she stopped herself just in time.

Tom cocked his head with an amused expression on his face. "I've traveled these moors and hills often enough to know where I am, Sally, and also where and how I'll find shelter for the night in the turf-cutting season. The tunnel we followed must have turned and climbed. We've come out close to the cavern entrance, but on the northern side of the hill."

"So we can probably avoid poisoned rat carcasses, or more dangerous infected survivors with sharp teeth and claws," Sally interrupted, genuine relief in her voice. Perhaps

Tom had said all he felt he needed to say. He certainly didn't object to Sally speaking out, but turned to face west where higher hills topped with clouds hunkered to challenge them.

"We'll not need to climb them. At least, not to the top," he amended. "And we won't reach them before nightfall anyway, but I'm not even going to try. We have a few hours of good daylight left, and I know a family not far from here who have always proved friendly to me in the past."

He moved off down the slope with a practiced, effortless side-to-side rolling gait perfectly suited to swallowing mile after mile of rough, trackless countryside using a bare minimum of energy. Sally had to follow, or lose sight of him. There was really no decision to be made. Her chances of survival alone and unprotected in such unfamiliar surroundings were not good. Yet even as she lengthened her stride to catch up with Tom, a faint mean voice in some dark corner of her mind whispered that he had no right to assume the leader's role, or that she was ready to follow blindly wherever he went. She'd managed to look after herself for many years and valued her independence. The doubt at the back of her mind refused to go away, but she realized that for the moment, she depended on Tom's knowledge and skills, and he clearly had a definite destination in mind, somewhere safe. She was happy to tag along; the mean voice at the back of her mind felt wrong to her generous spirit and caring nature.

As she joined Tom at the top of the hill, their shadows fell onto a faint animal track, long and spindly, distorted by the sun's angle. The track meandered down the slope into a lush green valley where a glint and a sparkle suggested a stream where they could refill their water skins. The opposite side of the valley was too distant for her to spot a trail, but the gradient didn't look too demanding. They should be able to aim for a pass between the shoulders of two peaks.

The wind was at their backs. Sally was grateful, as it increased noticeably in strength before the first hour had passed. She hated to think how much more difficult the trek would have been if they had had to battle against a headwind as well as the slope and the uneven ground.

Whatever wild animal had made a track of sorts as far as the stream had apparently not been tempted to cross it. They were entering a trackless, untamed wilderness. Rosebriar and tanglethorn flourished all around, slowing their progress, forcing the choice between making a detour, or slashing a path through the undergrowth.

"This slope is steeper than it looked from a distance!" Sally grumbled as they paused to drink and catch their breath. She looked back, and was surprised to see how high they'd already climbed since fording the stream.

"The stiffest test is still to come" Tom replied. "The bushes and briars that have slowed us until now won't hinder us above this point, but the bare rock of the mountain can be treacherous, especially when wet. Be careful where you place your feet."

Sally picked her way carefully, but the sharp rocks began to trouble the bare soles of her feet and she had to stop and ask Tom for something to protect them. He rummaged and found a pair of skins he'd adapted at some time to fashion a boot of sorts. She leaned against a tree while she laced them up, and nodded. "Much better! I'll be able to make much better time now... Ah! Wait just a moment!" She gazed excitedly up at the tree. "Hoist me to the lower branches, Tom. This tree is a Mountain Balm; I can use its leaves and flowers to cure a number of maladies."

In seconds, she'd stripped half a dozen boughs of every leaf and flower she could reach; not one missed the gaping neck of her carry sack. She scrambled down with a sincere word of thanks to Tom for the loan of his broad, strong back, and tied off the bag securely.

"What will it cure?" Tom wanted to know.

"It can be drunk, and will lower a high fever, ease a cough, even warm a chill. It may be made into a paste and will reduce a swollen joint as well as prevent the stiffness that follows bruising. I've never heard of it saving anyone's life, but it's very useful for lots of minor injuries, and I haven't had any in stock for...oh, a long time, anyway." She fell into step alongside Tom and noticed at once that he seemed anxious, agitated. He glanced over his shoulder every few minutes until at last Sally could stand it no more. She stopped from one stride to the next and turned to confront him. "Enough of this! You're making me nervous, constantly turning around as if you think someone's chasing us, and I'm certain we'd make better progress if you stop doing it! What's the problem? Who or what are you afraid of?"

They had reached a point where the track they were following became easier to follow. A number of side trails merged with it and ran together following the easiest passage between two looming masses of granite almost completely shrouded in heavy cloud. The wind took on a further edge of sheer savagery as the broad flanks either side of the pass funnelled the wind and made it difficult for them to stand still. Sally had to place her ear close to Tom's blue lips to hear what he was saying.

"The strengthening wind could not have come at a worse time for us! Rain will surely follow the wind, and at this height, it might well turn to snow! At very least, even if it falls as rain, with the power of the wind behind it, it's going to hurt like the lash of a Roman slave master. I don't dare *think* of how much more dangerous it will be if we are caught in the open in snow!"

She nodded her understanding. Any attempt at conversation would have been impossible as well as exhausting. They turned to carry on, and as they did, the first stinging spray of rain arrived, striking them from behind, driving them forwards. It was mixed with sleet and could be felt even through the furs, which were soaked through in seconds, causing them to become twice as heavy.

Visibility was immediately hemmed in on all sides. Tom was leading at this point, and Sally realized there was a problem he was unaware of. She raised her staff and managed to poke him—none too gently—between the shoulder blades. "Tom, I can barely see you from here! Grasp hold of my staff or we may lose each other!"

Tom took hold of the toe of her staff. The staff itself was worn from being planted into rough ground on a thousand journeys over the years, fire-strengthened and smoothly sharpened for occasional use as a spear or other defensive weapon. This was the first occasion on which Sally had allowed anyone else to touch it. She hoped its magic would not wane as a result.

Tom took a small extra fur from somewhere about his person and indicated to Sally that she should bind his right hand to the end of the staff so he wouldn't lose his grip due to its smoothness. Using the force of the wind on their backs as the only clue they had for the present, they resumed their journey in what they hoped would prove to be the right direction.

Chapter Six

Sally never knew quite how they managed to fight their way through the remainder of that short winter's day on the lea slopes of the spine of mountains that divide the eastern counties of England from the west. When she thought about it, she realized that they must have escaped the worst of the wind and the accompanying sleet and rain. It was coming from behind them, and as they fought their way down the western slopes of the mountain range, the worst of the storm would be blowing over their heads without touching them. That was no doubt the truth, but only of small comfort to Sally, who thought she'd probably spent as much time on her arse or on her elbow as she had on her feet as they slipped and slid their way down the treacherous, icy slopes of smooth granite that gave them little or no purchase or grip for their feet or their hands.

Gradually, the slopes became less rocky, but beneath their feet now was a treacherous combination of liquid mud and slippery grass and vegetation, all concealed beneath a layer of sleet and snow, which was beginning to settle. After one fall that left them winded but unhurt, Tom managed to gasp in Sally's ear, "We are through the worst, believe me. We are sliding around on mud and grass. The mountains themselves are now behind us!"

"Tom, we are soaked to the skin. I swear there are even patches appearing in your woad! We've managed to get through the mountains, but unless we find some sort of shelter very soon, we're likely to die of exposure to the elements!"

Tom clung to Sally as if he were afraid of being blown off his feet. "The wind is not as strong now we are out of the pass. Can you not sense that for yourself?"

In truth, Sally had paid little attention to the weather conditions, but it was true. The sleet had turned back to rain and was not driving as fiercely now they were out of the funnel effect of the mountain pass. Visibility was also far better, particularly to the west, the direction they wished to travel.

Tom relaxed his grip and allowed Sally to take a small pace away from him far enough to focus on his face—and particularly his lips—but still close enough to hear whatever he said.

"We need to keep going before we freeze to the spot! But we won't have far to travel. I have a friend who scratches a living on a hill farm close by, if I can find the path in this filthy weather! Listen for running water—if you can hear it over the din of this storm! The stream will take the easiest way off the hill, and leads straight to the farm."

The rain continued to ease as they stood, ears at full stretch, seeking to hear the unmistakeable cadence of a flowing stream. Again, Sally forced herself to relax with her breathing mantra, forcing herself to concentrate. *Breathe in through the nose, out through the mouth...*

The rain had almost stopped. When she opened her eyes, she saw a dark line, unnaturally straight, a short distance away to their left. Silently, she touched Tom's shoulder and pointed. "Could that be a line of bushes or trees growing close to the stream?"

"Quite possibly, Sally. I think your eyes are sharper than mine. I'm not sure I would have spotted that if I'd been on my own."

Sally counted two hundred paces as they forced their way across the waterlogged mud. They had to go around a number of dangerous areas where the soil had dissolved and formed boggy ponds too deep to ford on foot. Within half an hour, they had reached the line of hardy bushes, which proved to line both flanks of a small stream currently bursting its banks with the runoff of extra water from the adjacent hills.

"This may not be the stream that leads directly to the farm," said Tom thoughtfully. "But even so, sooner or later it will join with another and together they will eventually lead us to my friend's farm or another farm in the area, and I have no doubt that we will be allowed to beg for sanctuary. I know the people who have chosen to live off the land in this region, and they are all good people who would not dream of turning a traveler from the door, even a stranger."

They crossed, as it could only become deeper and more difficult to negotiate further down the hill, and followed close to the flow, trusting it would eventually lead them somewhere.

The stream meandered down the hill, always following the line of least resistance, which made walking alongside it much easier. There was still plenty of light left in the day when they came to a small outcrop of trees, and the stream flowed directly through it.

"We should stay close to the water rather than take a long hike around the woods," Tom said in answer to Sally's unvoiced question. "We cannot tell how much time we might lose if we do not."

This sounded logical.

"Is it also possible that someone living out here might choose to build a home within the woods as a natural protection against the weather?" she asked, and was relieved at Tom's smile as he nodded to her.

"You think logically, and you are right. I've never come to this region from the east before, but I think I recognize where we are."

Sally was glad of the opportunity to stand and catch her breath. Although they'd been traveling steadily downhill, the uneven ground had made it treacherous in parts and demanded total concentration to avoid falls. She controlled her breathing—long, slow breaths to ease the sound of blood pounding in her ears—and while they rested, she concentrated on listening to the sounds of nature all around.

Suddenly, she heard a familiar call—the sound of the unseen bird she'd competed with in the forest at the start of her journey. It sounded close, and immediately, she mimicked its call as she had done previously.

"La-la-la-la la, la, LAH-LAH!"

The bird responded immediately, sounding louder, but whether it was closer to them or just angry, feeling challenged, was something Sally could not work out. She laughed at the reaction she had provoked in the bird, but her laughter dried when she saw the concern in Tom's glance.

"How did you do that?"

Tom's face was difficult to read at the best of times, mostly due to layer upon layer of woad applications, which seemed to flatten every conceivable facial expression into an impassive mask. Despite this, it seemed to Sally right now that he was displaying a mixture of emotions, none of them positive. Shock, fear, possibly even tinged with anger? Sally was confused.

"It was something that happened before we met..."

In a few brief words, she described her song-duel with her unknown competitor on the first day of her journey, and how it had led her to experimenting with inventing words to go with simple melodies. Tom nodded his understanding, and Sally felt a sensation of relief as she saw him relax and smile once more.

"For a moment, I thought you were displaying arcane witch powers, communicating with wild animals and able to command them to do your bidding, even to the point of ordering them to attack and kill others." He cackled.

Sally was about to reassure him that she would never dream of anything so wicked and unnatural when she caught a faint but unmistakeable call from somewhere further afield. She held her hand up to Tom for silence and listened, hoping it would be repeated. In her experience, this particular animal was *very* vocal, and most unlikely to make a single call without repeating itself.

"*Cock-a-doodle-doooo!*"

The unmistakeable clarion call of a rooster. Though some still lived in the wild, it was almost certain that this was the stud male in a flock of hen birds, and that in turn meant...

Without thinking, Sally cupped her hands to magnify whatever approximate reply she could make, and tried to reproduce the call.

The answer was immediate, and louder, but Sally had no way of determining if that meant it was closer. Tom, however, seemed certain of the direction and began to lead off, half-left and forward of their position on the bank.

A few minutes of struggle through the undergrowth of untamed woods brought them to a track of sorts. Sally knelt to investigate; immediately she found the cast of several different animals. In the gloom of the woods, and with rapidly fading daylight, closer identification was not possible. All she could decide with any degree of confidence was that they all appeared to head downstream.

"Then downstream we must follow!" cackled Tom, who now seemed to have recovered all his natural good humor.

Sally stopped occasionally and sent out a *cockadoodle* challenge; each time, it was answered, and before long they found themselves at the edge of a glade that had been extended by someone who had chosen this as a central point for a home. A pen could be seen, from which the strident challenge of the rooster that had led them this far could still be heard. From another small, windowless building came the muted low of a cow, probably uneasy because its sensitive nose told of an unfamiliar smell, the sweat of an unknown intruder close by. The largest of the buildings had to be where the smallholder and any family or co-workers ate and slept at night.

Tom turned to Sally. "Lend me your staff. I'll explain later, but for the moment, I want you to stand and say nothing unless someone addresses you directly. Not all communities regard women in such honor or with as much respect as my people do. Be guided by me, for your own safety."

Without waiting for a reply, he squared his shoulders and tramped off directly toward the house, swinging the staff authoritatively and calling aloud. Sally gathered her wits and her hemline and scurried to follow, dropping into a submissive—she hoped—role two or three footsteps behind him, as if she were a servant rather than a companion of equal status.

The door was opened by a man, taller than Tom and heavily built. He wore trews tied off at the knee and a short-sleeved vest top, but the feature that demanded the most attention was his enormous gingery beard, which barely allowed space for his mouth and eyes. His eyes flicked from Tom's diminutive form to Sally and back again in silence. He seemed to be waiting for Tom to begin the conversation.

"Hail, and good fortune on your house, friend! We are two travelers who have sore need of a corner in your meanest animal shelter for the night, and a chance to dry our soaked clothing. We have little to bargain with other than the poor skills that the Almighty in His wisdom had seen fit to grant us, and must beg of you to extend your charity for the night."

"You seem to have little in the way of clothing, traveler." The houseman's reply was slow but clear, and had a distinctive edge to it. His eyes were very expressive, and sparked with hidden humor as he continued. "Your manner of speech marks you, I think, as a Brigante, whom I know still prefer to wear woad and consider it clothing enough for most purposes. Yet, I see you travel with one who is not of your tribe. Come inside, I beg you, and remove your wet clothing. I'm certain we can find you some suitable attire to cover you modestly." This last word was spoken after the slightest of hesitations, and a direct glance in Sally's direction "And until the clothing is ready to wear, we can no doubt pass the slow winter hours with tales of your journey in these parts, or perhaps an exchange of news from near and far."

He stepped aside to indicate they were welcome to enter the main building. Tom made a point of leaving the staff he had borrowed outside the door, a practice which was generally accepted as evidence that the staff bearer carried no weapon into the host's dwelling. Sally had heard of this custom, but her infrequent and restricted traveling prior to her present journey meant that she had never seen it in use.

The dwelling was bigger than any of the houses in Sally's village, and was not divided into rooms, but there were areas of the open space that were clearly defined for cooking, for sleeping, and for everything else. The short wall of the rectangular building immediately opposite the single access and exit door was heaped with furs, evidently for sleeping. A cheerful fire blazed in the angle between the sleeping area and the longer wall on the left. This defined the cooking area, which generated warmth to the sleeping area without the danger of dripping live coals to start a disastrous fire in the night hours, while the occupants slept. Close to the fire, a woman Sally thought to be somewhat younger than herself was trying to feed a small child. The child seemed listless, uninterested in the food being offered. A moment later, when Sally heard a telltale cough, she knew exactly what was wrong with the child.

She caught Tom's eye. He too had heard the cough and was already turning to Sally to make sure she had not missed the sign. Remembering Tom's word to remain silent and speak only if spoken to directly, she nodded. Tom turned once more to their generous host.

"My fellow traveler, as you so rightly say, is not of the Brigantii people, but of another tribe who may be distant relatives of ours, the Parisii. She has already proved to me several times on our journey that she is a skilled healer, and also one who could probably charm the birds out of the trees if she had a mind to it. I myself have witnessed only a few hours ago how she called to a wild bird in the woods, and it responded to her immediately, following us through the copse of trees we left not far from your refuge. We are eternally grateful for your hospitality already, and would consider an evening of storytelling and an account of our journey to this point to be an extremely fair exchange."

Perhaps Sally made an unintended slight movement, or maybe Tom caught something of the distress she felt at the child's obvious discomfort. He paused a moment, then continued.

"As I said, amongst her people before we met, and on a number of occasions over the past two days, I have witnessed with my own eyes when she has treated both humans and also certain wildlife for illnesses, and seen them cured only a short time later. I am certain she recognizes the symptoms your child displays and knows how to cure it. Will you trust her judgement and allow her to demonstrate her knowledge of medicines and herbs? I have tasted some of her brews, and you have my word also that she is neither witch nor charlatan, but a woman wise beyond her seeming lack of years who can offer your child a swift and effective cure that will allow *both* of you a night of unbroken sleep. I have contributed little to our quest so far, and I will offer to stand watch over your child through the night if you will accept my companion's offer and allow the child to be treated."

Tom glanced briefly at Sally, and risk raising an inquisitive eyebrow. She nodded. There seemed little else required of her at that moment, and she was confident of easing the little one's bronchial problem. She had a good selection of powders and herbs with her should the host and his wife not happen to have one or more of the necessary ingredients on hand.

The eyes half hidden by beard were unmistakeably moist at the unexpected offer made with such freedom and confidence. There was a quaver in the host's voice that he strove to control as he replied, "Our daughter Rosann has indeed been unwell for several days. I am known as Simon, and my goodwife, Ellen. We would be grateful to know your names that we might include them in our prayers tonight and beg blessings on you both from above."

Tom glanced at Sally and spoke first. "My name is Tom, and as you guessed from my speech and my preferred travel wear, I am of the Brigantii. I met my travel companion while cutting the last turfs of the season before journeying home to my people, but I will allow her to speak for herself, for there is much we have yet to learn of each other. We have been traveling the road together for less than three days, and we have had little time to exchange family histories on the way."

"Tom of the Brigantii, our sincere thanks for this. But you must first divest yourselves of your sodden clothing, else I fear you may both become ill!" Ellen said firmly, lying the child in a half-sitting position amongst a banked pile of fur to prevent her from choking on the mucous rattling in her puny chest, making her every breath a struggle for survival.

Sally had become so accustomed to the dampness of her clothing she had almost forgotten how heavy and uncomfortable it was. She unlaced her fur boots and stepped out of them, wrinkling her toes with the pleasure of freedom for her feet. Until now, she hadn't even been aware of how tired and tender they had become during the long day's trek through the mountains.

She began to pick at the knots on her shoulder straps, but Ellen laid a restraining hand over hers and led her to a corner of the sleeping area furthest from the light of the open fire. She drew a small screen forward.

"You may stand here and disrobe out of sight of the men folk," she whispered. "I'm sure I can find a robe of my own, which you can wear until your own clothes are dry."

Living on her own for so long, Sally had never given conscious thought to questions of modesty or pride, but she had already guessed that their benefactors were a God-fearing couple with strong religious beliefs, and had a different view of the common temptations and failings associated with gazing upon another person in the vulnerable state of nudity. Not trusting her voice to express gratitude without bursting into tears, she nodded her thanks and accepted the armful of robes and other clothes Ellen brought out of a neatly stacked pile of feminine garments. A clean, rough towel was laid uppermost, and she used it to dry herself thoroughly before dressing. A comb fashioned from an unidentifiable bone of some sort took the worst of the tangles out of her hair, completing the transformation from sodden tramp to young lady.

When she stepped from behind the screen, she almost fell to her knees from laughter. After seeing Tom dressed in nothing more substantial than woad and loincloth for the past three days, she had somehow been unable to imagine what a few scraps of clothing might do for his overall appearance.

Tom had opted to remain barefoot, at least while they were indoors. Apart from anything else, none of Simon's footwear approached his size even remotely. His loincloth, one long continuous piece of material, hung to dry in several long loops. He had found one of Simon's vests with no sleeves. It hung almost to his knees, and made a search for further garments to cover his nether parts unnecessary. He was clearly uncomfortable wearing borrowed clothing several sizes too large for him. Sally had to choke back her laughter and attempt to put Tom at his ease.

"Simon, is there a chance Tom might have some hot water, enough to bathe? From the little he has told me of his people and the manner in which they clothe themselves, I guess that this would be his greatest desire at the moment."

Simon glanced in Tom's direction and nodded. Tom hopped and beamed, and was effusive in his thanks. Ellen had already placed a pot on the fire for Sally to use in mixing medicines. Now she added a few larger pots around the flanks of the fire to heat some for Tom's use.

"It is not far from the time I would bathe anyway, and if I am to apply a fresh layer of woad, I will have to scrub the old layer off first. If only you or a close neighbor had a steamhouse I could use."

Sally looked from her companion to their host and his wife, puzzled by the unfamiliar word. "Steam house?" she said, pronouncing it as two separate words. The image of a building with wispy, nebulous walls started to form in her imagination.

Simon shook his head with obvious regret. "I have heard tell of such things, but have no clear idea of what they are or how they are used. Perhaps you could explain for us, Tom?"

"The steamhouse is a sealed building that is heated slowly until water turns to steam. The steam softens your skin and makes it possible to scrape away all the dirt, and even deep-seated dyes such as woad can be removed if you sit in there long enough. It will also cure many illnesses, including stiff limbs and chest ailments."

"I regret such things are not possible out here far from any villages. My nearest neighbor lives to the west, directly on the line you wish to follow. It will probably take you at least a day and a half to get there. I will give you a token to bear with you, which he will recognize as coming from me. He will give you a courteous welcome and help you on your way."

Tom begged some cold fire ashes from Simon and sat just outside the front door while he scoured his body free of as much of the obstinate blue woad as he could. Simon took a rough cloth and began scrubbing the area in the middle of Tom's back, which he was unable to reach for himself.

Ellen drew Sally to one side and offered her the first pot of water, which was now simmering, close to a full boil.

"Perfect!" said Sally. "The water should not be allowed to boil. That would kill off many of the healing qualities contained in the plants and herbs I am going to use. Let me have a closer look at Rosann. I need an idea of what truly ails her and what combination of medicines I might use. I may need to ask you if you have certain things to hand, should I find myself short of supplies."

"Living out here, as we have chosen to do, we have learned to keep our supplies of medicinal herbs and such things in good order," Ellen replied. "What do you need?"

"I have arrowroot and comfrey to ease the discomfort. If you have some chamomile, it will help her sleep. But I think you said she cannot take solid food? Is that since she was taken ill, or is she too young to have started solids?"

"In truth, Sally, she will soon pass fifteen moons, but every time I try to give her something solid, her body rejects it."

"Then you are still breast feeding? You still have milk?"

Ellen's eyes flicked to the men, sitting and talking to each other on the far side of the room. She appeared slightly embarrassed at the question, but nodded silently in response. Neither Tom nor Simon had noticed anything so far, wrapped up as they were in tales of recent events in the wider world.

"With your permission, I will paint the medicine directly onto your breasts, and you can feed her in the most natural of all methods!" Sally exclaimed.

Ellen still looked embarrassed, Sally thought, but she took Rosann and turned her back on the room before loosening her gown. Sally now realized that their host and hostess had already shown that they were followers of the recently imported Christian religion that had been around since the advent of the Roman occupying forces. There was that strange tale the traveling priest had once told—of a man looking at a woman, and knowing it was wrong—and something about angels with fiery swords chasing both man and woman from a perfect garden? She'd never understood that, but if this new religion taught that looking at another with no clothes on was wrong, perhaps she wouldn't bother going next time the priest came round.

But you've already decided, you aren't going back, a certain non-Sally voice reminded her.

Well, maybe I won't bother going anyway, wherever I end up and whenever the priest comes calling, she told herself with an illogical feeling of satisfaction in not losing an argument with her inner emotions.

Rosann was hungry, and lost no time pumping the milk from Ellen's breasts, and with it, the medicine painted on her mother's skin. Sally repainted further doses on each breast as Rosann worked on the other, and when she let the nipple slip for the final time, she was already sound asleep. Her breathing had improved, as had her skin color. With a further glance at the men folk, who were still talking quietly, Ellen flashed Sally a tired but grateful smile and wandered over to the darkest edge of the sleeping area, furthest from the flames of the fire. There she curled her slim frame protectively around her daughter and they both slept.

When she wandered back to where the men were sitting, there was a further surprise awaiting Sally. Tom's deep blue loincloth had dried quickly, and he'd lost no time redressing in the manner he felt most comfortable.

By contrast, there wasn't the least trace of the woad coloring left on his perfectly scrubbed baby-pink skin. The incongruity of this was further enhanced by the solid, stiff, and unyielding blue curls on his head. His hair actually looked as if it had been sculpted and glued onto his head, almost as an afterthought.

Tom must have caught the gleam of mischief in Sally's eye because he turned to address Simon while she was still preparing in her mind a witty barb to fire at him.

"Simon, my new and valued friend, I fear I must try your patience and your charity with one last favor I would beg of you."

"Then go ahead. We have until now done little more than anyone would do for a traveler in poor weather!"

"When I roam this far from my village to cut turf, I carry few supplies, and never any of the sacred woad. Now I am obliged to ask you to spare me some cast off clothing, perhaps too small to fit you, for my protection on the road until I can anoint myself once more in woad. I have nothing I can leave in trust other than my word, but I shall soon return to arrange for the cut turf to be carried back, and I will make sure you have an adequate supply as token of my thanks. Once dried, the turf burns slowly, but it is also excellent for building walls and roofs, or repairing small holes where the winter's wind may come calling."

"The turf you speak of, dug from the moors and the wet bogland, is something I recognize. We call it peat. But I had never considered its possibilities as a building block until you named it. My neighbors and I will have to experiment with that idea when the sun returns. Your tribute I will gladly accept, but I believe your companion may have already earned your room for the night with her medical skills. If she has indeed cured our daughter's eternal coughing, I stand in her debt forever."

For all his size, Simon could move as easily and as silently as any cat. He slipped over to inspect the dark side of the sleeping area. He stooped briefly to kiss both sleepers and hesitated a moment further to check on Rosann's breathing before flowing back to his feet and leaving as gracefully as he had arrived.

"Powerful medicine, or perhaps a powerful healer?" he said with a sincere note of respect in his voice.

"The healing power of nature's own plants is all I ever use, and I was taught by a village elder, who received her knowledge in like fashion."

"And every healer I've ever met will sooner or later say something very similar." Simon laughed. "Why are you all so modest about your skills? I am just glad to see our daughter breathing easily, and my wife able to sleep alongside her. She has had little or no sleep for almost a full week."

"But we must travel onwards at day break, and need our own sleep," Tom said.

"I shall make sure that there is sufficient medicine for all of you before we leave," Sally added, rising to her feet and reaching for her gather bag.

"It is still possible that you may become infected by being so close to Rosann all the time. I will leave two portions—a strong one for yourselves, and a weaker portion for the child."

Brushing aside Simon's protests, Sally quickly prepared the two draughts of medicine and poured them into two jars of different colors to avoid confusion. By the time she stumbled toward the pile of furs in the last fading flames of the fire, Tom was sound asleep She sank, exhausted, onto the nearest corner, pulling at a loose fur until it almost covered her. She was asleep before she lay flat.

Chapter Seven

They were all up at first light, and Sally's first waking thought was to check on her patient. Rosann lay clear-eyed and smiling in her mother's arms. Her temperature had dropped to something acceptable and her breathing was clear, untroubled by wheezing or rattles. She was a different child altogether.

To escape from the effusive but sincere thanks of both parents, Sally scurried off to rummage in her bag for something interesting to add to their morning tea. When it was ready, the aroma from the pot filled the room and even masked the ever-present smell of smoke.

"What did you use this time?" Tom asked. "It smells really...healthy? Is that a word I can use?"

"It's as good as any other, I suppose." Sally laughed. "I used the last of my dried blackcurrants to sweeten it, and that plant is used in many different medicines. It will also give us plenty of stored energy, which we will need if we are to walk all day."

Simon had disappeared outside for a few minutes, and now returned with a jug covered with a clean cloth.

"The weather is holding. It may be cold, but there is little wind and no sign of rain-bearing cloud. I believe you will make good progress today, with good fortune possibly as far as one of the mining settlements along the banks of the Mersea river. You might even be able to ease your feet and beg or work for a ride down to the harbor at Birkenhead Priory, or the Sacsen village of Leverpole if you land on the north bank."

"You seem well informed of communities that are some distance from here, Simon. Have you ever made journeys of that distance yourself?" asked Tom.

"When I was much younger, before I even met the glorious Ellen, I roamed from Cumbria in the north almost as far as the old Roman settlement at Deva in the south. I hired myself to anyone who needed muscle and brawn for harvest time and other farming work, and learned all the skills I now use each day to live and work my own farm without relying on others, except possibly when it is time to reap wheat and other crops. I raise mostly animals, though, and I can manage them without hired hands." He pulled the cloth from what he was carrying to reveal a jug filled to the brim with sweet, frothy milk. "Still warm; less than five minutes ago it was still inside the cow!" he announced proudly. "It doesn't come any fresher than that."

Ellen filled four bowls with firm, plump strawberries. "They're still full of juice. They were the last of the crop. I picked them about ten or a dozen days ago, and there are never enough on the few bushes we have to be able to preserve them for the winter, so we might as well eat them before they start to dry and shrivel."

Rosann was given two large berries to suck or chew upon. She amused her captive adult audience by managing to smear most of the fruit on her cheeks, her clothes, and the furniture while at least giving the impression that she was genuinely trying to put it in her mouth.

"Is there anything you lack for the next stage of your journey? You will need to stop and sleep at least one night on the open heath, and that's if you're lucky."

"We don't want to carry more than we must," said Sally. "And our water containers are full. We can eat along the way, for the bushes are full of fruit. I sense the season is no further along here than in my home valley, and you also have the mountains to protect you from the east wind, which shortens our growing season."

"I would like to beg one thing," Tom said suddenly. There was a look of doubt in his eyes, as if he considered his request impossible to fulfil.

Simon looked at him with open curiosity, and nodded to encourage him to continue.

"I have never thought of this before, and if I had not been

traveling for a number of days with you, Sally, I might nev-er...yes, I'll keep to the point. He took a breath and addressed Simon. "I know a great deal about turf and its many useful properties, but until I met Sally and watched her use contain-ers and pots of different sizes for her medicines and other plants, I never thought about this." He paused again, and con-tinued slowly, "If it's possible to find a pot—an old one, even one with a few holes in it—that might even make it work bet-ter."

Sally's face was clouded with doubt. What use could there possibly be in a pot which had *holes* in it? Tom caught her expression, and treated her to one of his merry giggle attacks.

"It's alright!" he said when he had managed to control the fit. "It really is! And I'm pretty sure this idea of mine *will* work. What I'd like to try and do," he said, seriously, "is find a way to carry a couple of *live coals* with us on our journey. Then we can pause for something warm in the middle of the day if it gets really cold, or we can carry it all day and not have to start fire building from scratch every night. So I'm thinking of a pot—even one with holes in it—on the end of a strip of cloth, with a piece of turf inside it. If I swing it from time to time, like the boys who help the priests with some of the services, it will keep the coal glowing all day. I'm sure it would work."

He was so pleased with his idea he was literally hopping with excitement, and when neither Sally nor Simon raised any objection to trying the idea, he was beside himself with glee.

Building the simple idea took no time at all, and by the time Simon had knotted a lanyard securely around an old, cracked pot, Tom had pried a suitably-sized turf from the fire base, one with plenty of embers still glowing. Small sods to be used if necessary as extra fuel during the journey were secreted in some of the folds in his loincloth. With embraces and sincere good wishes all around, the travelers set off westward bound once more, refreshed from a good night's sleep and a better breakfast than they had expected, ready to face whatever the day might bring.

Chapter Eight

Ellen insisted on providing them with some travel fare as they stood outside the door and said farewell. These were the sort of things that took up little space but provided plenty of nourishment—dried apples, nuts, some cereal that she insisted would make a tasty porridge, especially if they could bargain or barter for some fresh milk along the way. Ellen's final contribution was of a more practical and personal nature.

Despite Simon's best efforts, it had proved impossible to find protective clothing remotely close to Tom's size. He was, quite simply, swamped in what he wore, holding up a pair of shorts that drooped past his knees. This was going to be a major problem and would hamper their speed.

Ellen took out a needle and thread, and in less than two minutes, had sewn in the waistband of the shorts so that they became a snug fit, then performed a similar miracle with a fur-lined vest. Tom's good humor was immediately restored, and he responded by blessing Simon and Ellen several times with the turf embers, mimicking the action of the priest using a censor during one of the Solemn High Feast Masses.

Tom's humor was infectious, and Sally found herself laughing as she danced rather than walked over the easy terrain that unrolled before them. Tom capered like a child with a new toy, but when she thought about it, the censor he was using to carry the coals was just that. And with his diminutive form, it was still sometimes difficult for her to remember that he was a fully grown man, almost certainly older than her despite his lack of inches.

The minutes flowed by as easily as a fast-flowing stream, and they made good time. Sally caught herself humming a melody as they tripped along, and once more, the words suggested themselves, this time inspired by Tom's antics.

Bless the flowers and bless the trees. Bless the birds and bless the bees.

Yes, she decided. She was quite pleased with that one. She'd have to remember it for another time, when she could sit down and work on it a little bit.

"Tom, Simon gave you a token of some sort to pass on to his farmer friend?"

"You were busy checking Rosann at the time, and I never thought to show you afterwards. Yes, I have it here, look." From somewhere in his borrowed clothing, he brought forth a short length of rope that had a pattern of knots tied along its length. "Simon told me that each of the knots has a special message to those who know how to read them. The advantage is, nobody else would ever know."

"So all we have to do now is find the right farm." Sally tried to sound encouraging, but even to her ears it sounded a bit of a flat statement, and she didn't think for one moment it would fool her companion.

"Simon must know this heath better than I do; he lives here all year round. He seemed certain that we would be spending at least the one night on the heath before we reach the farm, so we won't even see it before tomorrow."

"That's why Ellen wanted to make sure we had enough trail food for today. Look, she even gave us some cheese and bread. But I think the bread must be eaten today or it will spoil."

The trail got easier as it left the hills and wound down more gentle slopes toward the glint of a river running almost at right angles to their direction of travel. Tom had a word of caution for Sally. "For us to see the river from this distance, it has to be a wide stretch of water, difficult to cross without a boat or skiff of some sort. On the other hand, I think it can only be the Mersea, and we can choose not to cross it here, but follow it on the northern bank until it flows into the sea at Leverpole."

"And what then?"

"What do you mean, Sally? Neither of us can swim, and unless you had thought to try your hand at joining the crew of a ship sailing from the 'Pole, that is your journey's end."

"And what of *you*, Tom? Where does *your journey* end? How far out of your way have I dragged you already? Surely your people are counting on you to return with the fuel they need to see them through the winter months?"

"You're just like *all* women, I see!" Tom teased. "Full of questions, then you ask them all at once, and tell us men we never answer. I tell you, we never get the chance." His mischievous eyes, even deeper blue than his habitual woad, sparkled as he spoke, and robbed his words of any possible offense. He sat on a rock of convenient height from the ground, and nodded to Sally that she could rest on a nearby log. "If I am right, and the river we see close to our horizon is the Mersea, then our ways will continue to run together the rest of today. It might even be a good idea to make a detour this afternoon and head direct for my village instead of building a bothie for the night. It would not add a great deal to your journey tomorrow."

"How can you be sure of your directions? This heath looks exactly the same to me whichever way I look."

"I can't explain it. I just know somehow. Have you noticed how the same pair of swallows return from the south and take up the nest they built the year before, or even several years on the run? Perhaps it's something we heath dwellers are born with. We don't travel as far as they do."

Sally thought about this. Everyone knew that when the swallows gathered in huge flocks and disappeared to the south, winter was approaching. She had always assumed that the reason for them leaving was to follow the sun to somewhere warmer, and Tom's explanation sounded logical, fitting as it did with her own observations.

"In that case, I can only say I trust your home feeling, and I'll be happy to follow where you lead."

Tom swung his censor a couple of times to make sure there was still life in the turf ember, and was rewarded with a thin plume of sweet peaty smoke. He looked at the sun in the sky; it was past the zenith, well into the latter half of the day, but Sally suddenly realized that he wasn't checking the time of day. Somehow, he was using the position of the sun to help him decide which *direction* he should be heading to reach his village.

This would be a useful trick, if she could only learn how it was done. She had lived alone for many years. She valued her independence, and she had no wish to rely on someone else to avoid getting lost on her travels. But was it the sort of knowledge that could *be* learned? Perhaps it was an inborn race memory, passed from one generation of travelers to the next, impossible for an outsider to learn?

So many new, original thoughts, emotions she had not known existed, the skill of talking to birds—was it also possible to communicate with other animals? What a useful skill *that* would be!

Having observed Tom taking stock of his surroundings and checking one final time against the sky, Sally was very aware of the difference it made to their trek across the moorlands, slight though it was. The sun was still warm enough to be felt on bare skin, and she could sense that it was reflecting on a different area at the back of her neck instead of on her left cheek.

When they had walked the best part of an hour, Tom paused and appeared to sniff the air in the immediate vicinity. Sally tried copying his actions, but could detect nothing unusual. The heath undulated away to a vague horizon every way she looked. The delicate scent of heather—another very useful healing plant—was all she could smell.

She wondered just how far across the heath their paths would "continue to run together," as Tom put it. There was no obvious sign of any settlement to be seen, large or small, all the way to the horizon. On the other hand, Tom was now striding out with what could only be described as a more confident manner. She could only guess that he had recognized some small detail in what looked to her like a totally featureless landscape, something that told him exactly where they were. Could it be that they were now close to Tom's home, closer than even he had dared imagine?

Suddenly, he broke into a trot, increasing his speed to a dead run as he approached a mound that might have been slightly taller than its neighbor. At the summit, he began to swing the censor in full circles above his head, faster and faster until his muscles rippled with the effort and the contents of the pot flared into hot coals. Flames sprouted from the cracks, and a thick, dark smoke formed a perfect circle just above his head.

Panting, he placed the censor carefully on a flat rock at his feet, ensuring that there was no possibility of the extra flames catching on a tinder-dry sprig of heather. He turned to face west. From where Sally stood, he became a black silhouette against the low angle of the blood-red sun behind him. He raised his hands to form a natural soundbox, amplifying his voice. The sounds that came from Tom's—throat? Lungs? Somewhere else?—didn't sound like anything a human larynx ought to be able to produce, and seemed to last an impossible time. How could he make such a loud noise, and for so long without pausing for breath?

Sally was forcibly reminded of the moment Tom had, quite literally, popped out of nowhere to stand in front of her a few days earlier. Seeming to spring direct from amongst the heather plants where there was no cover, no possible hiding places, half a dozen replicas of Tom were, quite simply, there. Sally blinked, wanted to rub her eyes in disbelief, but was afraid the gesture might have been misunderstood. If Tom had been one of *seven* identical siblings, surely he would have told her this remarkable fact by now? She had to get a closer look. Almost unaware of her actions, she began to sidle closer to the strange meeting. She was still too far away to hear what was being said, and as it was most likely in their own local language, she probably wouldn't be able to understand it anyway, but she simply *had* to learn whatever she could from this first meeting between her companion and those he had referred to as his people—often, and with self-evident pride.

As she approached, she became aware of subtle but distinct differences in the appearance of each of the apparitions. They were all of similar build to Tom, but even at a distance of maybe twenty-five or thirty yards she could now see differences in age, in posture. It was almost certainly the complete coverage of their wiry, muscled frames with the shocking blue woad that gave them the illusion of being identical. She'd led a fairly sheltered life, in a part of England rarely troubled by marauders, but she could still imagine what it would be like for any force of ordinary men facing a horde of screaming blue-painted demons, all identical, all running at you straight from the depths of your worst nightmare.

As she stood and gaped, there was another unexpected development. When they rose from nowhere, each of the woad warriors carried a weapon—a spear inches taller than himself, each with a cruel-looking, well-honed metal head.

Tom ended his short speech to them. With one accord, they all dropped to one knee and grounded their spear tips in salute. Tom seemed to have some authority over them, which they appeared to acknowledge without question. Again, he swung the censor over his head a few times, releasing another trail of smoke. Within the censor, the embers flared up briefly and settled to a healthy, all over cherry glow. The experiment had worked.

Now, he caught Sally's eye, judged where she had paused, and glanced briefly at where she had been standing. He smiled at her, and her heart skipped a beat as she recognized the same fervor in his gaze he had shown her when they had made love that night in the cave. Now she understood why the unnamed traveler from the north had described the experience as "laughing together." Would they have the opportunity to repeat the thrill of the ride to ecstasy and beyond before their paths must part? Deep inside, she knew that this must happen all too soon, and for one moment, she asked herself if she would be prepared to end her journey here, and stay with him—that was, assuming he might consider asking her...

Tom relaxed, and made a soft, courteous gesture, inviting her to come and stand at his side. "I have traveled the last few days with a companion, a skilled medicine woman named Sally. Tonight we will feast in her honor, and recount the tale of our travels together!"

The six almost-lookalikes instantly formed an honor guard around them, and at the same instant, another thirty or more sprang up in an outer circle and closed ranks, ready to march on Tom's command.

"By what magic do you command your people to appear?" she murmured to Tom, keeping her voice low enough to ensure that the conversation was private. The preparations to move off were almost complete, and she was afraid he might not have time enough for a proper reply.

"There is no magic in it, Sally, just an ability to be one with the heath upon which we live and depend upon for what we need in life."

The expanded numbers had formed into half a dozen reasonably straight lines and were now facing a few points north of the setting sun on the western horizon. With a silent gesture from Tom, who was still using Sally's staff as a symbol of office, they all moved off in silence at a steady, ground-eating jogtrot that was considerably faster than the formal tempo of an army cadre. As an added plus, Sally soon discovered that the springy, tough heather was flattened by the passage of at least three pair of feet before she trod in them herself. In fact, the minimum effort she had to expend herself to place one foot in front of the other was helped along by the faint pressure of the heather, recoiling to regain its natural shape and form close to the ground. The miles sped by, and as the last light of day leaked from the sky, Tom stopped and repeated the same impossibly loud wordless call he had used earlier.

The response was different this time. The glow of perhaps as many as a hundred small fires lit up the base of a roughly circular natural dip in the landscape immediately before them, and the tantalizing aromas of roasted meats along with other foods being cooked rose directly from the cooking fires to greet them.

"The fastest runners peeled off even before we moved away from our last stop. Many scouts have kept track of us since the morning we left the cavern. My people are prepared for us. Now, let us see what delicacies they choose to offer on my return."

Chapter Nine

Sally felt her gastric juices reacting to the scent of food cooking, and hoped the sounds she could clearly hear were not loud enough to attract the attention of the honor guard that surrounded them.

The travelers were led off to one side just before reaching an open space where the feast was set. Tom showed no surprise or protest, so she followed his lead.

They were led to a stream, which widened and deepened at one point to result in a pool, roughly circular and about three body lengths across. When Tom smiled and began unfastening the clasps holding together his borrowed clothing, she realized the purpose of the detour.

"A bath!" she purred, following Tom's lead with enthusiasm. Even the thought of cold water on her skin didn't dampen her pleasure.

The water was clear, and she could see the smooth, pebbly base. The current flowed over it, carrying no trace of mud. This had been carefully lined with stones to keep it clean...and the water was *warm*! Not a great deal above skin temperature, perhaps, but enough to make it a pleasure to stand in mid-stream and enjoy the luxury of running water caressing her skin as it flowed, turning the simple process of bathing into a truly pleasurable experience.

She turned to Tom with a question on her lips. He seemed amused at her reaction, and laid a reassuring hand on her now-bare shoulder.

"The water flows direct from a separate source to that which we use for all other purposes. It's one of the reasons we keep the location of our settlement hidden, because if our neighbours knew of this, we'd be in constant dispute for the right to live here."

"The water flows from a crack not far from here, and is always warm, even in the coldest months of the year. Snow and ice may be all around, but never form in a wide area either side of the hot stream. It has a certain bitter taste to it, and I don't recommend you drink from it. Still, it doesn't do any harm. Many of us have swallowed the odd mouthful without coming to grief, but it's bitter nonetheless!"

"Do you know how...?"

"How it is heated? No, not really. Some say it must lead from the lair of a dragon, but if that were so, the beast would need somewhere to enter and leave his lair, and we've never found any cave or other hint of an opening to an underground chamber, so I think it unlikely a dragon is involved—unless it's a truly magical creature that can pass through a solid stone wall at will to get in or out, which I think is unlikely."

"Where does the water flow to from here?"

"Very good, Sally. You think of such things, such practical matters, which many would never consider." He beamed, and continued. "We have done some minor digging, and led the outflow to join our main supply stream beyond the settlement in order to keep our drinking water clean and safe."

She stepped further into the pool, where it was deep enough to cover her as far as her breasts, and allowed a pair of naked young girls to apply sweet smelling liquids to her skin and hair. It was an unaccustomed, luxurious feeling to have another attend to her in this manner, like a queen or other important female whose least wish was treated as a command.

She felt the tiniest pang of regret when her ministrants took her by the elbow and escorted her out of the pool, scrubbed cleaner than she could ever remember being at any time in her life. They led her back to the bank of the stream. Someone had thought to provide a selection of garments for her to try on, and she was soon dried off and freshly dressed in long robes that clung seductively to her body, touching her in all the right places but allowing her the freedom of movement she needed to be at her ease.

Two spaces had been reserved in the circle where the

welcome feast had been set out, and as soon as Tom appeared with Sally's hand resting lightly on his arm, the crowd fell silent, waiting for his word.

"My friends, my Brigante tribesmen, hear me! I left you some time ago to cut and store the turf we need for the months ahead, and I return with a companion, a wise woman skilled in the lore of medicine and healing. Sally by name, and mayhap a distant relative, for she is of the Parisii tribe east of the Dragon's Spine. She has helped me many times in the few days we have traveled together, and is under my protection while she is our guest. She may have time to answer questions regarding health tonight or tomorrow morn, but she is on a longer journey, and I have said my people will be glad to offer what assistance is possible. Now, let us eat and be thankful!"

The standing crowd responded by saluting with the open palm of their right hand placed across their hearts. Sally had to think for a moment before she realized that she had seen this form of salute in pictures of the invaders from Rome who had run most of the country for many years before returning to their native land, leaving behind most of the major roads that were still in use hundreds of years after the breakup of the largest single empire the world had ever known. She wondered if the Brigante tribe were even conscious of where their salute came from. Probably not, she decided. Her own people had only very sketchy memories of the Roman times, passed on by word of mouth and probably much altered over the years.

A small group gathered close around Tom as the meal came to an end. Sally thought these were likely to be the more important people in the community; they all seemed older than her, though the ever-present woad still made such judgements uncertain. Tom's lack of blueness didn't seem a problem, as he conducted himself with the ease of an accustomed leader amongst equals, and he took control by referring to his current state with a slightly self-mocking sense of humor.

"My people, I thank you for welcoming me home in such a warm fashion, especially in my current state of undress! I will perform the sacred woad ceremony tomorrow, but in a few words I can tell you how I was forced to alter my appearance to such an extent that your scouts on the borders of our land failed to recognize me until I was close by."

Briefly, he recounted the details of their joint journey thus far, and although Sally thought he made too much of her contributions, she was gratified to see the positive response his account inspired in all who sat close enough to listen. Around them, she was vaguely aware of small groups settling to provide song, dance, and other forms of entertainment. Storytelling seemed to be a strong favorite, to judge from the number of groups who chose to sit in silence at the feet of a single speaker. She noticed that many of these seemed to describe the story they were telling as much with hand gestures as with words.

A light touch on her arm, and Sally realized that her attention had wandered. In fact, she was fairly sure she might have dozed off. Tom's familiar, deep blue gaze held a touch of concern as he asked, "Are you alright?"

"I...think I must be more tired than I thought," she admitted.

Tom nodded, and clapped his hands. Two females stood and approached, helping Sally to her feet.

"Our honored guest is tired. Please show her where she may rest tonight." He paused, then turned and spoke directly to Sally, but in a tone of voice that suggested that he was addressing the rest of the group through her. "I shall use the remainder of this evening to prepare myself for the Ceremony of the Woad, which is central to our beliefs and customs. I regret not spending the night in your company, but as you are tired, I hope you may forgive my absence. I will feel the pain of our parting tomorrow far less if I am able to offer you my blessing on the next stage of your journey in our traditional manner."

Sally felt a serious inner conflict. Her sensible, thinking brain insisted that this was the most logical way to round off what had been a long, tiring day of non-stop travel. Her heart was screaming for the caring touch of this diminutive colossus of a man who had awoken a range of emotions in her that she had never thought to experience.

Her body had the final say. Her head felt suddenly as heavy as a giant pumpkin, and she all but fainted into the supporting arms of her aides. As they led her slowly to a small building away from the laughter and song of the continuing party, the last thing she was conscious of was the

anxious concern in Tom's eyes as he watched her all the way
to the door.

It was neither sound nor light that roused Sally, but an
inner survival instinct, the result of so many years fending
for herself that ensured the transition from deep sleep to fully alert was made from one breath to the next. The merest
trace of a cooling whisper of moving air caressed her cheek,
suggesting that this could easily have disturbed her rest. She
continued to lie still, feigning sleep, a ploy that had certainly
saved her from rape, abduction, and possibly worse on more
than one occasion.

There was a suggestion of a scratch or creak, which could
have been a timber easing its position in a fitful wind, or the
incautious movement of someone in the room. Sally turned
once more to her tried and trusted breathing mantra, forcing
her nerves to attune to the tempo of her heartbeat, and
reached—it was the only word she could use to describe what
she did. Her hearing became super-sensitive as she imagined
her ears lengthening, quivering, straining to identify any
sound however small that didn't belong in the room. By now,
her eyes were half-opened, searching the part of the room she
could see as she lay on her side.

The instant there was a blur of slow, surreptitious movement at the edge of her field of vision, she was ready. With a
tiny *yip* of ferocity, she raised her knees under the sheet,
connecting hard enough to drive the wind out of her assailant. Continuing the same fluid movement, she flung her
body off the bed and wrapped a long tress of her hair around
something that felt like either a wrist or an ankle, trapping
whoever dared invade her privacy. To be attacked now, in
the first place she had thought to be truly safe since her
journey began!

"Peace, I beg you!"

The greatest shock so far.

"Tom? Oh, Tom, what have I done?"

"My pride has taken some injury, Sally, but nothing more
important."

"You said you would use the night for preparation!"

"And so I did, my sweet. The first glimmer of dawn is in
the east, and the night is almost over. Open your eyes fully
and look at me."

Sally did as she was bid. Tom turned and murmured a

few sounds that meant nothing to Sally, but when he added a few passes with his free hand, the embers in the fire bed glowed and burst into flame, illuminating the room and its occupants.

Tom was restored to his preferred smooth and seamless covering. He was such a bright blue Sally thought it deserved to be given its own unique name to honor the first time this exact shade of blue had ever been seen anywhere in nature.

"I could not bear for you to leave at sunrise, perhaps never to return, without speaking to you. If I had known more of the fighting qualities of the Parisii women, I might have approached the intended meeting a little differently."

Tom was still technically her prisoner, as his wrist was tightly wrapped in her hair. Sally released it with a smile, and kissed the back of his hand, running her tongue over each knuckle. When she reached the last joint, she looked up, directly into his eyes, and breathed, "I can tell you the answer to your question now, Tom. Your freshly-applied woad has no special taste, or not on the back of your hand, anyway..."

"Are you still decided that you will not return from this journey?"

Curled as she was in the arms of the only person who had ever shown her any affection, Sally found that she was without words, and not entirely because she was exhausted from the unplanned but very welcome time of "laughing together" she had enjoyed with Tom. She had no wish to walk away into the unknown, on her own once more, but she had to be honest with him. An insincere promise was not the way to build any relationship, especially if she wanted it to develop into something permanent. Yet, something warned her that there was a purpose to her quest, something she had yet to learn, but something she sensed would prove a watershed in her life. With a gentle kiss, she pushed herself away from him until she was half-sitting in the bed and could focus on his face in the flickering firelight.

"You have made a lonely girl into a happy woman, Tom, but I feel that there is some purpose to my journey, something that has yet to be revealed to me. I must continue, at least until I reach the west coast. You have already hinted to me that I have not a great deal further to go in order to achieve that."

Reluctantly, it seemed, Tom nodded, perhaps sensing Sally's line of thought. "This, then, is what I feel I must do, and I hope you will understand. Once I have reached the town of which you spoke—Leverpole?—and spent some time there to find out what is driving me to carry on my quest, I will either return here or make sure a message is carried to you before the next full moon. You are the only person who has ever shown me kindness and consideration, Tom, and I believe we could be happy together, but there is something unresolved in my stars, and I swore by all the gods there may be that I would do my best to discover what it is. Can you accept that?"

As well as being a difficult thing to say, this was probably also one of the longest speeches Sally had ever made. Tom bowed his head briefly, but when he raised it again, there was still that devil-may-care glint of humor in his eyes. "I would never force my worst enemy to stay if he wished to leave, and I can find no reason for treating you any less fairly than that," he answered. "So, perhaps it is best we break our fast, and I will arrange for a detail of my people to escort you as far as the river, and make sure you can get safe passage on a vessel of some sort heading downstream. There is no good reason I can think of for allowing you to tire yourself by walking the remaining distance."

Relieved to see that Tom was prepared to take his disappointment stoically, Sally had just one further thought. "Tom, the token Simon gave you to be passed on...?"

Tom smiled once more, this time a smile with a hint of self-satisfaction or even smugness to it. "Not forgotten, dear one, not by me anyway, and it pleases me to know that you also have the gift of being able to think of others as well as yourself." He nodded to where his loincloth still lay in a heap with her clothes at the foot of the bed.

"I used the rope as a belt on the trews I wore yesterday—Ellen's stitching was good, but they had begun to loosen by the end of the day and needed some assistance to stay in place. My scouts have already told me that the farmer concerned *is* the one I was thinking of. At the moment, he is using some good grazing land for his horses, hard against the Mersea's banks. We can deliver Simon's message, and ask about river transport for you at the same time."

Breakfast was a short affair that day, without even the time set aside to heat a warm drink, which Sally did not like. She was accustomed to the first drink of the day being a hot one, and missed the few moments of reflective silence she always enjoyed while drinking whatever infusion happened to take her fancy.

"I need to allow time to get my men there *and back* on one day, if it is at all possible," Tom explained patiently when Sally asked him why the rush. Now it was Sally who felt obliged to apologize. She hadn't considered the practical problem of walking there, resting the company of men, and returning on the same day. She, on the other hand, could relax in the luxury of being a non-paying passenger on a boat floating downstream with time to rest and recharge her energy before embarking on a new stage of her quest, one which at the present was both unknown and unknowable. Should she be excited or terrified by this? There was no way of telling, at least not at this very moment. But the least Tom deserved some encouragement, a happy memory of her to hold during the cold winter nights that were fast approaching.

Before she could blink, four Brigantii appeared at the door of the building where they had broken their fast. Sally thought it might be a communal kitchen, as it was all on one level and appeared to contain nothing other than the kitchen itself and a number of long tables with benches. She was fairly certain they were young, a fact born by their conscription of the power required to take up long shafts and pull a two-wheeled cart, in which she was apparently required to ride with Tom as her companion on the way.

Tom waved back at the community as they reached and rounded the first gentle bend on the road, cutting off their view of those left behind, then concentrated his attention on the road ahead. These might be relatively peaceful times, it was true, but there were still odd bands of bandits roaming the countryside, and the four young men pulling the wagon would be defenseless if he failed to keep a weather eye open for every possibility.

Chapter Ten

As they left the tribe's unique half-buried lodgings and headed west, Sally realized that they were now following the first distinct track she'd been able to make out since they began crossing the heath

The bogland had firmed considerably. It was now more like the solid ground she was accustomed to in the Dales, and easy to follow. She had to assume it was made by human rather than animal traffic, and used far more frequently than the much fainter trails they had attempted to follow further east.

The cart ran smoothly, and the enthusiastic young men between the shafts made light of their task, laughing and joking as they ran. The miles fled swiftly past. Tom took his responsibilities as lookout seriously, swaying with an easy balance as he constantly scoured the way ahead for any sign of potential trouble.

After a short while, Sally felt bold enough to clamber to her feet and join him, one hand on the coaming of the wagon, the other wrapped around Tom's waist. Tom's reaction was to clasp his arm firmly over hers and return the secretive embrace. The only drawback to this arrangement was that they were in full view of a number of people on every side, and thus unable to caress each other in a more intimate fashion. A few miles on, Sally suggested that they might sit down and conceal themselves long enough to exchange a few more leisurely kisses in relative privacy.

As they slid below the rim of the cart—and, for the moment, out of sight from the runners and the rest of the vanguard—Tom suddenly put one hand across his eyes and winced in pain. An involuntary tightening of the muscles of the hand around Sally's arm made her aware of his discomfort.

"Tom! What's the matter? Are you in pain?"

"Nothing more than a sudden ache behind my eyes, Sally, together with a touch of dizziness. Give me a moment and I'll be fine again, I'm sure."

She placed her hands tenderly on his cheeks, cupping his head firmly as she gazed into those wonderful blue eyes, but this time with the dispassionate concern of a healer. Even the whites of his eyes had a tinge of blue to them, a blue which deepened as it reached the iris. The black pupil in the very center of each eye seemed extremely small by comparison.

As she studied him, the pupils of both eyes changed suddenly to a vertical lens shape, splitting the iris from top to bottom for a few long seconds before reverting to their small, perfectly round shapes. Had she imagined it? She didn't think so. From memory, the only time she had noticed this distinctive lens shape in nature was in the eyes of the few semi-domesticated cats she had been asked to cure, usually in an attempt to appease a tearful child who had become attached to a family's mouser.

She continued to assess what she could of Tom's general state of health. His skin felt dry, too dry, especially for one who had so recently been anointed with a crushed seed mixed with oil product such as woad. If anything, she thought, his skin ought to feel damp, even greasy. He was also too warm to the touch for her liking, and his body had not produced the sweat reaction she would have expected in anyone running even a slight temperature. This was another symptom she could not explain or ignore, and because she couldn't do so, she grew steadily more and more concerned for Tom. What if he were really sickening with something serious? Would she have the skills, the knowledge, and the drugs or equipment to cure him?

It was only now that Sally realized there was a problem with her usual method of checking on a patient's condition. This was particularly the case if she was going to have to check Tom for any signs of the mysterious ailment that had laid her low, though she would never begin to guess just how close to death she had been. How was it going to be possible for her to check Tom's skin for any discoloration or telltale bruising against his deep blue skin? There was simply no possibility of any blotches or other signs being visible.

She thought furiously—bruising, tenderness, swellings...what else was there to guide her?

"Tom, listen to me! Do you have any sore places, in the joints, perhaps, a tender area on your body you hadn't been aware of before? Any lumps or swellings? Particularly if it's something that has shown itself suddenly, within the last few days, with no apparent cause. Think, Tom. This could be very important!"

The perpetual light of humor in Tom's eyes, which Sally had thought until now was an essential part of his very nature, seemed to have died. His tongue rasped dryly across his lips as he attempted to speak Automatically, Sally reached into a corner and found a waterskin. She moistened all around his mouth while he summoned the energy to put his jumbled thoughts into words. He took the skin in both hands and gulped greedily for several seconds, then nodded his thanks.

"Sally, it sounds to me as if you have a particular illness in mind. You have just described everything I would have told you about how I feel right now. How is this possible?"

"Tom, it's possible you may be smitten with the same illness as I had; the symptoms are very similar, if not the very same. I was lucky. As a medicine woman, I had the knowledge and the skill to heal myself, but sadly, I was unable to prevent the deaths of many others in the village where I used to live."

Sally's eyes moistened; she bore down ruthlessly on the tears that threatened to choke her and shook Tom gently to gain his full attention. There was a glazed, distant look in his eyes she didn't like. "Tom, listen to me! I managed to cure myself by a combination of luck and some knowledge of plants and healing. Some of the signs are bruises, swellings, and discolorations on the skin, but I cannot tell if you have any because of the woad you wear. I have a blending of the herbs and essences I used on myself, but your body is going to want to resist them. It will be necessary for you to sleep while the medicines take effect. It's vital that someone stand watch over you, day and night, while your body is defenseless. Do you understand?"

"Sally, will you not—"

"No, Tom, I could not trust myself to do that! Once you are asleep, there is nothing I can do to change the course of events. The medication must be allowed to fulfil its natural function. My presence would make no difference at all to that, and I have not the strength of will to stand idle and watch your body fight for survival. I have sworn an oath that I will see my quest through to its end, whatever that might be. I must see it through. I sense there is a purpose to it that has yet to reveal itself. There is...something that tells me that my journey is not yet over."

She lay on the bed of the wagon and put both arms around his shoulders as they swayed onwards.

"Until we met, Tom, there was nothing that would have persuaded me to think about returning along a path I have already traveled. Most of the people I knew—possibly all of them—are dead, and I've lived alone for far too many years. Yet this much has changed for me, after meeting you. Once I have reached the coast, and this town you mentioned..."

"Leverpole," Tom added as she hesitated. He was weakening rapidly, Sally thought; speaking the single word cost him some considerable effort.

"Leverpole," Sally repeated, as if tasting the word for some subtle flavoring. "Tom, I promise this. Unless I find a very good reason to remain in Leverpole, I now have a choice that you have made possible. I am willing to retrace my steps as far as I need to in order to find you and your proud people. I will find a way to send a message to you through your farmer friend, either by delivering it personally or through a trusted message carrier. You shall have my message by the next time the moon has run her race 'gainst the sun, showing her full face."

Tom's eyes were still clouded. Sally sensed he wasn't hearing all she said, and she had grave doubts about how much he understood or could take in. She untangled herself and staggered to her feet. This was only possible because the wagon was moving at quite a sedate pace as the two-man yoke team had been trotting for... Sally looked at the sun. For some time now. She still wasn't very good at judging the passage of time.

They must be getting tired, she thought. Time for a

change. She put two fingers in her mouth and whistled once sharply. The vehicle came to an immediate, shuddering stop, and even the Brigantii on the outer rim of the honor guard, which seemed to swim or glide through the heather rather than walk or run, heard the blast from Sally's lips and stopped dead in their tracks.

"We need to speed along. Tom has taken ill!"

She had barely finished speaking when four of those closest to the wagon had replaced the two who had been between the shafts for the first part of the journey. The shafts were long enough for them to be able to pair off without treading on each other's heels, and Sally felt the increase in speed as soon as they started off. The fresh volunteers found an efficient pace and rhythm within seconds.

Tom was still conscious, and Sally was reasonably sure he was still aware of what was happening around him, but his breathing was becoming labored and his eyes were bloodshot. The woad prevented her trying to judge his health from other natural signs such as skin color. As she gazed out, scanning the horizon for any sign of their destination, Tom tugged at the hem of her dress to catch her attention. She was on her knees, giving him her undivided attention immediately, cradling his head on her elbow.

"You must remember to give this token to...Simon's friend, once we reach the farm." He pressed the length of knotted rope into her hands. "This person does not know me personally, though I have traveled across his lands many times. He may not be inclined to offer assistance to a stranger. We cannot take anything for granted; there is much unrest in the land at the moment."

Sally took the water gourd and helped Tom to sip at it. "You must promise me that you will do exactly what I tell you now."

"I'm listening."

"Good. The medicine I've prepared was in case I needed it myself, if the disease returned. It cured me, and I believe it will work for you too, but it is a mild poison and your body is going to fight it. That is why you must sleep through the healing period, and I have another medicine that will help you to achieve that."

"And I suppose it probably tastes foul, too." Tom's sense of humor had not deserted him, not yet, anyway

"You're going to need all the humor you can find to come through this, Tom. Yes, the medicine does taste vile. It was all I could do to choke it down, but I believe you will do it. It's the only thing that will save you, if you have indeed caught the disease from me."

A call from one of the free running Brigantii had Sally back on her feet in an instant.

"There is a building of some sort, hunkering close to the bank of a river up ahead of us, Tom. Can we have reached the farm we seek so quickly?"

Tom was back on his feet, perhaps a shade more slowly than usual, but for the moment, at least he appeared to have shrugged off any sign of his health problems. His eyes were clear as he scanned the horizon.

"That is the farm. There can be no doubt. Send our fastest runner to announce our arrival," he called to one who jogged alongside the cart, clearly waiting for instructions.

Sally stood behind Tom, using her whole body to support him lest he stagger and reveal his weakness, something she sensed he would do anything to avoid.

Where they seemed to have traveled fast and light earlier in the day, the final miles seemed to drag. Despite his attempt to put on a brave face, Tom was unable to remain on his feet for long, and slumped back to the corner of the wagon as the young bloods pulling them redoubled their efforts and the wheels spun faster.

They had covered perhaps half the remaining distance when a call came from a sharp pair of eyes far ahead of them. Sally's eyes were good, but even so, it was a few minutes before she could make out a plume of dust that grew against a cloudless sky, thickening by degrees as it approached at a speed that was far in excess of the fastest runner. A dark smudge at the center of the cloud solidified as it came closer, but it remained unidentifiable until it was within perhaps five hundred paces of the travelers—a human figure perched upon the back of a horse.

He made no attempt to slow down until he was within twenty or thirty paces of the cart, but skidded to a stop under full control of his steed when it seemed a full speed, disastrous collision was inevitable. He leapt sideways from the horse's back, holding the reins lightly in his left hand. Sally noticed that he spurned the use of either saddle or stirrup, and had apparently ridden at a breakneck speed to meet them without needing anything more than the reins to guide his mount.

"Your envoy, your runner, messenger, call him what you will! He said that you were on your way, and had need of assistance for someone taken ill?"

There was the slightest of inflections on the final words, making it sound as if a question was being asked. Since Tom was suffering another bout of wheezed breathing, and nobody else seemed willing to respond, she found herself elected spokesperson by default.

"The leader of this group, who took me under his protection when I was in sore need, has become ill. We have traveled far together, but our acquaintance is still new, and this morning he told me that he knows you by reputation only, and in all likelihood, you do not know him. That is why we were given this token by someone else who knows you both. I am assured it contains a message that you will recognize, but your mutual acquaintance has not told us what that message is, only that he hoped it would make our journey easier if we chanced to meet you on our quest."

For a moment, Sally cursed herself. Until now, she had deliberately avoided using the term "quest" in speaking of her journey with others, and she hoped her momentary lapse in using the more formal term might go unnoticed. Nobody reacted, as far as she could see, and she breathed easier.

Don't let that happen again! she scolded herself. It might not be so easy the next time. *If there* is *a next time,* she added, still chiding herself mentally. All this had happened in the blink of an eye, and she found herself leaning down from the cart to pass the knotted length of rope to the horseman. Before placing it in his hand, she straightened slightly and waited until she had the rider's full attention and her gaze locked on his.

"The person who entrusted us with this token assured us that only the person for whom it was intended would be able to read its message. You have shown that you are a person of honor by riding as you did to offer assistance. However, we are still strangers, and I would ask you therefore if you are the person to whom the message ought to be delivered?"

The horse nickered, as if it understood the question and had found something disturbing in it. The rider patted the side of his mount's neck lightly, and nodded his approval of Sally's caution.

"We rarely chance the featureless, trackless heath to the east, and there is but one person I know who does. He lives in the shadow of the mountains and has red hair—some would call it rust-colored, due to the amount of rain that falls on him and his demesne each and every day. His name is Simon, and as he has sent you with a token, he will not have told you my name. Therefore, my lady, know that I am called Bryn, and I would not hesitate to offer what help I can to any traveler, sick or hale, who asks for it."

"We are grateful. It was indeed Simon who gave us this token, and at the same time, a warning that there are still many who are wary of the habit of admitting one's name to a stranger. I return your trust by giving my name—Sally. The person who has fallen ill is the leader of this group, Tom of the Brigantii."

"Here is our first mystery, I see, for you are most certain-ly *not* of the same tribe, yet you say you have traveled to-gether for some time. But that must wait. How ill is your pa-tient?"

Sally was unprepared, and thought for the moment that this Bryn person might have arcane knowledge, a soothsay-er, a wizard of some sort. "How could you ...?"

"Know that the patient was close at hand? Why would a tribe such as the Brigantii wish to use a wheeled cart, unless it was to transport either someone who is unable to walk, or possibly for heavy goods? And at the speed you were travel-ing, you aren't carrying heavy goods, not in a single cart. Many wagons would be needed if goods were being trans-ported, either to build a new home, or to trade at a market."

"You judge wisely, Bryn! We will speak of this later, but our first concern is for the patient, Tom. Come, I will intro-duce you."

Tom's condition had worsened, and it was obvious that he was in some pain. There was little that could be done oth-er than to find a few scraps of clothing to keep him warm for the remainder of the mercifully short distance that had to be covered. They made all possible speed to Bryn's farm, where a sickbed had been prepared as soon as the first message had been relayed.

Sally's request for warm water was answered immediately, which she took for another sign of thoughtful readiness on Bryn's part.

"I have mixed a medication that has proved effective in the past. I hope it will work for him also," she explained as she went about steeping the ingredients to produce the liquid. "But it is vital that someone watch over him all the time until he wakes. He may even appear lifeless for a time, but do not be fooled! It is the body's way of dealing with this mixture."

Briefly, she listed the special need for constant supervision she had already gone through with Tom, and suggested that two or three of the traveling party might be the best choice. The crucial step could no longer be postponed; Tom had started to drift in and out of consciousness, and it was vital she persuade him to take the bitter medicine while he still had the conscious reflex to swallow it.

Cradling Tom's head in her arm once more, she stroked his tight, blue, waxen curls and persuaded him to struggle into an almost upright sitting position.

"Tom, I know this is not going to taste good. I've treated myself with it, remember. But you have to take the full dose, and then I have a more pleasant tasting drink for you that will help you sleep while the medicine takes effect. Come, now."

To her surprise—and also to her great relief—Tom made no protest, but drained the whole draught she offered him in one long, single swallow. He handed her the cup and winked. "I learned a long time ago that if you know the drink is not going to taste pleasant, it's better to take it all in one swallow. You don't have time to notice the taste or regret your choice. But you were right; it is truly foul!"

"I have also heard others say that if a medicine tastes foul, it must do you some good—else, why have it at all?" Sally replied with an encouraging smile that cost her dearly. Lying was not one of her talents, even when it might be justified by claiming it was necessary to reassure nervous patients. In this case, she had no feel for just how sick Tom might be, or even if he was in reality suffering from the same mysterious illness that had laid her low. What if she was treating the symptoms, but not the disease? Would Tom survive at all? As quickly as they intruded on her consciousness, she banished these dark, despairing thoughts of failure. Failure was one thing that must not be allowed to happen!

As she watched, Tom started to shiver, though the sick room was well ventilated and at an acceptable temperature. She decided it was time to administer the other draught, the one intended to help him sleep through the healing process. As she had promised, this was far more palatable and came in larger quantities, so Tom took the cup trustingly and toasted Sally over its rim before draining it in a single swallow.

He'd had nothing to eat, and the medicine clearly worked best on an empty stomach.

"A far more pleasing brew!" He tried to make a joke of it.

Sally frowned at him. "You should be more serious about this; it might even kill you!"

"So, if I find myself in Valhalla, I shall steal a mount and ride the world with a sword in my hand until I find my Sally again. Life without you would surely be an eternity of punishment."

More than a little shocked at this sudden, public declaration, Sally reddened and withdrew from the immediate circle, allowing two young girls from the household to finish the task of making Tom comfortable for a long, uninterrupted sleep, and hopefully making the first steps along the road to recovery.

His breathing remained calm, even, and free of wheezes or other signs of the encroaching illness. Had the preventative medicine already begun to take effect? Sally doubted if this was possible. More likely, his body was automatically closing down organs it would have no immediate use for once he was asleep and totally dependent on the healing skills of someone else.

Sally spoke quietly with the three volunteers who had insisted on the honor of keeping a watcher's brief over Tom as he lay in his comatose state, and drew lots amongst them when they could not agree who should be first.

She left them to organize themselves and stood outside the single-room building, separate from the main building, which had been set up as a sickbay. For the first time in several days, there was nothing urgent demanding her immediate attention. She wondered how soon she could continue her journey without appearing ungrateful for the assistance already offered so freely, even discourteous?

Bryn was suddenly at her shoulder, and appeared to read her mood accurately.

"I have read the message from Simon," he began, casually, as if this were an everyday occurrence needing no particular skill. "And I sense that there is much more behind this that you have not told him regarding your journey. But I think I am right if I say that you feel you must continue this stage of your...journey..." He paused, giving the word he had chosen the lightest of stresses to suggest that he thought the word itself a significant choice, then continued. "Must continue as soon as possible."

Grateful that she had this opportunity to speak about it without needing to raise the subject herself, Sally nodded. "Do not think me ungrateful for the kindness and aid you have already shown two complete strangers, Bryn! If circumstances were otherwise, I would happily spend time here, and know you better, but as you have so wisely seen, there are other forces in play, and time is of the essence. For reasons I cannot understand or explain, I must complete this *journey* as soon as I possibly can," she concluded softly.

Bryn stared hard. Sally matched his stare, but said nothing.

"You are a determined woman with hidden depths," Bryn murmured.

Sally relaxed fractionally, sensing that she had the advantage. "I will promise you this much," she said slowly. "Until Tom took ill, I had no plans to return east. I had even thought to continue westward by sea, if nothing persuades me to remain in Leverpole. Yet his welfare now depends on my skill in blending a remedy. I have promised him that I will return, if only to let him know my decision. This promise I now extend to you as well. As our host and provider, we owe you that much."

"Am I right to think you wish to travel on in what remains of today?"

Startled, Sally nodded. She hadn't known how to broach this subject, but Bryn's shrewd guesses were beginning to convince her that he could read her mind. His next comment almost completed the process.

"Your thoughts are your own, healer, but your face, and especially your eyes, reveal much that you seek to withhold from the rest of the world, though there are a few of us who see more clearly than most the things that throb and churn beneath the surface—thoughts and emotions, for the most part. I can arrange for a small boat to carry you swiftly downstream, a journey of no more than perhaps one hour. I will send an oarsman, as I have need for some supplies I cannot produce myself, nor barter for them with chance travelers. He can obtain what I require if he stays in town three days, no more. What say you? Can you hope to have an answer to your personal petitions by then?"

"If I have not found a definite answer and need more time, I will ensure I get a message to your oarsman before that time," Sally replied, and felt immediately as if a heavy weight of responsibility for her actions had been lifted from her shoulders.

"Then we must eat. I cannot allow you to leave my home on an empty belly! While we eat, the boat can be made ready and I will have someone make up a travel pack for you—dried foodstuff which will not spoil. You may find that a township the size of Leverpole is not as open and friendly as small villages; folk will expect to be paid in coin rather than bartered goods."

Sally knew of the custom of exchanging gold and coins, of course, but had never found it necessary to use such methods of payment. "Sire, I thank you for all you have done."

"I have dealt with Simon of the Brigantii many times over the years, and we have even exchanged coins and other tokens from time to time. The least I can do is supply you with a small amount of coinage that you may find useful. You may return what you do not use when you come this way again, or I shall no doubt come to some arrangement with Simon if, for any reason, you do not..." He stopped abruptly, not wishing to end his sentence with any suggestion that Sally might not be able to return. "Come! It is time we eat if you are to go further this day. 'Tis already close to noon, and I have not eaten since I broke my fast before dawn."

Chapter Eleven

Sally and Bryn ate in the main farm building while the boat was made ready to carry her on the next stage of her journey. She felt slightly guilty about seeming discourteous by insisting on traveling instead of staying to thank her host—and Tom's saviour—in a more fitting manner, but the compulsion to continue was almost a physical force, one which she was unable to resist or gainsay.

The boat bobbed gently at a small quay built straight out of a sand dune that started life as a small hill covered with elephant grass behind the main farm building. The grass thinned as it approached the crown, reminding Sally of the way in which the hairline on certain middle-aged men she knew had receded as they grew older. This picture the comparison of life and nature created in her mind made her smile.

Bryn handed her into the boat, and gave the rower a few final words of instruction while she settled herself in the pointed prow, facing the rower.

When he finished giving instructions and moved to the prow to release the mooring, Bryn dropped to one knee and placed a small Hessian sack in Sally's hand.

"Here are the small coins I promised you. Be careful people don't try to cheat you of their value. It is not a fortune, but it should be enough for you to live on comfortably for several days. With a strong rower, and with the assistance of the current as you travel downstream, you should be in Leverpole within the hour, perhaps a little more. There is plenty of traffic in the harbor, but my rower knows where to moor while he carries out my business. He will show you to a hostel where I believe you can safely lodge, and he will call on you before he leaves."

"Bryn, you are far too kind. I can never hope to—"

"Please, not a word more, else you may discover that I am in truth a hard taskmaster and a greedy usurer who charges excessive rents on his loans! Now, off with you, and Godspeed your return!" Without giving Sally the opportunity to protest, he cast off the rope that restrained the skiff from being taken by the current, and the distance between shore and boat widened in an instant.

There was much to distract Sally's attention during the journey, both on the river itself and along both banks. She thought the river to be about half a mile wide at this point, though bends, creeks, and bays both natural and carved by hand meant that this could only be a guess.

There was plenty of traffic on the river, too. They passed and were passed by many other craft of similar shape and size to the one she traveled in, and when she thought of how swiftly the current was taking them down the stream, she realized how much faster this particular form of transport was, as well as being more convenient. When she thought of how long it would have taken her—possibly traveling alone, which might not have been a particularly wise thing to do in unknown territory—she shuddered. How could she possibly have even considered doing anything so rash?

As the river widened and the details of the buildings and communities along the banks became more difficult to make out, Sally switched her attention to studying the other vessels skimming around her.

She took her bearings from the sun, which was now beginning to approach the western horizon ahead and to her left. The silhouettes of tall ships with full sail were etched black against the sun. They were so many, it seemed incredible to her that they avoided collision as they jockeyed for position in the river mouth, some arriving, others leaving. Soon she found the explanation when she observed a small craft pull alongside one of these large vessels close by, and a passenger swiftly scaled a dangled ladder, carrying a leather satchel. She watched him greet a uniformed sailor, presumably the captain of the vessel, and immediately start pointing, giving directions. Of course! The harbor must have a number of guides, or pilots, familiar with local currents and tides, who would guide ships to a safe mooring. Even to her, with no knowledge or experience of rivers, ports, or harbors, this was a sensible safety precaution.

As she watched that particular ship, all the sails were suddenly furled simultaneously at a command she was too far away to hear. She happened to see the main anchor released, falling with a visible splash. After a few seconds, it bit in the river bed and the ship ceased to move. Evidently, this was their allotted anchorage for the night, in mid-stream.

Along with a ragtag of small crafts similar to their own, they followed close to the northern bank of the river on their right. Small craft, it seemed, were not considered to be a significant hazard in the harbor, but were left to their own devices and allowed to ply in and out of the various docks unhindered. The rower seemed to know exactly where he was headed, so Sally sat back and allowed him to complete the task without interfering, though she was also ready to assist if he should suddenly ask her to do something.

The rower rested on his oars a moment and stared hard at a number of mooring posts as they floated past, propelled by the fading strength of the current. Sally divided her attention between watching him and glancing at the riverbank, trying to guess what he was looking for. Almost every mooring seemed no different to the one on either side of it, but then she noticed that each one had a slightly different symbol on it, either a number or a letter, most likely. Sally had never had the chance to learn her letters, but this didn't seem to be the case with Bryn's rower.

A grunt from the stern of the craft caught Sally's attention once more. The rower had selected the mooring he wanted for the night, and was now approaching a private jetty. One large ship was already in position, showing riding lights at prow and stern. All was dark and silent aboard; she was going nowhere tonight.

As they came alongside the stone built pier, Sally could see a set of rough steps rising from the water's edge to the jetty itself, some six or eight feet above their heads. The rower's eyes flicked sideways as he maneuvered with his sculls, and she realized that he wanted her to take hold of the rope she could now pick out, hanging from what must be a mooring post or something similar just out of sight on the platform of the jetty itself. She caught hold of it as the next surge of the tide bobbed her close, and with a grunt of satisfaction, the rower shipped his oars and hastened to take the rope. Seconds later, he had secured the rowboat with an efficient set of knots and turned to help her negotiate the slightly treacherous, seaweed-strewn steps.

The sun was very low by now, but the jetty faced west and had the advantage of its light for as long as possible. Every building, and even the meanest piece of equipment casually tossed in a corner, discarded after use, was diffused in a soft, golden light, which made everything it touched glow with a faerie magic.

"Master Bryn suggests you take lodgings at that hostelry, close by so you can find your way back to this mooring if there is any sort of emergency." He pointed to a particular building that was well lit and no more than fifty paces from the jetty. "The mistress is someone he had dealt with in the past. Her name is Tess O'Reilly, the widow of one of his closest friends. He says you will be safe enough in her tavern."

The tavern backed onto the docks, and there was an unmarked private door, which Bryn's rower knocked upon with the familiarity of one who had performed the same task countless times. A young boy opened it almost immediately, and the assorted scents and aromas of a busy kitchen welled out into the evening air. Words passed between them that Sally couldn't catch, and they were invited to come in from the chill. The young lad disappeared briefly, and returned with a matronly figure in tow. Sally thought she was probably a few years older, but that could have been the effects of running a busy inn.

"Sam tells me that you travel under the protection of his master, my friend Bryn, and seek lodgings for a few nights."

"That is correct, milady."

"Oh, go on wit' yiz! There's no need for formal titles, for sure, and certainly not one I can't claim to deserve, d'y' know! Tess O'Reilly, that's me, though I've answered to less polite names in me time! Tess to you, mi dear, and your name would be?"

"Sally. Sally of the Parisii, some distance to the east of here."

"I recognize the old tribe name, Sally dear, but we haven't used them in this region for many generations now! Still, there were some of the Parisii people lived at a distance to the north of Leverpole, in Northumbria if my memory serves. Come, come, and I'll show yiz a snug room. Have you no more belongings than that one bag? I'd have thought a lady of your standing might have several changes of wardrobe, even when she travels light."

Tess kept up an unbroken stream of rapid-fire chatter as she took a candle from a wall bracket and led the way through the hostel, passing but not entering a well lit room where Sally saw a large crowd sitting, drinking from glasses and tankards, and singing.

At the top of a second flight of stairs, she stopped outside a door with some symbols scratched on it. Without appearing to look in Sally's direction, Tess remarked, "D'yiz not have y'r numbers then, darlin'? Sure, an' tis no disgrace, you're in good company. This is room number one, the first one on this level, and easy f'r yiz t' find, even without the number on the door, d'y' know!"

"No, I don't...didn't..." Sally felt confused. Whether she knew or not—and she didn't—why was it so important that Tess should have to ask? What was she supposed to know?

Tess paused with her hand on the door latch. "Is there a problem? You seem—blaithered, d'y' know..."

"That's just it, Tess. What am I supposed to know? That's the third time you've asked me!"

"Sure, Sally, it's me that should be sorry! 'Tis just me style o'spaikin' now, an' there's them that say I still sound like I only come off the Dublin packet boat yistiddy, d'y' know! There, I've said it again! What a terrible country wench I mus' be soundin' to one as talks so noice as ye does!"

Boat, thought Sally. Then that must mean... Suddenly, her brow cleared. "You mean, you were born...somewhere else, Tess?"

"Sure, an' that's a fact! There's many more came the short sea trip from Ireland, both before me and since. People still say we talk twice as fast as everyone else and make half as much sense, d'y'know, but yiz'll make yiz own mind on that, too! Is this the first time y've met one wit' an accent such as me own?"

"'Tis the first journey I've made in my life, Tess. From where I grew up on the other side of the mountains far to the east of here, our journey must have taken us seven or eight days and nights, and I have never heard any speech or accents that were not local. We of the Parisii tend to settle close, and do not travel greatly."

"Well, now, and isn't that something?"

"I...suppose it is, but..."

"Ah, Sally, I'm sorry. That wasn't a question. It's just my way."

"Tess, it's alright. I must learn to listen carefully to what people *mean*, not just the words they speak. Yet, I fear that may not always be easy..."

"Listen, I'll take you through into the public room now and serve you a meal. I'll sit with you while you eat. Some of the sailors who come in here when they're on leave can get a bit...noisy at times, but they'll leave you alone as long as I'm with you, you can be certain o' that!"

Tess would hear none of Sally's protests, but took her by the arm and continued to talk at what seemed an impossible speed while chivvying Sally through the narrow corridor from the kitchen to the public room. Before Sally could raise as much as half a protest, she found herself sitting in a curtained alcove barely big enough for the table and two chairs it contained. The curtains were drawn back, and she had a good view of almost the entire public area.

Two tall glasses of drink arrived at the table as they did, and Tess eased herself into one chair, leaving Sally secure with her back against a solid wall. Anyone wishing to approach or talk to her would have to deal with Tess first.

Sally sipped cautiously at the drink placed before her, which had a creamy foam layer. She was surprised to feel tiny bubbles form and burst in her mouth; the drink was pleasantly sweet, and tasted strongly of apples.

Tess caught the expression on Sally's face and burst out laughing. "Sally, Sally! Haven't you ever tried a drink wi' a bit o' fizz in it? This one's called cider, and popular wi' many o' the female drinkers here in my tavern—them as don't take the gin, that is, but I didn't rate you as one o' their class, or lack o' th' same, if yiz know what I mean!"

Sally didn't, but after the misunderstandings she'd already had with taking that particular phrase too literally, she decided to remain silent this time.

"Won't y' intro-dooce me t' y'r new friend, Tess?"

Tess froze a moment, her glass halfway to her lips. Sally saw she closed her eyes briefly, as if in real physical pain, then continued to take an extraordinarily long time taking a delicate sip, replacing her glass, and wiping her lips with a dainty lace napkin before acknowledging the speaker's existence for the first time.

"Why, if it's not Mr. Finnegan, himself! And who's the last skipper had the pleasure o' tossin' y' off his roster f'r bein' pissdrunk on duty, then?"

"Now then, Tess, me darlin'! Yiz'd not be believin' all the tales told 'round the alehouses an' gin-soaks in town, surely now? And such a pretty guest y're entertainin' it's ashamed y' should be f'r denying us all the hop-portunity t' get t' know her the better..."

A hairy hand with grey-green, misshapen talons where others have nails started to wander across the table in Sally's direction. Frozen with fear, she watched it approaching until Tess picked up the candlestick from the center of the table and scored a direct hit across the wrist, producing a sharp yelp and a string of curses.

"Be on y'r way, Mick, an' know y'r place. Leave y'r betters to enjoy a meal in peace!"

The unwelcome visitor took Tess' none too subtle hint and left, nursing a hand that quite possibly sported a couple of shattered bones.

"Do you have many...customers of that nature?" Sally gaped as Tess calmly refilled both glasses as if nothing untoward or unusual had occurred.

"Ach, Mick gets a bit, what shall we say, a bit *too* friendly when he's had a drink or several, but there's no real harm in him. Not like some o' th' cutthroats I have to toss onto the street from time to time."

Suddenly, there was a resounding crash from the front of the house as the doors flew back. A dozen or so burly men charged in, carrying cudgels and brass knuckles, overturning tables and screaming curses as the patrons in the crowded tavern scrambled desperately to get out of their way.

Tess blanched at the sight and stood to block off the alcove. "Sally, get under the table and stay there! I'll keep them from you if I possibly can. Don't let them see you!"

The biggest and meanest of the intruders halted in the center of the wrecked scene. Half of the newly arrived force remained guarding the door; the remainder strode purpose-fully to strategic positions around the walls of the room. He picked up someone's pint glass from the nearest table. Amazingly, it was still upright and seemed to have survived without spilling. He emptied it in one steady swallow, belched crudely, and looked around the captive audience.

"Greetings, citizens, from your local Muster Crew, with our regular offer of a life of adventure to those who take the king's shilling, or a reg'lar flogging to them as don't take our generous offer immediately, and a promise that they'll finish up crewing on someone's ship before the week's out anyway, so why refuse the first offer? Because the next one won't be any improvement."

"Nay , it'll no doubt be the same at best, but wi' extra floggin' thrown in free an'gratis!" interrupted another of the vicious brood who stood by the main door.

"You can stop threatening my customers, so you can!" Tess snarled. Under the table, Sally caught her breath. She would never have suspected that the innkeeper could be un-afraid of such large, well-muscled, and plainly armed bullies. She concentrated as Tess continued.

"You an' y'r press gang have bled me of reg'lar customers each week for several months now, and none of those you frog-marched out of this tavern have ever returned to regale us wi' their tales of fighting pirates and sailing to faraway lands where the sun always shines. Most likely on account of there bain't no such places, 'cept in your pipedreams!"

"Have a care, innkeeper, or I'll make sure you're first into the hold next time we come a-lookin' for vol'n teers." He leered, but Tess rounded on him so fiercely he backed off a step.

"Muster men ye call y'rsel—hah! Ye're nought but a crowd o' bully boys lookin' f'r smaller, weaker men t' pick on, selling a body for the price o' a glass o' gin! We all know ye by other names, too, and yiz aren't welcome in *my* tavern!"

A knife appeared in her hand. Fast as lightning, she sliced off the ponytail that held most of his hair off his face, tempo-rarily blinding him and causing a roar of laughter from the tavern customers. This was too much for the rest of the press gang, who had been forced to stand and watch their leader's public humiliation by this arrogant slip of a woman. With a concerted yell, they drew their weapons and began bludgeoning all and sundry. The patrons were defenseless; they had come for an evening's entertainment and song, and had no weapons of their own to hand.

Tess crashed to the floor, bleeding heavily from the mouth. Sally had seen the leader of the press gang strike her across the face with the back of his hand; she was out cold. A second later, the table was overturned and she was confronted with the man-bear himself, who howled in triumph.

"Well, lookee here! A bonus on the evening's crop, me lads. A tasty morsel we can share around before I get a goodly price for her from any one of half a dozen ship's masters looking for a strumpet t' pleasure 'em on long voyages!"

His gang looked up as he dragged Sally from her knees and flung her over his shoulder.

"Bind the strongest amongst this sorry bunch—no boys, no old men—and meet at the usual place. I'll attend t' the Jane first, an' if any of yiz wants a share after, yiz c'n draw lots."

Sally couldn't move she was clamped so hard in his grasp. She was barely able to breathe. With her last remaining strength, she managed to sink her teeth deep into the flesh at the back of his neck, and she tasted blood. He howled once more, this time in pain, and Sally felt his arms loosen slightly as he shifted his balance.

She had no time to take advantage and wriggle from his grasp before a blow to the back of her head sent her spinning into a black hole of pain and oblivion.

Chapter Twelve

Sally opened her eyes and immediately decided that it wasn't a good idea. Colored lights whirled before her vision, throbbing rhythmically in time with the waves of excruciating pain that threatened to burst her temples, or her eardrums, or both. She closed them again. It made absolutely no difference; the same lights danced mockingly, out of her control, against the same blackness. Had she lost her sight altogether? Surely not. She'd seen the appalling state of penury blind people suffered, shunned as useless by every village and hamlet, forced to wander from place to place begging what alms they could until they died of starvation or neglect. Some had been sent—or more often brought—to her seeking possible cures, but blindness was one of the illnesses she had never been able to cure or even alleviate.

She had to discover what had happened to her while she was unconscious, what damages had been wrought upon her body, where she was—a hundred questions flooded through her mind.

First things first—there was no profit to be had from letting herself be ruled by blind panic. She had to lie still, take stock, relax.

Discipline and training took over automatically.

Breathe in through the nose, hold it; breathe out through the mouth.

She felt the familiar relaxation of over-tensed muscles rippling gently inward from her toes and fingertips gradually, as if the blood flowing in her veins was easing each knot of resistance it encountered, massaging aches and pains out of her system.

When the garish, soundlessly popping colored lights had stopped exploding inside her skull, she decided to chance opening her eyes once more. She felt the muscles controlling her eyelids move, but the blackness was absolute. As far as she could tell, there were no bindings on her eyes, but wherever she lay was an enclosed space of some sort with no windows, and no stray leaks of light to indicate a door or other means of access—*and exit,* she had to remind herself. *If someone can get in, then I can find a way to get out.* Unless she told herself this, and believed it, she had no chance of ever escaping...wherever she was.

Time to begin a few experimental maneuvers. Stretching her arms, she discovered that someone had tied her hands together at the wrists. The bindings were tight, and in the dark, impossible to study, but her jailer had been careless, or perhaps just ignorant. He, or she—though Sally thought that was unlikely—had made the mistake of crossing the wrists and binding them one on top of the other. The knots themselves were inexpertly tied, and in very short time, even working blind in total darkness, Sally's hands were free.

Her feet were still tied to something or other, but in such a way that she was unable to draw her legs up to her chest or even close them together. Following a swift search patrol, her sensitive fingertips reported that she was lying on a rough blanket, which covered a flat surface—possibly a bed?

Stroking her hands across her body, she discovered that her clothing was in shreds. This could only mean one thing. Against her will, while she'd been unconscious, someone had physically attacked her, abused her unresisting, limp body as a rough bully of a child might take pleasure in deliberately destroying a toy. She felt suddenly sick, violated. Her hands, exploring her thigh region, confirmed that there was something unpleasantly sticky clinging to her flesh. She fervently hoped it would prove to be blood, once she could find a source of light to inspect herself, but feared it was almost certainly a different bodily fluid, and not one that belonged to her.

Her probing fingers massaged some life back into her legs. They confirmed that there were tender spots on her thighs, further evidence of the violation she suspected. She felt physically sick, and had to repeat her breathing mantra to calm herself before completing her blind investigation of her lower limbs.

At full stretch, she could just reach first the one ankle, then the other. Both were bound to some sort of post, suggesting that she was as she had suspected lying on a bed or something similar. But whoever had imprisoned her and tied her to the bed had made an error in her favor—they had *not* removed her boots.

And had therefore not found her workblade, a thin, extremely sharp knife that she habitually carried tucked inside her right boot, to use if she was foraging for medicinal plants deep in a forest. With this, the straps around her ankles parted as soon as she touched them, and she spent a good ten minutes roughly massaging some circulation into her deadened feet before even contemplating moving off the bed to explore her immediate surroundings. She needed to move silently, and dared not risk stumbling due to poor circulation.

Cautiously, she moved to one side of the platform and swung her legs out in front of her. With her knees against the edge, she slowly lowered her feet, and was rewarded when her heels touched a smooth, solid surface before her legs reached a true perpendicular. Whatever she was lying on was, she judged about the height of a typical bed, a comfortable height off the ground to avoid the worst chills rising from the ground during the coldest months of the year.

What next? she wondered. Sitting there, still in total darkness, she concentrated on the senses that did not rely on the presence of light—touch, smell, and hearing.

She concentrated on listening, and slowed her breathing as she tried to identify anything in the immediate vicinity. There was a high-pitched whine, which seemed to emanate from a region just behind her ears. She tried to ignore it, seeking for the least creak or noise from anywhere close by. There was nothing.

How big was the room? Without getting off the bed and moving about, there was no way of knowing, but if this was a locked room, there might be a guard alert for the least sign of her awakening, and she dared not risk giving herself away with a noise that could have been avoided.

She held her knife firmly, placing thumb and forefinger at the very butt end of the handle, and allowed it to dangle. Holding her breath, she tapped the blade firmly with a fingernail, creating a low musical chime. It didn't die off immediately, but seemed to shimmer, not quite visible, in the utter, formless black. There was the faintest of echoes, she decided, suggesting that the room was not oversized, but at the same time, it wasn't a tiny cell either. Possibly it had not been intended as a prison. If that were the case, it might just make it easier for her to escape from it.

There was little more she could learn sitting there. A voice in her head advised her, *If it feels like a bed, treat it as a bed. For now, at least, it* is *a bed.*

Sensible advice, maybe, but where had it come from? Whose voice could it possibly be? And why did it come to her in just this fashion, right now?

But in a lightless, unfamiliar environment of unknown dimensions, which might be filled with lethal traps or dangerous, noisy obstacles that might betray her to a watchful, listening foe, how best to proceed with the exploration of her surroundings?

Slowly and carefully; that was the *only* way to do it, the only advice she could offer herself. Carefully, she placed the knife between her teeth and inched forward until she could feel her knees on the floor. Step two involved stretching both arms in front of her to make sure that she was not sitting immediately opposite an unseen obstacle. She could circle both arms freely through open space, so she reached downwards and lowered them, seeking to place her fingertips on the flooring as close as possible to her knees. Again, she achieved this without problems and spread all four limbs to broaden the base. *One step at a time*, she thought, *and don't get careless! You've made a good start. Don't risk it by being impatient!*

She raised one hand, gripped her knife by the handle, and made a few cautious sweeps of the quadrant she could reach ahead of her and off to the right. Transferring the blade to her left hand, she repeated the same exercise on the opposite side. Allowing for the length of the blade, there was no obstacle she could touch within a couple of arms' lengths, and that was good.

Carefully, she lowered herself still further, left arm, right arm, until she was spread-eagled comfortably on hands and knees, her breasts barely touching the flooring, reminding her of the fact that someone had destroyed her clothing. *That* was definitely going to cost someone dearly!

She had to stop before carrying on; she had to be clear, calm, fully alert to every little nuance of sound or motion around her. She couldn't afford to be distracted by the furies of anger, hatred, revenge...

Now she concentrated on her highly sensitive nose, and the sense of smell that had been one of her most valuable tools in all the years she'd practiced as a medicine woman and healer. Her nose confirmed what her fingertips had already suggested, namely that the flooring was some rough form of timber rather than stone or other material. Conclusion—some sort of building, as opposed to a cave or grotto well away from any human other than the animal who had raped and caged her before going away and leaving her bound and helpless—or so he thought. Cautiously, one limb at a time, she began to spider her way across the floor inch by painful inch, trying to steer as straight a course as possible, while at the same time attempting to estimate how far she had traveled.

With her nose and the sensitive skin of her cheeks close to the floor, Sally was suddenly aware of the faintest hint of an eddy of movement of air. It had to be coming from somewhere! Despite all her attempts to stay calm, her heart pounded with anticipation. She had her knife; there were very few locks that would withstand her determined efforts. If she could only find the door with the slightly imperfect seal that allowed this whisper of a breeze to enter her prison cell...

She concentrated as never before on the caress of air on her cheek. On her right rather than from the left, she decided, and turned her head slightly in that direction. She opened her mouth and held her breath, trying to taste the air as well as feel its passage. Nothing ventured... Scarcely daring to breathe, she continued to inch her way forward, trying to aim slightly to the right of her original direction. Without a light source, this was a combination of luck and blind guesswork.

On her seventh attempt to spider her way forward, the cautious sweep ahead with her knife resulted in the lightest of scrapes as the very tip of the blade made contact with something solid where previous sweeps had only indicated free air. Had she reached a wall—or was this an object, perhaps some piece of furniture standing free in a larger space?

She felt exhilarated at this first success, but refused to allow herself to get carried away. She had to find out as much about the geography of the room as possible, using whatever senses she could, but she had to remain calm.

She stretched her arm once more, slower than she had done on the previous sweep, and touched the tip of her knife against a solid surface before her arm was fully extended. She applied the least imaginable degree of extra pressure along her arm and concentrated on the extreme tip of the knife. Was it her imagination, or did she sense the knife biting just a fraction deeper as she leaned on it?

With infinite patience, she adjusted her weight balance until she felt in line with the blade, then crabbed forward once more, inch by inch, until she was kneeling upright and her right flank, shoulder, and cheek were all flush against an unyielding surface. Her fingertips confirmed once more that it was wooden with an open, rough surface. It appeared to be more or less vertical, as she would have expected of any well-constructed wall.

She tried pressing her ear harder against the wall, willing her senses to pick out a voice, even with mumbled indistinguishable words, or at very least a noise she could identify. Apart from a few odd creaks suggesting natural tiny movements of timber settling in the frame, there was nothing obvious.

Back to tracing the leak in the structure that had admitted the suggestion of a draft. She gripped the knife firmly in her left hand this time and used her right to support her balance as she sank to her knees and lay flat on the floor again.

There it was again! It was definitely somewhere in front of her on her right. She eased the knife against a point where the wall met the floor, and slid it forward an inch at a time, seeking a slot, a seam, anything suggesting the bottom edge of a door that might admit a breath of air.

Another inch, and another. Was that a faint trace of a scent she could almost recognize, or just her imagination? She inched forward, and tried the knife blade again. This time, it slid forward smoothly, vibrating slightly in her hand as it rubbed against at least one surface, but for the moment, she couldn't tell if it was the bottom edge of the wall/door, or the floor beneath the blade.

She eased the knife to the left. It ran unchallenged for a

couple of feet before coming to a stop. She thought for a moment, and grinned as the answer suggested itself. By now she had developed a method of dealing with the total dark, utilizing the sensitive pads of her fingertips. Now she placed her right hand against the point where the hilt of the blade rested against the door, withdrew the knife, and turned it through ninety degrees. After one or two fumbles, she managed to insert it once more to the hilt, and started to run it upwards. It slid without hindrance, and she rose from her prone position to kneeling before she encountered some resistance. It didn't feel like a solid, immovable barrier this time. There was a degree of give when she tried exerting a little more pressure.

She paused a moment, and tried to imagine what this might suggest. She was wary of trying anything that might load her knife's blade and snap it. It was, after all, her only possible escape tool. She'd been working blind for long enough to work things out using her other senses, and this had to be some sort of lock arrangement, the most likely being a lift latch of some sort. Surely she could lift it with her knife blade without snapping the steel...as long as she was careful!

Ear pressed flat against the door to catch any sounds that might help her, she applied some pressure and increased it a little at a time, sawing the blade back and forth in an attempt to cut into or through a rope fastening. The knife blade seemed to be cutting into something, but resistance soon built up and her only option seemed to be to try once more to lift whatever was holding the door closed rather than cut through it. Now she prayed to *all* the gods, equally and without preference or prejudice; she could use some assistance in her present predicament, and she wasn't particular where it might come from.

Slowly, she increased the pressure, and was rewarded when she felt the bar lift in response to her efforts. Suddenly, it rose more freely, a good three, maybe four inches. She hadn't planned this, but it worked in her favor. Applying pressure to the knife in the crack, her shoulder was jammed firmly against the door, and as the latch reached its upper limit, she tumbled inelegantly to her right. Instinctively, she continued the tumble into a controlled roll and bounced to her feet, ready to defend herself should it be necessary.

It took her a few moments to adjust to the fact that she

had *not* been struck blind, something that she as a healer had begun to wonder about after discovering evidence of several heavy blows to the head. The lighting was sparse, but sufficient enough to seem almost painful following the length of time she had lain unconscious, plus however long had passed while she had been occupied with breaking out of her prison. Catlike, silent, she padded her way from the open space in which she crouched defensively, back towards the door she had successfully broached.

She realized that if someone were to look in and check on the prisoner right now, the game would be up. After a long, careful inspection of what she could see from where she stood, she turned to the open door and closed it carefully, not allowing it to boom or slam, and quickly replaced the latch to secure it. So far, so good. Now she had to rally her thoughts and plan her escape. Wherever she was, she wasn't out of the woods yet. By the looks of things, she wasn't even outdoors.

She crouched in some comforting shadows close to the door she'd tumbled through and studied the enclosed space around her, trying to make sense of what she could see. It seemed to be designed for storage. The door to whatever it was she'd recently escaped from was flush against a long, unbroken, slightly curved wooden wall. There were windows in it, but strangely positioned close to the ceiling. Apparently, they were intended for someone to look in from above. They were clearly not intended to be of use for anyone inside the structure at Sally's level. They were also far smaller than any window she had ever seen before, and round, not the square or rectangular ones she had seen used in the towns and villages she had visited.

Sally couldn't see any doors or archways that might be exits, an escape to the outside world. Suddenly, she felt a stab of longing for the sun, moon, stars, and the freedom of nature, an environment she understood.

Her prison cell seemed to be built in one corner of the roughly rectangular area. She tried to estimate its size— perhaps fifty feet across, maybe three times that in length. Long, serried ranks of goods were stacked evenly throughout the open space, each stack about twice an average person's height, spaced in six long rows with narrow passages between them. Most of them were covered with a heavy piece of fabric and efficiently roped down, as if to prevent pilfer-age.

No, that didn't make sense. If this wasn't intended as a security measure, could it be a storage room for things intended to sell? The problem with this was different, but equally as persuasive. Suppose a customer wanted to buy something. Why hide the goods under a piece of fabric? And how would one remember exactly where the item had been stored?

Hmmm. Not security, but secured nonetheless. Not for selling either, but sheeted and protected for some other reason.

Transport! That ticked *all* the boxes, but it still looked like a building, fifty feet wide and at least three or four times that in length. It was far too big to be used as a wagon of any sort; the weight alone would force the wheels into the ground.

Diagonally opposite the corner where she was crouching was the only feature of the alien landscape that just might lead somewhere. It was a staircase of some sort, flush against the wall and with looped rope as a handrail on the other side. Something she recognized as a door was at the top of the staircase. It had a fan-shaped window inset toward the top, and if it was locked or secured in any way, it could only be from the outside. Sally's heart sank momentarily. She was far from keen on going through the same time-consuming, nerve-wracking escapology using only her trusty work blade.

She had no other choices, or none that she could immediately see. Flitting like a shadow from one tethered stack of nameless goods to the next, she crossed the width of the storage area, moving forward every time she came to the next alleyway between the ranks. As she placed her foot on the first step and reached for the rope handrail, she noticed that it appeared to sway just slightly, enough that she almost managed to miss it. She all but sprinted to the top of the stairs, pausing two steps from the top to stare through a convenient round window level with her eyes.

The view was slightly distorted, as the glass was quite thick. What she could see outside the window, however, changed her view of the geography of the room and explained both the secured, roped and sheeted goods, and their even distribution for optimum balance as well as capacity.

This storage unit was never going to have problems with the weight of goods causing wheels to stick in the mud of a road. The slight sway Sally had noticed was also easily explained by the view outside the window. She had been carried off and left in the brig of a four-master sailing ship, fitted for service as a cargo transport.

Chapter Thirteen

For a moment, Sally froze with the shock. If she was on board a ship, that could only be because she'd been brought to the ship unconscious, then left inside a locked cell after someone—more than one someone, she suspected—had used her body as a plaything, a tool for self-gratification. Just thinking about it made her sick, and she felt her anger creeping back. That was a luxury she couldn't afford, she scolded herself, and took a couple of deep breaths before peering once more at the slightly distorted view outside the grubby pane of glass.

Only a small segment of a wide vista could be seen. There were a few small boats, and a shoreline in the distance. The boats she could see were all in motion, but the shoreline in the distance remained constant. There was a slight up-and-down swell under her feet, which was only noticeable if she really concentrated on it, and after a minute or two, she decided that this was probably because the ship she was on was still moored at a quay and had not yet set sail. And that meant just one thing—Sally's only chance of escaping her current predicament was now, before the ropes were cast and the ship left the quayside and sailed away.

Thoughts of Tom and his silent battle with the mysterious ailment she was convinced she was quite possibly responsible for crowded into her mind. Her glib promise to return and continue ministering to him would be an empty, broken promise if she allowed herself to be carried away from Leverpole, and this thought spurred her into action.

She gripped her knife blade firmly, but caution made her

stop and reconsider. If she were someone's prisoner, then whoever was responsible would be sure to look in and check on her before leaving port.

Bullies never worked alone, she told herself. There was bound to be more than one person in any party sent to check on her before they left port, and she had neither the skills nor the strength to take on even a single opponent, not under any circumstances. Taking on and beating more than a single person was therefore out of the question. Force was not the solution. With a pang of regret, she nodded to herself and looked to sheathe the blade.

The only available place for it was the concealed sheath inside her right boot. She left it there and inspected the rest of her clothing—or, more correctly, what remained of her clothing. The rough treatment her unconscious body had been subjected to had effectively reduced her clothing to rags. She couldn't appear in public in such a state, and this had nothing to do with female modesty or personal pride. The clothing was simply too badly damaged to remain attached to her, useless as protection against the elements, or for any other purpose, unless one counted starting a fire with it.

Beneath the steps there was a partially cleared area resembling a workspace with a few single items lying on or near a table of some sort, presumably not a part of the ship reserved for storing goods, but for carrying out any of the small tasks needed to make transportation possible. She edged carefully down the steps, noting that the slight rise and fall motion was becoming more noticeable. She hoped this didn't mean that departure was imminent.

Under the table, she discovered three or four reasonably clean and empty sacks woven of some intensely strong fiber, probably a cotton mix. She picked up one that seemed slightly bigger than the rest, turned it inside out, and shook it vigorously to rid it of the dry flour or whatever had last been inside.

Out came the blade once more. Three careful slashes in the base of the sack and just below each corner resulted in a rough but serviceable smock, which she pulled over her head, ignoring its scratchiness and discomfort. From the wreck of what she had been wearing, Sally managed to find a length of cloth that was barely long enough to plait into a serviceable belt, which she tied off around her waist. Knife back in boot—*now* she felt as ready as she'd ever be to take on the rest of the world, if necessary, in order to keep her promise and return to her patient who hovered between life and death a few miles to the south.

She returned to the top of the stairs and immediately breathed a sigh of relief. There was a handle this time, indicating that the door was intended to be opened from the inside as well as the outside, and there was no sign of a hole for a mortise key or any other security measure. Now, if she could just slip outside unobserved, surely her luck would hold long enough for her to slip overboard and onto the quay. After that, she was quite willing to take her chances in a foot-race with anyone from the ship who might try to pursue her, though her lack of familiarity with the outlay of this port might be a distinct disadvantage. *Get through this door first; worry about other things later if and when you have to,* she told herself, and laid one cautious hand on the heavy cast-iron ring that would open the door.

She eased the door a few inches, just wide enough to slip her slim frame out sideways, then turned and eased it just as carefully closed. No alarms sounded, there were no voices raised in challenge or defiance, and Sally was able to absorb as much detail of the vessel as her senses could record for as long as she dared to stand in one place. She couldn't see anyone, but that didn't necessarily mean she wasn't being watched by someone else, someone more skilled at concealing himself.

She glanced around her, and decided that a mare's nest of tangled ropes that lay untidily in one corner would make an ideal place to hide while she sat and planned her next move. What was even better was the fact that the ropes were almost the same color as the sackcloth she wore, and the camouflage was as close to perfect as made no difference—she hoped.

Once again, she concentrated on trying to glean any information she could possibly turn to her advantage from what she could discover through her senses. She'd been forced to do without the advantage of sight for a sustained, stressful period of time. How long she couldn't even begin to guess, but since the present position of the sun seemed to suggest it was not yet noon, she had to guess and hope that no more than one night had passed. Her stomach sent out a disgruntled rumble, but she ignored it. She was used to living off short rations, and the occasional skipped meal was nothing to be concerned about.

Her nose was full of the salty tang of the sea, another new experience for her. This was overlaid with the other scents and aromas associated with a busy port—tar, horse dung, the unmistakeable—and, curiously, not totally un-pleasant—smell of gently rotting seaweed exposed on the stanchions and pillars with every low tide. Then there were the other smells, less easy to put a name to—warehouses containing exotic spiced goods from far away, freshly tanned animal hides on their way to traders in other ports, freshly cut timber stacked neatly on the quayside, the sap still bleeding from the woodcutter's axe, the heady perfume redolent on the air.

And the air itself! The oxygen-rich, charged air that Sally's healing mentor had insisted was so good for many chest com-plaints and a surprising number of minor illnesses.

"Send as many as can afford the time to take the air at a coastal town, Sally. You'll be surprised at how many of them come back to thank you, after even a few days rest some-where they can take the waters!" one old crone had cackled to her, and Sally had tried to follow her advice, although from where she had always lived and practiced in the York-shire Dales, it was a long and difficult journey to any coastal region, and only a few had decided to invest the time that would be needed to follow her advice.

There was no time to think, no room for hesitation or un-certainty. She wriggled around in the ropes to see what ac-tivity was taking place on the land side along the quay.

There was nobody within sight on the ship itself, which cheered her immediately. She had no illusions about her abil-ity to fight her way off the ship and win her freedom in heroic fashion. A narrow plank was laid from a point on the deck where a section of guard rail had been removed, sloping slightly down to rest on the quayside. As Sally watched, a man with a piece of sacking protecting his shoulder from fric-tion burns came out of a doorway carrying a wooden crate and made his way down the plank.

As he reached the end of the plank, a second man, simi-larly dressed, emerged from the same door and followed him, crossing the quay and heading for a line of low buildings opposite. A third person followed, and Sally decided here lay her best chance. After all, she argued to herself, where did one hide a tree? In a *forest!*

She snatched up a random piece of sacking, abandoned at the side of her hiding place, and quickly gathered together some of the loose detritus that collected in every odd, unpoliced corner of any ship. To finish off, she threw in the remnants of clothing and twisted the cloth to resemble a sack. Stealthily, she approached the section of the deck where this activity was replaying itself, and waited out of sight of anyone coming through the door. Timing was everything. She'd noticed that in every case, the one porter had reached at least as far as the bottom of the plank before the next one pushed the door open. She would have to leave before the next one got that far. At the same time, she couldn't get too close in case he turned round and saw an unfamiliar face where he'd expected a close friend.

She held her nerve, and waited until the next porter was perhaps three paces from the end of the plank before she stepped on at the top. It might have been because her light build and fake load weighed very little compared with the other muscled and well-built porters who were obviously chosen for their brawn, but her slightly premature entry to the line failed to intrude upon the other's consciousness, and he continued to stomp rhythmically across the quay without looking back.

Sally hurried down the plank, all the time straining to hear the telltale *thuink* as the door slammed shut behind the next carrier. She had both feet firmly planted on the quay before she heard the sound, and eased off her speed just a fraction. She didn't want to draw suspicion from a landside observer by appearing to find the job a little *too* easy, any more than she wanted to catch up to the man in front. She was certain this was *not* a job that women would ever be hired to carry out, and there was no way she could explain her way out of it.

She plodded along, following the same line as the man in front, trying to imitate his tired, heavy gait. As she approached the line of buildings, which she realized was a destination of some sort, she started to look for an opportunity to leave the line without being missed. She couldn't even begin to think of what the situation might be if she was obliged to enter the building, but she thought her chances of escape would be far more limited if she did.

She was approaching a narrow passage about twenty paces short of the door the man in front of her was about to enter. A lightning glance over her shoulder—the man behind her had his head down, oblivious to his immediate surroundings. It was now or never. Holding her breath, she stepped sideways into the alley, and breathed a prayer of thanks as she found a space where she could crouch between two untidy piles of rubbish until she heard the plodding steps of the next porter trudge past.

As soon as he had passed, she was away like a startled rabbit, fleeing further down the passage, seeking a safer hiding place. The burden she'd used to blend in with the porter line was no longer needed, and she could move more quickly without it. After counting the fingers of one hand, she stopped and flung herself flat against the building on her right, looking back toward the quay and remaining immobile until she saw another muscled figure slouch past the alleyway. She was now much closer to the rear of the building than the front, and was confident that she could reach the corner and duck completely out of sight behind it on her next run.

At the end of the passage, she crouched low and poked her head around the corner, keeping flat against the angle of the building. Once again, her luck seemed to be holding. There was nobody in sight, nothing to prevent her walking straight out of the docks unchallenged.

A low, rumbling growl from behind warned her that her situation might yet be compromised by an unexpected problem, one she couldn't talk her way out of.

She knew enough about the dangers of confronting an ill-tempered dog; she'd treated and attempted to treat a number of animals brought to her by villagers. If she was brutally honest, she'd have said that most of them were probably suffering the effects of old age more than anything else, but they'd been brought to her generally by or on behalf of a young child, who regarded the animal as a pet, loved in the same way as a younger sibling.

A large animal, which to Sally's frightened eyes seemed to be the size of a small horse, stood with hackles raised a few paces behind her. It might have been her imagination, but she was certain she could smell its foul breath as it panted, tongue lolling and drooling saliva, mouth open, cruel teeth glinting in the early afternoon sunlight. For the moment, it remained unmoving, as if studying her, waiting for her to make the first move, challenging her as if defending what it perceived as its own personal space.

It growled again. Instinctively, and without thinking about it, Sally found herself copying the sound as best she could within the limits imposed by her own vocal cords. The dog stopped in mid growl and appeared confused. After a few seconds, it seemed to alter its position, easing some of the tension in its posture. When it sounded off again, to Sally's ears, it was a much less aggressive noise, more like a piteous complaint, reminding her of the irritating sort of people who wasted a great deal of their time and that of others moaning about the fact that nobody liked them.

She was too worldly wise to think that she had somehow made contact with the emotions of a half-wild animal, but for the moment, it seemed less likely to attack than it had scant seconds before, so she must be doing something right. Cautiously, she tried once more to copy the dog's sounds as accurately as she could. Her lips were painfully dry with fear and tension, but she dared not show her tongue long enough to moisten them, lest the dog interpret the movement as an indication that she might be getting ready to launch an attack.

The exchange of greetings continued for a few more rounds, and then the dog surprised Sally by doing the one thing she hadn't expected of it. With a short, pitiful-sounding whimper, it lay flat in the dust and stretched its snout toward her as if begging for her to reach out, touch...

Did she dare trust this animal whose background and temperament she didn't know the first thing about? Her choices were limited—reciprocate, trust, accept the invitation, or turn and attempt to flee? She knew that she could never hope to outrun a powerful four-legged creature on her two spindly stumps. Slowly, she lay prone, as close as she dared, and stretched her neck until she really *could* smell the dog's breath, which wasn't as unpleasant as her fevered brain had told her it was bound to be. She held her breath and closed the final inch between them until her nose touched lightly against the very tip of the offered canine snout.

As soon as the contact was made, the dog whined once more, but this was more of a sound that Sally recognized. The dog rolled onto one dusty flank and raised its front left paw in the air. The sign was unmistakeable; this was an animal in pain, begging for help! Had it somehow sensed that she was a medicine woman, healer, and a person to be trusted? How could that possibly happen?

Little bit of bread and nooooo cheeeeeeese.

The distinctive melody of an unseen bird's game with her in the earliest days of her journey suddenly trilled in her inner ear. For a moment, she was perplexed, and glanced swiftly around the eaves of the building looming over her to check if it might be a real bird rather than an apparently random memory. Seeing nothing of any consequence, she lowered her gaze to the animal that lay before her, all its earlier aggression and threat removed. She held eye contact and found herself uttering gentle, wordless murmurs of sympathy and trust as she reached her right hand toward the injured paw. The dog sighed, reacting almost as a wounded human might do, expressing relief that someone was prepared to offer much needed treatment to ease the pain of injury.

She eased her head back from the nose-to-snout physical contact in order to concentrate on the limp paw. She noted that his powerful nails were fully sheathed, secured deep inside the pad. Feral or not, this dog had no intention of attacking her. She placed her left palm lightly on the animal's long, slender nose, and let it rest there a moment before applying the gentlest of pressure to the offered paw, raising it slightly for a closer inspection. This produced the feeblest of whimpers, and she felt obliged to wait a few seconds longer before gazing at it with a professional healer's eye.

Deep in the center of the paw, right in the most tender part of the flesh, there was some sort of object that was definitely not canine—a foreign body, thin, surrounded by dried blood in a variety of shades. This object, whatever it was, must have been troubling the patient for some time.

Clearly, it had to be removed, but how to go about it was something she needed to think about. She recalled how she had observed animals dealing with cuts and slashes by licking at them. That was something she could at least try, something the dog might recognize as an attempt to help. She continued to caress the animal's muzzle with her left hand while she sucked at her cheeks, trying to produce extra saliva. Scraps of knowledge she'd picked up over the years flashed through her mind as she did this. She was sure that someone had once told her that there were certain healing properties in every animal's spittle, including humans. If only her mouth wasn't so dry, mostly from a degree of fear she couldn't quite shake off.

She allowed a few drops of spittle to dribble past her lips and fall on the center of the injured paw, and waited for a moment for any reaction from the dog before she began to massage around the wound entry mark with the extreme tip of one finger. She was careful not to touch the wound directly. Gently, without haste or any sudden movements, she worked away from the center until all the dried blood had been removed. Now she had to have complete trust in the animal as she adjusted her sitting position and lay down as close as possible to the dog's flank. She placed her mouth to cover most of the underside of the paw and began to lick at the wound itself, running her tongue across and along it. She could feel the dog react by relaxing still further; her body told her that the dog had relaxed so much, it might even have drifted off into a light doze.

That could only make the next, most difficult part of the job easier. She sat back on her heels and eased her knife out of its sheath. Her heart hammered wildly in her chest as she lay the knifepoint as close to the foreign object as possible, slightly to the right of what she could see of it. One thing she was sure of—this object was deeply embedded in the flesh, and a certain amount of pain was inevitable for the patient. She had to be ruthless, she had to be decisive, she had to be fast, and she had to be prepared for the animal to react unfavorably to the pain, perhaps even turn on her despite all her good intentions. The rapport she had managed to build up so far would count for nothing if this powerful beast decided to exact revenge for the hurt she could not avoid inflicting on it.

With one final non-specific prayer for a positive outcome, Sally suddenly bore down hard on the blade, turned her wrist a fraction and pulled away, feeling something dislodge and fall free of the flesh, caught on the tip of the knife blade. The dog stiffened and howled, sounding in that instant more wolf than dog, and struggled to rise to his feet, but Sally had anticipated this reaction and was ready to counter it, tossing her knife a few feet to one side where she could retrieve it when circumstances allowed. She raced to get both arms around her canine patient's shoulders, at the same time attempting to immobilize his powerful back legs by entwining her own around them.

It was a natural instinct for the dog to attempt to bite a living thing that tried to hurt it, and Sally had to be extremely inventive and supple to avoid being seriously hurt by the dog's perfect set of teeth as he twisted his neck almost in a full circle both to the left and to the right. Sally was too quick for him, keeping her head right when he snapped to his left, and vice-versa. A certain element of sheer luck and good guessing were also involved, but no more than she deserved for her prompt and courageous actions.

Once her patient had calmed down and all the twisting and turning had ceased, Sally sensed that she could at last initiate the final stage of recuperation, the stage of rest and convalescence.

She took his head in both her hands and cradled them together gently under his chin, not giving him the opportunity to look away

She was still conscious of the need for stealth. She was, after all, somewhere she wasn't supposed to be. Furthermore, she was presuming an unheard-of ability to communicate with a wild dog. That was something nobody would accept was even remotely possible. If Sally's experience with the superstitions still common in most communities was any guide, this was a guaranteed, swift solution for anyone who felt an urgent desire to be burned at the stake with the crowd screaming, "Witch, witch, witch!" in her ears.

Chapter Fourteen

Once Sally was reasonably certain that the dog had recovered from her rough emergency surgery, she loosened her grip around his neck and pulled her water gourd out. It was one of the few things her unknown attackers had not either destroyed or stolen. She wanted to feed it to the dog, but it wasn't obvious how to go about the task, which was essential if the patient was to make a speedy recovery.

Pouring a few precious drips into the palm of her hand, she attempted to slide them into the corner of his mouth. About half went in, and he seemed to get the general idea. His tail almost wagged as he staggered to his feet, with the left front paw held off the ground.

Sally touched his nose. It was dry and far too hot. She wondered if it was just a reaction to the injury, or if he was running a fever from some other cause. There had to be some way to get some hydration into him. Right at this moment, that was what he needed most. She tried tipping the gourd, aiming the thin stream of water directly at his gaping mouth. Again, most of it seemed to end up inside the dog rather than spilled on the ground.

As she sat up to ease cramped muscles, she caught sight of her knife lying where she had tossed it. The object she'd removed was still glued to the tip of the knife by a tiny drop of congealing blood, and proved to be a rusted fish hook. Sally understood just how painful this must have been, and spent several minutes caressing and comforting her grateful patient. She kissed the wound, as she had "kissed it better" for an injured child many times in the past, and had to suppress an inclination to vomit when she tasted the pus that her spittle released from the wound. Eventually, she was able to rinse her mouth with the last few drops of water from the gourd and cradle Dog's head in her arms while they both recovered.

"Where do we go from here, Dog?"

Sally had spent most of her adult life living alone, and talking to herself had become a habit. The fact that she had been almost continuously in contact with other people in recent days hadn't changed the habit formed over a period of years, and she certainly didn't feel in any way self-conscious about communicating with animals. For her, it was as natural as breathing.

On this occasion, she was merely voicing her thoughts, and wasn't the least disappointed when Dog failed to respond. She'd have been far more surprised if he *had* answered, she thought, and grinned at the scene that flashed across her mind. Her and Dog sitting on stools with a cosy camp fire between them, a drink in hand/paw, calmly discussing the next day's travel plans. She giggled aloud, and Dog's head swivelled round with a peculiar expression in his eyes, as if this was something totally outside his experience. He said nothing, however, and she continued to fill in the blanks on his behalf.

"I came to Leverpole by river. If we follow the river and keep moving upstream, sooner or later I should be able to find Bryn's farm, and the only people in this region I know, and who know of my existence. If we're really lucky, I might even come to the part of the harbor where Tess O'Reilly has the tavern I was supposed to sleep at. If Bryn's man hasn't left yet, we might even be able to sail upriver with him. I just wish I knew what day this is and how long I spent locked inside that prison cell."

Dog looked away, almost as if bored. This person was not talking about *him*, that was quite obvious, and he had a typical dog's attention span, almost zero. He lifted one rear leg and began cleaning his nether parts.

Sally's stomach sent her another reminder of the fact that it had been some considerable time since she'd last eaten. She acknowledged the fact, but as she had neither food nor the wherewithal to buy or barter for supplies, she ignored the message and stood, prepared to take the first chance that presented itself to slip away from the docks area to the relative safety of Leverpole's crowded, anonymous back streets where she sincerely hoped the press gang would not find her before she reached either the tavern or a track that followed the line of the river and led to the sanctuary of Bryn's farm.

There was nobody close at hand, and the few people she could see around the docks all appeared to be going about their own business. She judged them to be far enough from her to be unable to recognize her, even if they were actively seeking a runaway. *And for all I know*, she thought, *they haven't even discovered I'm not where they left me.* With this small crumb of comfort to brighten her spirits, she laid her left hand on Dog's shoulders and moved away from the rear of the building, aiming for the outskirts of the dock area and the jumble of streets that gradually melded into a potpourri of small houses and a sprinkling of shops and businesses.

The morning reluctantly became early afternoon, and a tide at low ebb meant that the docks area was thinly populated with no ships queuing to be loaded or unloaded. It was ridiculously simple for Sally and her new canine companion to wander unchallenged through the unguarded dock gates, past St. Nicholas' church and the Tithebarn toward the center of town. Industrial and commercial premises rapidly gave way to houses in a wide variety of styles. Some were clearly the random, unplanned efforts of the less well off and looked as if they would fall apart with the first blasts of a winter gale; others were large, well-built mansions erected by professional architects following the instructions of rich and influential merchants.

At last, Sally felt she could relax. The danger of being recaptured had become almost zero once they'd passed the dock gates. Now they were an ordinary woman in a cheap, common robe accompanied by a dog, and there was nothing remarkable about either of them to attract unwanted attention.

Was it possible to find the way to Tess O'Reilly's tavern? Depending on how long had passed since her abduction, it was still possible that Bryn's rower—how she *wished* she'd thought to ask him his name!—hadn't returned to the farm yet. It would be so much simpler if he was still there, and she could avoid the inconvenience of walking the full distance without knowing exactly where to find the farm other than the simple fact that it came right down to the river's northern shore and should be easy enough to find. Such was her theory, anyway.

She arrived at a junction where four well-trodden paths met. Vehicles and pedestrians jostled and feinted to gain advantage over traffic moving in the opposite direction or turning left and right. Nobody seemed prepared to give way and allow another a second's advantage to make a turn, or use the smallest of gaps to complete negotiating passage, but as far as she could see, there was a general mood of tease and banter in the insults and curses being hurled between the combatants.

Two gentlemen who were clearly better dressed than most stood deep in conversation and slightly withdrawn from the general melee. Every so often, one or other would gesture toward the chaos of the junction and make a point that invariably drew further comment from the other. Sally decided from their dress that they must be important local dignitaries of one sort or another. Sooner or later, she had to pluck up the courage to ask someone for directions, and she thought she had a better chance of a truthful and courteous reply from two stylish gentlemen rather than a cheeky street urchin, or a semi-coherent drunkard stoned on poor quality gin and draped around a piece of street furniture.

They stood outside a hostelry, which sported a large sign with an ornate crown painted upon it. From their gestures, Sally thought they had finished discussing the traffic chaos and re-directed their attention to discussing the market, which was doing a roaring trade on the corner diagonally opposite them. Sally positioned herself where they could see her, and waited politely for them to reach a convenient pause in their discussions. After a minute or two of gestures and comments in which both gentlemen seemed to be agreeing cheerfully with whatever they were discussing, one opened a small ornamental box—Sally thought it might be made of brass—and invited the other to share some of its contents. It contained some sort of powder. Sally watched, incredulous, as they both shook a portion of the powder onto the backs of their gloved hands, and lifted their hands to their mouths...no, not their mouths. They both lifted their hands *past* their mouths, nodded to each other, and simultaneously *sniffed* the tiny mounds of powder into their nostrils. The powder was a dark brown, and Sally could see it clearly against their spotless white gloves. One moment it was there, the next it had all disappeared, leaving no trace of any residual stain on the material. The owner of the tin replaced it in a waistcoat pocket, and Sally seized this opportunity to catch his eye.

"Excuse me, sir. I am not familiar with this town. Could one of you please tell me which of these roads will lead me to the river? I have been wandering, and lost all my sense of direction." Sally squared this with her conscience by reminding it that most of what she had just said was true.

The gentleman nearest to Sally, and not the one she had actually addressed, turned with a genuine smile on his face and beamed at her. "Allow me the honor of answering your question, dear lady. My friend and I have always agreed that we lay up treasures for ourselves in the next world when we perform small acts of kindness and consideration for others whilst here on earth. It will therefore be our greatest pleasure to assist a young lady, especially one who considers us trustworthy enough to be relied upon for assistance in a town that boasts as many ruffians as it does true gentles."

"Sadly, that is true!" the other interrupted. "But you must never forget that, according to one learned philosopher, Leverpole is home to almost twice the number of four-legged rats as the two-legged variety!"

They both leaned heavily on their ornate, gold-capped walking sticks as they shook with laughter. Sally looked from one to the other. She understood almost every word that had been spoken, and from the way in which they were used, she could make a fair guess at the meaning of one or two words she hadn't heard before, but on the whole, she didn't think the comment had merited quite so much open and genuine hilarity.

When the two men of the world had regained control of their laughing fit, it was the owner of the small box who spoke first. "Be not afraid, young lady! What I said about the 'two-legged variety' of rat," he gestured over the heads of the crowd as if in explanation, "was not intended to be taken seriously!"

"Indeed, very few of your comments are *ever* taken that way," quipped his colleague, and they exploded into another paroxysm of helpless mirth before the speaker could continue.

"Be that as it may, and I'll not deny, there's some truth in my friend's statement, but there are far more *good* folk in Leverpole than...let's say, than those who are less than perfect."

"Ah, Duncan, you never cease to amaze me with your cheerful outlook on life, and the way you can always find something positive to say of your fellow man."

"Brian, 'tis always better to look for the silver lining in the clouds, or the rose sprouting from amongst a bush of thorns."

"Again, beautifully put! You have a way with words, 'tis no surprise that you have become one of this city's best known poets while I must apply myself to the mundane tasks of local government."

"And one of our town council members, one I can see becoming Lord Major before much longer, if there is any justice!"

"My friend, I fear we embarrass our damsel in distress! She has told us that she is in need of assistance and advice, and other than saying that we will help, we have not progressed beyond that stage as yet. Indeed, unless I misremember, we have as yet done little of any consequence other than praise ourselves." He turned to address Sally, and chose to do so in a style that was almost formal in nature, yet still managed to convey more than a hint of self-deprecation and concealed humor. "My friend Duncan values the beauty of words almost as much, I'd wager, as he loves his own life! My name, as you've heard, is Brian, and now you have the advantage of us, miss...?"

"Sally, medicine woman and healer; 'tis a well-respected calling in the small community I have lived in all my life until recently. Something happened in my community, and I was prompted in a strange sort of a dream to make a journey." She faltered, certain that if she started giving unnecessary details, she would either omit something vital, or bore her listeners with the length and nature of her account.

"And your journey brought you to Leverpole. What did you hope to find in this fair city?" asked Brian, who seemed the more practical of the two.

"For the moment, I cannot be certain, but I know that I

must return as quickly as possible to a farm not far from Leverpole, where a true friend I met along the way is seriously ill. He awaits my return to continue nursing him back to health so that he might travel onwards with me."

"Aha! Straightway there is more to the tale than first it seemed!" Duncan exclaimed with joy. "Milady Sally! This chance meeting, if indeed it or any other meeting can truly be said to occur by chance, is indeed truly fortuitous! For it so happens that your most direct route from here will be to forge across this busiest of Leverpole's roads, Linden Street, and continue straight on, following the road ahead at all times until it leads you to the river. I estimate it a distance of some two thousand strides. What say you, Brian?"

"If you mean two thousand paces of the Roman Empire measure, I'd say that was a very close figure, my friend. For a poet, you can still surprise me sometimes with your wealth of knowledge of science and so many other subjects!"

Sally listened to this swift banter without really understanding it all. She was used to people speaking plainly, and took everything she heard literally. Verbal games involving jokes, exaggeration, or making puns and playing with words was new to her, but she was beginning to understand it better, especially when it occurred between such close friends as Duncan and Brian. The idea of deliberately speaking a lie, or something she knew to be untrue, was something that would never have occurred to Sally; the very concept was alien to her nature and upbringing.

Brian caught her eye, and she smiled to show she was ready to listen.

"The most difficult part of getting to the river is probably going to be fighting your way across this junction," he said, seriously but with an amused twinkle in his eyes. Seeing he had her full attention, he continued, slightly self-consciously. "That is in fact what my friend and I were just discussing. This busy meeting of the four main routes into the center of town is always like this, as so many people come into town to do their business, and everyone meets here. Result? As you can see, total chaos! Nobody is prepared to wait and allow another to cross before him. Fights are common, and accidents, unfortunately, even more frequent. We have been trying to find a way of easing the problem, but so far nothing has helped. The press of the crowds is becoming more of a problem each day, and the people mill around like mindless sheep." He sighed.

Sally's imagination populated the junction with the bodies of sheep, all with human faces. She smiled at the mental image, but suddenly, a thought struck her. Of course! It was so obvious! She turned to look up at the two burghers of Leverpole, and before she could stop herself or think about whether it was her place to speak on the subject, she heard herself blurt out, "Milords, have you consid—"

She stopped in mid-sentence and hung her head. She had dared to open her mouth to begin a conversation without being formally invited to express an opinion! This was something she would *never* have been allowed to do in her small, isolated village community, where all the decisions that mattered were discussed and implemented by the men. Women were rarely, if ever, consulted on anything of import, and then only allowed to speak when spoken to, or invited to give an opinion. What had she done? Would they think her brazen, or worse? She dared not lift her eyes from the ground, and awaited their judgement.

"Sally, we like to think ourselves gentlemen—or gentlefolk, if you will! But lords we are not, and if you have some thoughts on this, for I suspect that is what you were about to reveal, then please, feel free to tell us."

Duncan leaned forward on his stick and bowed slightly to bring himself to her eye level, trying to present her with a less imposing, formal figure.

She glanced from him to Brian; the latter nodded and bent at the knees so that they were suddenly a close group that a casual observer might think were discussing a personal matter concerning nobody but themselves. Dog wriggled and lay flat on the ground between Sally's feet as if he were a co-conspirator with every right to participate in the discussion.

Sally took a moment to collect her thoughts, and said, "Your description of people 'milling like mindless sheep' made me smile, but it also gave me an idea. I have lived my life until recently in a small village far from here, and isolated from other small villages, none closer than two to three days' walk. For most of the year, our men farm the land and raise the animals we rely upon for food—cattle, poultry, and sheep. The sheep spend most of the year grazing freely in the hills and valleys, but when we have to herd them together for shearing, or for market and for slaughter, the men control them with special sticks called crooks, and have a special language of whistled commands, which they use to send dogs running to gather the sheep and move them in the desired direction. Do you think it possible—"

"To introduce some sort of control?" Duncan interrupted, his eyes shining with excitement. "Why, yes, Sally! I believe it might work! A signal to move or wait..."

"But the dogs," Brian interrupted with a worried look on his face.

"Oh, I don't think we'd need them!" Sally laughed. "People aren't as stupid as sheep! All you need would be some men with long staffs, like the shepherd's crook."

"And some agreed whistle commands!" Duncan concluded. "Yes, Sally, I really think it would work! And the dogs, are they specially trained? Is this the sort of dog you use?" He nodded toward Dog as he spoke.

Sally shook her head. "No, he's far too big and clumsy. He'd probably chase the sheep, or scare them up into the hills and we'd never get them to market! In fact, he's not really *my* dog. We only met this morning. I think he's a stray. The dogs we use are a much smaller breed, and yes, we train them, but I know nothing of how that is done. It is not considered suitable work for women."

"Hmm. Crooks and whistles. That sounds very simple, Sally. We are in your debt for this idea! I shall put it before the council at our next meeting!" said Brian. "It is poor payment for services rendered, but the least we can do is offer you a meal, and then to escort you to the river, if that is your destination."

Sally gasped. Every scrap of wind was driven from her body, and her hands flew to cover her face. She felt embarrassed. Her cheeks were surely on fire! As she struggled for breath, her hands fluttered down her flanks, a vain attempt to smooth the wrinkles of her sack-cloth emergency clothing.

"Your offer is far too generous, sir! I couldn't possibly—"

"Oh, but I must insist," Brian interrupted "Or perhaps that should be we insist," he continued, glancing at Duncan.

"Indeed it should, my friend." Duncan nodded. "I am certain that your present state of attire is not one you would have chosen if another had been available! I feel you have been the victim of some unpleasant incident that has made you a genuine damsel in distress in need of the assistance of a gentle-man—or two!" he concluded, receiving a nod of confirmation from Brian.

Before Sally could find a word of protest, Duncan had linked his arm under hers and raised his swagger-stick to force passage across the busy junction, ably assisted by his colleague.

As they passed the row of lime trees that marked the opposite side of the street and found their way into the market, the press of bodies eased. There were still plenty of people scurrying from one vendor to another, but there was also adequate space between the stalls and barrows for Brian and Duncan to flank Sally, and the three of them were able to walk freely, three abreast. Dog remained as close as possible to Sally's feet without tripping her, and his size was enough to encourage others to move swiftly out of the way.

Duncan looked up and signaled with his stick that he had a specific destination in mind.

"When the Romans retreated from this part of the country, they left behind plenty of well-made roads, and a few other things," he remarked. "One of them was a highly efficient water-heating system, which they used in building public bath houses. There is one here in our market, copied from the Roman bath house at Deva, which is as close to Leverpole as the Romans dared to come. They could never quite control the local residents."

Sally's senses were almost overwhelmed by the sights, sounds, and smells of each stall they passed. Barrows filled with fresh fruit and vegetables vied with more permanent-looking stalls selling hot, cooked food and drinks. Others traded in bolts of brightly-colored cloths or cooking pots. They passed a small smithie, where a muscular youth was repairing someone's sword.

Duncan stopped at a robust, stone-clad building, one of the permanent structures. "This bath house is owned by a friend of mine, Sally. I promise you'll be safe here. You need not worry about being attacked when you remove your clothing to bathe. I'll introduce you to Helena. She is the owner, and while you attend to your own personal needs, Brian and I will purchase a few trifles of clothing, which I trust you will do us the honor of accepting as a gift once you emerge, a bright butterfly escaping its chrysalis!"

The curtain almost in the corner of the building hardly seemed to twitch as Helena appeared and dropped a formal curtsey first to Duncan, then Brian.

"This is Sally, who is in sore need of the healing powers of a bath. Please help her with whatever she may require. We will return soon with a few purchases."

Dog padded into the building, Sally's inseparable shadow. He went to follow her into the bathing area, but she decided that some things were too personal to share. With a shake of her head and a short throat-sound, she pointed to a rush mat on the floor underneath a small table. Dog dropped his head, then turned and curled up under the table without further protest. Helena saw this exchange, which caused her eyebrows to shoot skywards in disbelief, but she made no comment and turned to lead Sally into the first of a nest of interconnected bathing rooms. Bowls of lightly scented luke-warm water were standing ready, together with soapwort and other plants Sally recognized as useful for basic cleansing. She smiled. She had a feeling she was going to enjoy this experience, make it last as long as possible...

The water in the ewers cooled as Sally sponged the worst of the dirt from her skin, and she wandered through to the next room where she discovered a pool of much warmer water, deep enough that she could lie in it, with a selection of sweet-smelling oils to use on her skin and on her hair.

A skin hung over the exit doorway. As Sally pushed it to one side, a small puff of steam greeted her. Helena had changed into a floor-length, toga-style dress and welcomed Sally with a graceful gesture.

This room was the hottest of the three. It was filled with steam, which puzzled Sally. The only water she could see was in a small bucket standing on the floor next to a pyramid of rough stones in the center of the room. Small benches were placed against the walls.

Helena took a scoop of water from the bucket and drizzled it over the stones, creating a thick, dense fog of steam. Sally felt the temperature in the room shoot up as the water hissed on the stones. Helena splashed a second scoop of water on them, and the temperature increased once more.

Sally could actually *feel* the pores of her skin opening, gaping wider than should have been possible. The sweat of many days' labor and endless travel was being efficiently pumped out of her system. Instantly, she felt revitalized, as if she had sloughed away every last cell of her old skin and stood now in a fresh skin, as pure and unsullied as a newborn infant.

A further surprise awaited her when she glanced at Helena. The bath house owner had discarded her garment, and now stood naked, holding what appeared to be a young sapling—a birch tree, Sally thought—in each hand. With a smile, she handed one to Sally and began to beat herself gently with the one she kept. Bemused, Sally copied her, slapping every part of her body with the flail. When Helena began to dance around the room, Sally again followed her lead. Soon they were laughing and skipping as they beat themselves—and occasionally each other—with the saplings until most of the leaves lay littered across the chamber floor.

Helena paused, and with obvious reluctance, tossed her branch into one corner and took Sally's hand, leading her into a final chamber, where a miniature waterfall tumbled in one corner and piles of thick, white towels were folded in neat bundles around the rest of the room. Helena stood under the waterfall for a few seconds, then ran out and began toweling herself vigorously.

When Sally imitated her hostess' lead, she realized why Helena had only stood under the water for a few seconds. It wasn't just cold, it was *freezing!* She was convinced she could *hear* her wide-open skin pores snap closed in protest. The friction generated by the vigorous toweling warmed her body back to a more normal temperature as well as dried her.

When they were both dry, Helena led Sally toward the final door in the nested system of rooms. Two full length robes of the same absorbent material used for the towels hung there. She handed one to Sally.

"Your friends may well be waiting for us when we leave. Duncan said he would buy you some clothes, so I've thrown out the sack you were wearing. I hope you didn't intend to keep it?"

Helena's voice had a pleasant, musical quality to it, and Sally realized with a start that she hadn't actually spoken in all the time they'd shared the final stages of the cleansing process—she couldn't recall Helena answering Duncan's greeting either. Her acute ear insisted that Helena was probably not born in Leverpole, but came from somewhere else, a part of the realm where people *sang* rather than spoke. Was that possible, or even likely? She wondered. She made a note of this curious but fascinating tidbit of information, along with the hundred and one other trivial details she'd learned since leaving her home. When would she find time to sit down and study each of them, giving them the time they deserved?

They went through the door, and Sally discovered they'd entered the first room of the maze. Dog still lay obediently under the table, which now held a selection of female garb. Brian and Duncan sat, looking slightly uncomfortable, side by side on a bench on the opposite side of the room. They were genuinely pleased, and, Sally thought, somewhat relieved to see Sally and Helena re-enter.

"Dog was quite happy to allow us to enter, but not at all keen on the idea of us leaving!" Brian said.

"Indeed, he stood between us and the door, and refused to allow us passage," Duncan agreed. "Did you not say he was a stray, and you've known him only a few hours? Have you trained him? But of course not, you haven't had *time* to train him!"

Sally looked at Dog, who uttered a few sad-sounding whimpers. She nodded briefly and turned her attention to Duncan. "Dog says he's sorry if you ..."

"He says *what?*" Duncan spluttered. "How can you tell what he *says?*"

Now it was Sally's turn to look puzzled. "Why, I simply listen to him. How else does anyone know what another says?"

"Sally, I know you said your life as a medicine woman has been quite a lonely one," Brian said, "but you appear to have developed a talent that few have ever even contemplated, and I know of none who have achieved it. Communicating with animals on *any* level is not a skill usually granted to an ordinary man or woman!"

"But I'm not...special!" Sally protested. "I'm just a healer, and maybe I'm good at that because I *listen* to my patients when I try to find out what's making them ill!"

"That would make it easier to *listen* to animals, as well as people," Helena offered.

Sally nodded. It made perfect sense to her. How could one tell what had made someone sick if he or she didn't, or wouldn't, listen when the person tried to tell you what was wrong?

"Brian and Duncan, I'm really, truly grateful for the clothes and the time you have offered me already today, but I know you're both busy men. Allow me to dress suitably, and we can return to The Crown to share a meal before our ways part."

Helena ushered the two gentlemen into yet another of the cells that formed the honeycomb layout of her business premises, leaving Sally with the luxury of a private dressing room. As she inspected the selection of clothes Brian and Duncan had provided, she could hear soft laughter from the side room, punctuated by the distinctive *clink* of coins being passed from hand to hand. She decided that her bathing experience had been worth every penny, however much it had cost!

The clothing might have been made for her by the most skilful bespoke tailor in Leverpole. A snow-white blouse with a lacy trim around the neck caught her eye, and a wispy purple chiffon scarf to complement it. Also, dark blue satin trews ending at the knee with leather drawstrings to secure them and a long-sleeved lime-green jacket decorated with a pattern of small yellow diamond shapes. Stockings in the same shade as the jacket, and a sturdy pair of brown leather shoes, which she sensed she could walk in comfortably all day, completed her selection, and she called to her benefactors to come and inspect the end result.

"I really don't know how to thank you," she began, but Brian would hear none of it.

"You'll need this to carry the remainder of the clothes with you," he said, producing a solid bag of impressive dimensions from behind his back.

"What? You mean, *all* of this is...for me?"

"'Tis my experience—and, I am sure, that of my friend, too—that a young lady will *always* carry at least one full set of clothes to change into," Brian murmured.

Duncan took his cue. "And as it is crystal-clear to both of us that you have spent most of your life thinking of others rather than yourself—"

"And have recently been subjected to some...misfortune, which I suspect included not a little violence against your person," Brian added.

"We could not stand aside and say 'let her sort it out her-self—it's not for us to interfere,'" Duncan added with a busi-nesslike manner that suggested he was not prepared to lis-ten to any argument or further negotiation on the subject.

Before she could protest any further, Duncan offered Sal-ly the crook of his arm, escorted her back to the Crown Inn, and demanded a private table of the barkeep. Dog padded obediently close to Sally's heel, curling up out of sight under the table they were offered. A meal was served almost im-mediately, and Sally was suddenly aware of how long it had been since she had last eaten. Despite her hunger, however, she was conscious of Dog's need for sustenance and fed him discreetly from her own plate throughout the meal, much to the amusement of both her new friends.

The crowds and the vehicles jostling for advantage on the streets when they left The Crown seemed more chaotic than before, if that was possible. Brian stood and surveyed the scene, possibly trying to envision how some minor degree of control might have a positive effect.

"We might try placing two men with crooks on each junc-tion," Duncan offered. "They could use the crooks to hold back the crowd while the cross traffic moves across the junc-tion, and take it in turns."

"And I'm sure I can persuade the council that it would be money well spent, hiring a couple of constables to bring or-der to the town on market days," Brian added.

Duncan flexed his shoulders and lifted his walking stick. "Let us see if we can force a path with our own 'crooks,' shall we?"

Brian caught the idea and copied Duncan's stance. They flanked Sally, slightly in front of her and the dog, and leaned on the nearest of those fighting to cross the still-chaotic junc-tion. The combination of the two well-dressed men carrying solid walking sticks, which they were clearly prepared to use as weapons if needed, was hint enough to persuade people in the immediate vicinity to move out of their way. As if by magic, a path of sorts appeared in front of them, and slowly, but without needing to use muscle or weapon, the trio—and Dog—were able to cross the junction unhindered.

Many fingers were pointed at the way in which Dog re-mained in close attendance to Sally with no apparent need for a restraining leash or even audible commands. As word

was passed from mouth to mouth through the press of bodies, the crowd parted more swiftly until it was no longer necessary to use the walking sticks to force passage. Duncan
and Brian reverted to the accustomed manner of using them
as accessories, which marked their rank as men about town.

"That worked even better than I dared think possible,"
was Brian's excited comment as they reached the opposite
corner of the square.

Sally had another thought. Where were all these strange
new inspirations coming from recently? She seemed to be
simply *bursting* with fresh ideas! "Gentlemen, do you think
people were looking at your style of dress, as well as the
sticks you were carrying? That might be something you could
think about if you're going to hire people to do this job."

"A simple idea, but an effective one, I think!" said Brian,
with more than a hint of approval in his voice

"I agree, and perhaps use bright colors, or ribbons or
something, on the crooks themselves, as if they were a
badge of office!" Brian echoed his friend's enthusiasm. Sally
tried to hide her embarrassment under her borrowed robes,
but there was nowhere for her to hide.

Duncan seemed to sense her discomfiture and made an
attempt to change the subject. "Did you say, you only found
this dog early today? A stray, here in town?"

Sally nodded. "Yes, he had a big, rusted fish hook lodged
deep in his paw, and I managed to remove it for him. He
seems...grateful, and has followed me since."

"Gratitude? An animal can't show feelings!" scoffed Brian
with a short laugh.

"Are you so sure of that?" Duncan said with a thoughtful
expression. "I don't think you should dismiss the idea completely, my friend. I have known animals, dogs especially,
who are clearly devoted to their masters."

"But in such...such a *short* time? Sally and her canine
companion seem to have become very close immediately,
and that isn't something I can recall ever hearing happen
until now."

"The circumstances themselves were unusual, though.
She removed something from his paw that had been causing
him great pain and distress! Did it appear to have been there
for some time, Sally?"

Sally nodded, shuddering as she thought of the layer upon layer of dried blood and pus that had been in the wound. She winced once more as she tasted the evil mix she had sucked out of Dog's paw after removing the hook.

"I've seen similar wounds before in my time as medicine woman and healer. I guess he was unable to move around without severe pain, and it was obviously a wound he'd been carrying for a while. I would certainly be grateful if somebody performed such a service for *me*."

"But, Sally, you're saying that animals can have emotions, feelings. What is it that separates man from other animals? Are you saying you think animals can have a soul?"

Sally had only a vague idea of the concept of a soul, based on the inexpert words of the traveling priest whom she'd only met a few times, and even he had seemed somewhat uncertain about what a soul was, never mind discussing who had one and who didn't. Reluctantly, she shook her head. She was genuinely unsure what she thought, and had no concept of how to tell a lie.

"That is a question I cannot answer, Brian. I simply do not know enough to give you an answer. You must ask a priest, or another expert. All I can say is, Dog seems to trust me and has followed me of his own free will. I have done nothing to compel him to do anything he doesn't want to do."

"Whether you grant him a soul or not, have you given him a name?"

Sally immediately felt uncomfortable. The tribal customs and the mystique surrounding names and name-giving were deeply ingrained in her upbringing and beliefs. She hadn't given thought to the idea of name-giving for her companion, and in her mind he was simply "dog."

Duncan sensed her discomfort and tried to create an escape route for her. "Here in Leverpole at least, it is a custom most people follow if they have a cat or a dog living with them. It makes it easier to call them home if they are on the street when you wish to close your door for the night!"

He said this lightheartedly, making it sound like a joke of sorts, and this confused Sally for a moment. Could these people really think that the sacred rites her tribe associated with name-giving were so trivial, something to laugh about?

She tried again. "Your pardon, sirs. But my tribe, and a number of others I have dealt with in my travels as healer, have ancient traditions, part of our beliefs, which places great importance on names, and we are usually very wary of admitting our own personal names to a stranger at first meeting, and perhaps not even on meeting them a third or fourth time. We believe that knowing someone's name gives you a power, or an advantage over them. For this reason, it is usual for people to *exchange* names at the same time, so neither has the advantage over the other."

"Sally, I think I see your problem," Brian interrupted. "For I can tell you, in my dealings with folk from other towns and different parts of the country, I have encountered a number of ancient traditions and beliefs that are closely connected with name-giving rituals and ceremonies. Your tribe is not alone. Nay, I venture to say, not even in a minority in this respect! Rest easy. If you had not considered naming the animal, I am sure that thinking of him simply as Dog is perfectly acceptable."

"A family may name a pet to amuse a child," Duncan said, "or to remember a family event. You may wish to do the same. Wait until a name suggests itself, perhaps an event that binds you more closely."

"Sally, we are close to the river now, and soon our ways will part," Brian said.

Indeed, Sally suddenly realized that the familiar blend of salt, ozone, tar, and rotting seaweed had become more prevalent while they had been strolling along the road, but she had been so engrossed in their discussions she had barely noticed the change until now. The crowds had thinned, and they were almost alone on the street apart from a ragged group of children running around kicking an inflated pig's bladder in some ball game of their own, and of course, the inevitable beggars pleading for alms on every street corner. Sally was generally almost blind concerning these people, but not because she didn't care. She never carried money; it was not the tribe's way of doing business. Therefore, she had nothing she could offer them, but she had on occasion passed one a draught of medicine to combat an illness she had seen developing through their symptoms, or a warm drink or something to eat.

Sally caught a certain look in Brian's eyes and realized she was keeping him waiting. Although he hadn't ended his sentence with a question, it was obvious that he expected her to speak next. It was equally obvious that the conversation still had some way to go before reaching a satisfactory conclusion.

"My apologies, for a moment I was caught in the threads of my own thoughts," she managed to stammer, and was immediately relieved to see a thoughtful and genuine smile on his lips once more.

"Duncan and I will leave you once we reach the river, as we both have some distance to ride home, and we must first collect our horses from the livery yard. You have been very useful his afternoon, Sally, and I insist you accept this small token of our gratitude." He produced a small purse and hefted it. There was a small but unmistakeable *chink* of coins inside it. "You may find that you need to replace—whatever it is you're wearing—with something more suited to city dwelling," Brian said, completely serious for once, and continued. "This does *not* represent a fortune, dear one, and if you are unable to return this way and repay it, it will be no great loss for me personally. 'Tis clear to me you have a specific reason for traveling all this way, and you have referred to at least one place you intend to visit when you return. Do you know how to get there from here?"

Sally nodded. "I was ferried downstream from a farm that nestles right on the banks of the river. If I follow the line of the riverbank, I cannot miss it."

"There is clearly more to discuss, which we have not had time for as of yet. But that must wait on another meeting, for the afternoon is upon us and you are short of travel time, young lady!" With these words, Brian pressed the sack of coins into Sally's hand. "This will buy you a couple of nights' bed and board, if you do not succeed in getting a ride part or all the way to your destination today. Think of it as a reward for your ideas, but if you insist on regarding it as a loan, anyone you ask will be able to tell you where to find Brian Stanley, if you should inquire after me. I hope we meet again. Until then, God with you!"

Sally embraced both men while Dog sat and watched impassively. With a final wave and another round of mutual thanks, she turned her attention to the well worn path that shadowed the meanders and bends of the river Mersea and strode off.

Chapter Fifteen

"We must have met the river upstream from Tess's tavern, Dog. We're not in the dock area anymore."

Sally had been walking for perhaps half an hour, and had not recognized any landmarks yet, but the track was leading her through a part of the town that was mostly houses, definitely not docks or small river trading businesses. Eventually, the track split, and she opted to remain on the right hand path, which continued to follow the course of the river and looked to continue to do so as far as her limited horizon. Fields replaced houses on her left, a mixture of grazing paddocks populated by horses and cattle interspersed with fields planted with crops of wheat and barley. This was now farming country; she felt she had probably left the town itself.

A small stream with a pebbly bed danced down from the field she was passing. Someone had sought to add their own finishing touch by adjusting the flow of a short natural fall over a few rocks to convert it into a miniature waterfall that appeared to leap from a small gap in a section of drystone wall, which she assumed marked the boundary of a farmer's field. As she stooped to refill her water gourd, Sally nodded her approval of this thoughtful detail. Someone had gone to a lot of trouble to complete a necessary job without damming or diverting the stream.

"Come, Dog, let me see that paw," she muttered. Dog had been half-lying on his flank, licking at the damaged paw. Sally spoke so softly she was barely aware of having voiced the command, yet he looked over at her, then rose and trotted across, favoring the damaged paw very slightly but not by much. A confused jumble of thoughts chased each other through her mind for a moment, and were gone.

DidIspeakaloud? Didhehearme? Isthisjustcoincidence?

For the moment, there was no test she could think of that might prove or disprove her questions. She'd have to keep an open mind, and observe Dog very closely over the coming days. Of course she'd heard even as a young child all the superstitions and folk tales about witches and their familiars, though these usually involved cats, not dogs, as well as shape-shifters who could become wolves, usually at certain times of the year or phases of the moon. She didn't believe for a moment that there was anything unusual, strange, or supernatural about Dog, but they *had* achieved a seamless, instant understanding upon meeting, and she thought once more about the exchange of growls that had been her first breakthrough in establishing contact.

How did one measure the intelligence of an animal? Of course, they could neither read nor write, but Sally had never learned her letters and numbers either. If she really concentrated, she could even put names to the numbers; one, two, three...sometimes as far as ten, which she remembered was the name for the number represented by one on each finger.

Without the sounds to communicate this, it was unreasonable to expect animals to be able to reason or add simple numbers, but in this they were in many ways no different to most of the people Sally knew, who lived full, if not always deliriously happy lives without this knowledge. Did that mean *they* had no soul, simply because they had never learned their letters or numbers? She shook her head decisively. No! That could *never* have been the intentions of an all-powerful God, who made the world and everything in it, and found it good... The phrasing from Scripture she had heard during one of the traveling priest's infrequent visits sounded in her head, speaking to her in his distinctive, reedy voice so clearly that she suddenly whipped around and scanned each direction. It had been as clear as if he'd been standing right beside her, speaking softly in her ear.

Dog had remained still, his injured paw resting on Sally's upturned palm all the time she had drifted off into her own thoughts. Now he chuffed—a peculiar sound, half sigh, half pant—and the slight ripple of tensed muscle that went with the sound was enough to bring her back to her immediate surroundings.

She raised the paw to inspect it more closely, gazing deep into Dog's eyes, willing him to remain calm, to trust that she would not dream of hurting him. No sudden movements, no negative thoughts...

Slowly, gently, she turned the paw to look at the wound itself. She could see that there had been a tiny spot of fresh blood following the emergency surgery she'd performed, but Dog didn't flinch, suggesting that it wasn't hurting too much.

She cleaned away the soil and dirt that had built up around the wound, and peered carefully into the deep gash left by the embedded hook as well as the extra damage she had been forced to apply with the tip of her blade in order to remove it. She splashed some water into the cut and inspected it once more. There was no dirt to be seen in the wound. The flesh was the healthy pink of healing rather than the angry red of inflammation. The dangerous yellow pus of infection had also disappeared completely, and the flesh showed signs of beginning to knit together nicely.

How can I stop the dirt from getting into this deep wound? she asked herself. If she'd been treating her own feet for a deep cut, or anyone else's for that matter, she'd automatically cover the wound with a strip of cloth and advise her patient not to remove the boot or shoe for a couple of days.

A picture of Dog wearing boots on all four paws popped up uninvited, making her smile. Such strange pictures she was getting in her mind these days! And yet, why not?

She rubbed Dog gently between the ears, and was rewarded with a grunt she had come to recognize as an expression of pleasure. She tried to copy it as best she could on the principle that if she was going to manage some limited communication with Dog, she had to practice every sound she heard him make and try to remember the correct situation that went with each sound she succeeded in imitating.

Gently, reluctantly, she ceased rubbing Dog's head and neck. For what she was planning, she needed both hands free.

She slid her knife out of its sheath in her boot and inspected the lower hem of the garment she had fashioned from a meal sack. It wouldn't cause a modesty problem if she trimmed an inch or two from the hem.

Carefully, she sliced through the material, which was easy enough to cut. She only needed a hand's span or so, no more than the width of her thumb. She showed the length of cloth to Dog, kissed him gently on the nose, and soaked the strip of cloth in the running water of the stream before tying it firmly but not too tight around the injured paw, making sure the underside was smooth and the knot used to secure the bandage was high on the lowest part of his leg. A slightly bizarre question popped into her head. Did dogs have wrists and ankles? She wondered, and grinned once more as she pictured Dog walking upright on his back legs, brandishing a stick similar to those affected by Brian and Duncan, neither of whom seemed to have need of a stick to assist their walking.

She sat and watched as Dog slowly raised his rear end, standing briefly on three legs before placing his front left paw on the ground. He stood still for a further moment, then bent his head and sniffed at the bandage. He looked up as if puzzled, then took a cautious step with the injured paw. He seemed to grow in confidence and took several paces, circling to his left and returning to sit in front of Sally. His tail lifted slowly and thumped a couple of times on the grass. This was the first time Sally had seen him do this, which she had been told was the sign of a happy dog

"Come on, Dog, we won't get very far if we sit here all day!"

Sally placed one hand on Dog's shoulder and began walking, with frequent glances to her left to assure herself that Dog was moving comfortably without limping. He seemed to be trotting along without any obvious discomfort, and she deliberately started to force the pace. Looking at the position of the sun, she decided they were now closer to sundown, and she still had to find either somewhere to buy a prepared meal or food she could prepare for them both. The weather was considerably kinder here along the coast, she decided. If necessary, they could sleep under a hedge, if she couldn't find a bed for the night.

Remembering the way time and distance had seemed to unroll so swiftly crossing the heath in her native Yorkshire, Sally began to hum a little melody in time to the rhythm of her stride. She wasn't really surprised when Dog adjusted his trot to match her stride, and before long, she was convinced that he was timing his panting to the pace she set. Was she imagining things? She glanced down once more, just as Dog raised his head and looked straight at her. She could swear that was a broad, wolfish *grin* he was showing her!

Determined to test this latest development, Sally deliberately increased the pace again. If nothing else, they would cover more miles this way, provided Dog could cope with the increased pace. Dog's initial response was to prick up his ears and throw his head back, running ahead and returning constantly.

He believes this is a game! she thought to herself. Darting ahead once more, he stopped, turned, and barked at her, a clear challenge. She responded by imitating this at a slightly higher pitch—fairly accurately, she thought.

Dog leapt high in the air and dashed away again. Sally really had to pick her pace up now to keep him in sight, and by the time she caught up with him, she was definitely panting herself. He sat on his haunches, licking his fur into place as if taking a well-deserved rest before streaking off again. There was no longer any doubt in Sally's mind. He was definitely trying to take charge, setting the pace instead of following her lead, and Sally didn't know whether to be annoyed with him or pleased that he had responded so positively after she had dressed his wound.

Dog seemed to have found a bottomless well of unbounded energy. He was constantly ranging ahead, sometimes at breakneck speeds, and the first few times Sally was expecting it all to end in tears, or at very least a serious accident. Away he went, back he came; soon he started adding to the game, punctuating each trip with a short, high-pitched "yip!" which Sally was absolutely certain was a deliberate tease, possibly even a challenge. There was a certain glint in his eye she hadn't noticed until now, a devil-may-care challenge issued to a poor, clumsy sluggard who could never match him for speed, having only half the number of legs.

He had just begun another sprint ahead and disappeared briefly out of sight around a bend that was sharp enough to foreshorten Sally's view of the road ahead. Suddenly, she heard a new and completely different type of yelp from Dog, and there was something about it that jarred and made her feel anxious for Dog's welfare. By the time his head and shoulders reappeared on the bend, she was already running. This time, he didn't continue back to her side, but skidded to an ungainly halt, threw his head back, and howled. Sally redoubled her efforts and was at his side within seconds.

"Dog! What's the matter? What have you seen?" The words tumbled out of her, interspersed with a whole range of the canine sounds she'd managed to get more or less off pat.

He looked up at her, glanced over his shoulder, and returned to face Sally squarely once more. This time, he hesitated briefly before locking his gaze onto hers, and produced a sound totally unlike anything she'd ever heard before—a long, wavering sound that warped up and down two or three octaves and made her flesh crawl. There was no way she was ever going to attempt to imitate it.

She was also convinced that this was not another variation on Dog's game of "tease," but something new and different. She bent down and laid one hand on his shaggy ruff, uttering small, throaty sounds she had learned had a calming effect on him. She could feel his tense muscles across the shoulders, but after a few seconds, he began to relax. She stood slowly, encouraging Dog to rise and stand with her. She took a few steps along the road until the corner straightened out again, and she looked up the road ahead to see what had caused Dog to react in such a strange fashion.

A short distance further along the road there was an overturned cart. Its load, most of which could be identified even at this distance as farm produce, was spread to all sides and some of it was still rolling. Evidently, the accident had only happened very recently.

A man Sally guessed to be a few years older than her was fighting what appeared to be a losing battle with a small horse that was still attached to the wagon by a tangle of straps and reins. Each time the terrified horse rose and plunged, the tangle became worse, and the man trying to deal with the crazed animal lost further ground in his one-sided struggle. Each time the horse rose in panic and crashed back to the ground, the wagon shifted slightly and released a few more pieces of its load, adding to the confusion and general disorder.

Sally reacted without thinking, and sprinted toward the accident. She desperately wanted to help the older man, who was visibly tiring with every lunge the horse made. She pulled up sharply just before she arrived at the scene and walked slowly until she was sure that she was within the horse's field of vision.

She stood completely still for a moment, steadying her own nerves with the breathing mantra she had discovered was at her fingertips at a moment's notice. It continued to serve her well whenever she needed it, and for that she was grateful. She imagined a narrow tunnel connecting her eyes with the horse's and focussed on them, willing with all her might for the horse to lock gaze with her. This seemed to work; the horse's front hooves pounded into the turf once more, and it ceased its wild leaps of terror, caught in the aspic of Sally's unblinking stare. The weakest of all nickerings burbled from somewhere deep in its throat and escaped through the nostrils. Immediately, and without thinking about it, Sally copied the sound, trying to force the sound through her own nose.

A swift passage of non-verbal sounds between horse and healer followed. Sally caught something of the horse's fear during this exchange and strove to counter it with calming thoughts of her own—a meadow filled with the sweetest of grasses, a golden summer sunset, the peaceful tranquillity of a snug, warm stable, any picture she could conjure up from her imagination that could possibly calm a horse.

Maintaining rock steady eye contact, she reached out her left hand and placed it under the tiny goat-style beard trying to grow on the horse's chin. Would he flinch at this initial contact? She was relieved when he didn't. Quite the reverse, he dropped the full weight of his head into her cupped palm, an action that surprised Sally just as much as it pleased her. She appeared to have gained his trust, but it was too early to take anything for granted.

Movement at the very edge of her field of vision reminded her of the presence of a third party witness to the scene as it unfolded. For the moment, she ignored him. If this situation should have a satisfactory resolution, anything she did right now might make a crucial difference, and in all honesty, she wasn't quite sure what she'd achieved so far, much less what else might be done to reach a happy ending.

You're beautiful, she thought, giving his chin the lightest of affectionate squeezes before moving half a step closer to ease her arm around his neck and comfort him further.

Instantly, she felt a wave of emotion from her new patient, unmistakeable feelings of gratitude and thanks. The feelings were so strong they couldn't be mistaken for anything else, but how was it possible for her to sense them at all, let alone identify them so positively? Another mystery to be pondered upon; such things caused disruptions in a predictable, ordered life, something Sally had taken for granted until very recently.

The horse seemed to have run out of matters to discuss for the moment and ceased producing all the small throat-and-palate sounds he had been directing at Sally. She eased him ever so slightly backwards by the simplest of maneuvers, placing her shoulder against his and giving just the suggestion of a shove. She caught the eye of the presumed horse owner, still agitated and hovering behind his animal. With a sharp glance, she hinted that he could use this opportunity to reach into the tangle of reins and harness and release the horse from the wagon. Fortunately, he grasped the idea at once, and completed the task in moments. Once the horse was free of all the constraining straps and harness, he shook his head proudly and let his full mane fly freely, resembling a golden halo when it caught the light.

"I am in your debt forever, sister," the man gasped. Although of the three he had probably exerted himself the least, Sally could see that he was a good deal older than she had first thought, and his breathing was still labored.

"Not so, sir! 'Twas by chance alone I happened to be close by, and once Dog showed me someone having difficulties, possibly in danger, I did no more than what any Christian would do for another."

"You are too modest. In all my days I have not seen anyone with such mastery, such control over a frightened beast! Might I inquire the name of the young lady who performs such miracles that I may thank her properly?"

"My name, sir, is Sally, and my home lies across the mountains, in the Palatine of York. Amongst my people, it is tradition for strangers to exchange names, that neither may feel at a disadvantage." Sally used a rising inflection to show that this was a question, neither a rebuff nor a suggestion that he was discourteous to ask so directly. She was still very aware of the fact that certain tribes had definite taboos regarding names.

"Then I will say that your custom has much to commend

it, and I could wish others would do likewise! My name is William, from the village of Hale. As you may guess, I was on my way home from market when my wheel caught in a rut and overturned the wagon."

"And is it also a custom amongst *your* people to give names to your animals?" Sally inquired.

"Since I own only one horse, there is no confusion, yet I hope one day to own more, and in that hope I call him Joseph, after Joseph the Worker, for that indeed is what he does without complaint every day!"

"What a good choice!" Sally said, and she meant it. It had never occurred to her to give a name for a particular skill or a trait of character; children were generally named when they were taken to church and christened at an age when they were far too young to have displayed any personality traits or special skills. "But, come now, let me help you gather together your purchases, for they do not seem to have taken any great harm from the spill. Road dust can be washed off, and I cannot see eggs or any other fragile items amongst the casualties."

Despite William's protests, Sally began plucking those things that lay nearest to her at once, and he was obliged to join her or seem churlish by refusing. The cart had taken no serious damage and was soon righted.

"We appear to be traveling in the same direction. Will you accept a ride, Sally? I can see that your...wolf of a companion seems to run easily, but is he lame? For I do believe I see a bandage of some sort on his front paw."

Sally was obliged to give a shortened version of the first meeting between herself and Dog, one that omitted the fact that she had been kidnapped by the press gang, imprisoned, and managed to escape their clutches by the narrowest of margins.

"That in itself is a wondrous tale for the telling around an evening fire shared with a few close friends," was William's comment when she had finished. Sally wondered what his reaction might have been had she chosen to tell the full story of the past two days in Leverpole, and decided that in this instance, it was politic to remain silent. William had, however, planted a seed in her mind, and she determined to observe Dog even more closely over the next few days to discover if a more particular name than the generic term "dog" might suggest itself as a suitable name.

"...so I have chosen to spend my time on the roads, serving no man but myself, and beholden to none." William had used the last hour of the day's good light telling Sally something of himself and how he made his living as a traveling Jack, sharpening knives and scissors, hiring sometimes on a daily basis when crops were due to be gathered or animals driven into folds for the winter.

"The depths of winter's the only time I sometimes wonder if I can continue this life, though," he admitted at one point. "At that time of year, nobody needs a Jack of all trades—and master of none!" he added with a negligent gesture, as if dismissing all his many talents in one fell swoop. "There have been times when I've lain under a thin blanket, beneath my wagon, or in it if the ground's too cold or snow has fallen, and thought summer's warm would never return to unfreeze my old bones. Yet there's nothing can compare with awakening as the sun peeps o'er the treetops on a clear Mayday morning when you could be forgiven for thinking you're the only person in Christianity awake to witness the sight. Sometimes it feels as if you own the whole world."

"You sleep in this wagon, too?" Sally was puzzled. "Where, then, is your bed? Or do you content yourself and make do with a couple of thin blankets, as you hinted a moment ago?"

This time, it was William's turn to laugh out loud, and he did so with such gusto and volume that Dog, who had been running easily at the side of the wagon, raced around behind them where the wagon was open at the rear and leapt gracefully aboard to see what the fuss was all about. A few cuddles and an exchange of grunts and growls seemed to reassure him that he wasn't missing out on anything interesting, nor were there any edible treats to be begged. Soon he was off again, exploring the way ahead and the fields on either side.

"As you can see, this wagon is comfortably big enough for two travelers—three, really, because as you can see, we were not crowded when your wolf-hound joined us, brief though his visit was." William grinned. "Over the years I have wandered, I have built storage shelves, cabinets, and other devices into my wagon, fitting it out exactly to suit my purposes. For the moment, you may continue to sit on that bench, but if you look more closely, you will see that the seat can be removed, and inside it is all the linen and bedding I will ever need, and most of the clothes I happen not to be wearing at this very moment. This driving seat I sit upon is another store, containing all my pots, pans, and tools of my many trades. There is also plenty of room for one or two to stretch full length on the wagon bed, and I have also a screen that can be fitted in an instant, day or night, if it looks like rain!"

"So you travel alone the year round? Is there no one place you call your home?"

"I travel the year around because that is what I choose, and I am never alone, though I may on occasion have no companion to spell me at the reins," he said with an air of mystery in his eyes. He seemed to be daring Sally to ask the obvious question, and almost pre-empted her question by beginning an answer to the riddle.

"What do you...?"

Somehow, from nowhere, a wooden flute appeared between William's fingers and he trilled off a complicated pattern of notes that seemed to hang in the air far longer than should have been possible.

"I always have my music with me, and when music is present, you can never be truly alone," he said when he eventually stopped to draw breath again. "Music and song are sometimes the best way to tell a story, especially a long one, or one that has great joy in it—yea, and deep sadness too sometimes."

He paused for a moment. Perhaps his attention had been caught by a particularly poignant memory, thought Sally. She was almost tempted to ask a further question when he continued.

"Perhaps you'll allow me to sing for you part of one of the traditional songs of the roaming folk? It may explain something of how I—we—feel?"

Sally nodded. She had always liked music, and her own recent attempts to invent new words and melodies to pass the time, especially while traveling alone, now seemed to make more sense.

William played a slow, thoughtful measure of notes on his

recorder, then placed it in his lap as he put words to the melody:

"Now the open roads are calling, and my old shoes are full of holes
And I have just carved my secret symbol behind a sign on this dusty road
I'll start from Preston and head for Chester
Forgotten now winter's bitter days
I'll sharpen tools and I'll edge your scissors
I'll sharpen sunshine to pay my way."

He played another verse on his instrument and laid it aside once more. Sally was spellbound. William's voice was perfectly true, but sounded as if it ought to be coming from a much younger man.

"That was beautiful! Is there more?" she asked, hoping to encourage him to sing more verses.

William smiled. "That is a very old song, and one with many more verses. I'm not sure if anyone truly knows how many, or has the wit to remember them all," he said. "'Tis but one of many songs that tell of a way of life some people choose to live. I could not live any other way. To remain in one unchanging town or village, seeing the same people every day, doing but one job again and again, whether it be farming, tanning, working in a smithie, or serving ale in a tavern, I know I could not stand the thought!"

"But surely you must have somewhere that you call home? I mean, where you were born, where your parents lived...?"

"My parents, and their parents before them, lived as I do now, on the road, constantly traveling. Our traditions say that we are what is left of a people once called Romany, who traveled throughout this country and many others from the frozen fields of the north, whence came the Viking invaders in their own good time, down as far as the sun-baked lands that border the Middle Sea around Rome, Greece, and other countries too hot for comfort! Myself, I'm content to live with the uncertain weather of this country, which has neither extreme of too hot or too cold. Now, if it would only rain a little less, this could be the perfect clime."

"William, can I ask you to play me just one more song?

You sing so beautifully."

For answer, William took his instrument in his hands as if to comply, but then looked to the sky and frowned. "Your pardon, Sally, but it's later than you might think, and I've a sense of rain in the air. We should first stop and make camp for the night, and I'll instruct you in how to erect the skin that will protect us tonight if the rain arrives soon after sundown, which I feel it may!"

Sally looked up. She was fairly weather wise, but could see no sign of rain in the offing. William was right, though; the sun was getting low, and she saw the sense of making preparations while there was still enough light to see by.

William pulled to one side of the track so the wagon was parked on lush green grass. As soon as the bridle was removed, Joseph tore hungrily at the nearest clump and was evidently more than content with his lot. William led him a little further from the wagon, and drove a sturdy spike into the ground to tether him for the night.

The skin he had referred to was rolled tight and smooth around two sturdy poles and carried lashed near the axle, underneath the bed of the cart. It was thin, but incredibly strong leather. The two poles slotted into two holes in the front corners of the wagon and the leather cover stretched over them, tying off at the rear to form a triangular shelter the size and shape of the wagon bed.

William soon had a cheerful blaze going, and they picked from amongst the produce that had been salvaged a few hours earlier to use for a meal. He selected some fried fish and a small amount of salted meat. These, together with cooked fresh vegetables, and one of Sally's refreshing non-medicinal teas, proved more than enough, and Dog seemed satisfied with the ham bone and a few scraps of meat.

"Can we reach the farm I seek tomorrow, William? For last time I saw him, my good friend Tom was seriously ill and he needs me."

"I know of one or two farms that are bound to the south by the river that flows past, the Mersea. One of them is owned by a man who calls himself Bryn. I think it likely that is where you are headed. It's perhaps an hour's journey from here, no more, I'll warrant!"

"You have been most helpful, William. Though I have wondered several times, why does walking this distance take so much longer than sailing? On my life, we were no more than half a day on the river."

"Yes, Sally, traveling *with* the current, and with a man in the stern using a paddle, I imagine?"

Sally nodded, and suddenly understood.

"So the speed of the water *and* the muscles of the rower took us quickly downstream. Oh, William, you must think me foolish not to see that for myself."

"Fear not, my lady. Indeed, it was not *so* obvious to one who has never sailed before. I *am* right, that was your first time? I thought as much."

Sally nodded.

"Now, let us hurry and crawl under the skin. I smell the rain, and it is close at hand. There is room for Dog, I suppose, but it might be better if he sleeps under the wagon where it will remain reasonably dry anyway. That will give us a little more breathing space, and avoid the stench of wet dog."

They barely had time to bank the fire for the night and call Dog back from wherever he'd been exploring before the first fat drops of rain began falling. Dog was content to be shown the ground beneath the wagon. He curled up on an old blanket William had tossed out, calling it ancient and threadbare.

"William, can I ask you to sing a verse of the other song you mentioned? I feel that the music and the rain between them will help me fall asleep."

Inside the shelter, it was almost pitch black, but Sally could just make out William's silhouette against the protective skin, picked out by the dying flames of the fire, which was being battered into submission by the strengthening squall of rain.

"As long as you don't mind me singing without playing the melody on the recorder," William murmured. "Not because I cannot finger it in the dark, but quite simply because I have put it away to keep it safe."

Sally agreed willingly, and watched William's silhouette as he settled and lie flat on his back. He hummed a short snatch, then began to sing softly:

*"I'm a free-born man of the Traveling People
Got no fixed abode with no man am I numbered*

Country lanes and byways were always my ways
I never fancied being lumbered."

"Well we knew the woods and the resting places
And the small birds' sign when winter days were over
Then away you'd jog with your horse and dog
Nice and easy, no need to go faster."

Another three or four verses followed, and William's sensitive musician's ears heard what he was listening for halfway through the fourth verse when the first soft snore could be detected in Sally's deep, regular breathing.

Chapter Sixteen

Sally woke the following morning to an enthusiastic washing of her face from the rough surface of Dog's tongue. She rolled onto her right shoulder to speak to William, and found that she was alone in the wagon.

The rain had stopped during the night, and the air smelled as if it had been scoured spotlessly clean. Even the salty tang of the air felt like a disinfectant, brought to her nostrils by the westerly breeze curling up from the river.

A cheerful, whistled tune hinted at how close William was. When she then heard the snap of a twig, it gave her a clue as to why William had risen with the sun, and what he was doing now.

"Off with you, Dog! I'm starving, and you're too big for this wagon anyway."

Laughter from outside the rain shelter told Sally that she hadn't spoken quite so softly as she thought she had.

"Do you know you mix words with dog sounds when you speak to the hound?"

Sally ran an instant replay through her brain. She realized that William was right. And had anyone other than William noticed, but been too polite to pass a comment? Even though she was alone in the solitude and dimness of the shelter, she could feel her cheeks redden with embarrassment.

She bounced out of the wagon, straightening the hem of her skirt, offering a silent word of thanks to Duncan and Brian for the selection of clothes. She shook her curls into place and gave them the briefest of combings with her fingertips.

William had placed two separate pans on the fire, both three-quarters filled with water and just about to boil. He looked up and grinned as she clambered awkwardly over the tail gate.

"The rear board comes loose, remember. You've no need to climb over it."

It was well-meant advice, but a second or so too late. Sally was by now committed to the climb, and dropped to the ground. "This is a new tea blend I've never tried," she said, offering William a handful of mixed herbs.

He sniffed them and looked her squarely in the eyes. "Are you saying you've never even sipped at it yourself? How do you know it won't taste awful, or worse, make one or both of us ill?"

"Because over the years I've learned from testing the brews on myself just what to expect from certain combinations. I don't need to taste something with fly agaric in it to know that even the smallest sip is likely to kill! I just learn to recognize the sight of it, and avoid even approaching it if at all possible. This is a new blend for me because it's made of local herbs and plants, many of which are new to me because they don't grow on Yorkshire's peat bogs. On the other hand, I've seen pictures in books, and remember what a number of teachers and mentors have instilled in me during my years of training to become a medicine woman."

"I understand, and please forgive me if I sounded rude. I never intended..."

Sally smiled. "William, life's too short to bear malice to anyone, and especially when it's not deserved."

"Well, if you place it in the smaller pot and leave it to draw for a minute, I'm just going to get something."

Before she could protest, or even ask where he was off to, William was gone. He was also true to his word, thrusting through the bushes less than two minutes later with another small pot in his hand.

"The poor cow's udder was over full, close to bursting!" he said, blinking his eyes in a comical parody of childish innocence. "And I do believe she thanked me, in her own fashion, for the favor. I'm sure she'd have found a way to express herself to you, considering the way you seem able to communicate with any animal you happen to meet!"

Sally laughed, but felt faintly embarrassed all the same.

She'd never suspected this new talent might lie latent in her, just waiting for the right stimulus to show itself before burgeoning forth fully-formed and ready to be used. She decided to try changing the subject. "Well, are you going to put half of that in my drinking horn, or are we going to cast lots to see who gets it?"

Sally had thrown in half a hint to a Scripture story she almost remembered the traveling priest retelling on his last visit, and wanted to test if William's casual reference to Christianity was sincere or empty bravado. William rose immediately to the challenge and passed her test with flying colors.

"I'm a bit more honorable than a Roman soldier, Sally! We chased them out eventually, didn't we?" He grinned, then added, "As a matter of fact, I was going to share it equally between us. Fresh milk tastes wonderful on a bowl of porridge oats."

Sally had to admit that the combination made very for pleasant eating, especially when topped off with a spoonful of wild honey William had chanced upon during his travels. Dog, however, decided it wasn't for him and shot off into a nearby copse to forage for his own breakfast.

"Do you have any idea how far we are from Bryn's farm?"

They were out in open country now, with the river still in sight on their right and tidy, managed farm fields filling the remainder of Sally's view. Dog loped easily close to the wagon, seemingly content to socialize, remaining close at hand rather than ranging ahead.

William rubbed one hand across his cheek, as if this helped him to think. "If I'm right, it may be closer than you think. I see smoke over to our right, and it has to come from a dwelling of some sort."

Sally peered against the bright sun, which was still low in the sky. She knew there was nothing wrong with her eyes, but they were apparently not as keen as William's.

Around the next bend in the road, a collection of buildings came into view and Sally recognized it. Their landside approach was from roughly the same direction as her previous headlong dash to reach the farm in time to administer the lifesaving medicine she had prepared for Tom.

Tom! With everything else she'd had to think about the past, had it really only been two days since she'd escaped from the ship's brig? However long it was, she'd barely thought of him, and the memory of his gentle touch was still there, feather light on her skin, provoking surprising, confusing, and powerful emotions in her, feelings she had never experienced before; she didn't know how she should deal with them.

Had he survived? Was he still clinging on to life in the coma she had induced? "William, I feel we should hurry! Something in me says that my...friend may be in sore need of my presence, and right soon!"

William said nothing, but lashed the reins several times on the horse's back to encourage his speed. The wagon jolted forwards until the wheels bounced on every rut and stone they encountered. Dog seemed to catch the sense of urgency, ranging ahead once more. At a bend in the road, he paused, sat, and howled back to them. As they approached, William slowed the cart to a walking pace once more. Dog sat where a side track forked from the main road, and Sally was certain.

"This is the path to the farm. I recognize the surroundings! We turn here."

Dog ran off before them once more, barking at the top of his voice. By the time the wagon reached the cleared space in front of the farm buildings, Bryn and several of his family and other farm workers were there to greet them.

By now Sally was beside herself with worry, and a healthy dose of conscience at the thought of what her actions might have done to Tom. She forced herself to be patient as Bryn welcomed them, and used an absolute minimum of time to introduce William, but declined to spend a moment more than that on explaining why he was there, or even how they had met.

"I will leave William to fill in the details, Bryn. I sense that the signs are not good for Tom. I must see him straight 'way!" Without waiting for Bryn's response, Sally flew to the cottage that had been set aside for Tom. A silent bluewoaded figure sat at the foot of the bed, watching over the patient. The guardian was completely immobile, and Sally might have thought him dead but for a flick of his eyes in her direction as she entered, the whites a shocking contrast to his skin. Details were blurred by the flickering light from a peat fire that also served to keep the room warm, but the only thing that concerned Sally was the state of her patient.

She dropped to both knees at the side of his bed and nodded her thanks to the guardian. He stood, bowed, and withdrew.

Left hand to his brow—cold. Dry, but cold. No hint of a raging fever to raise his temperature. Was that a good sign or not? Sally wondered, and moved her hand to lay her sensitive fingertips as lightly as possible where the main blood vessel should show itself at the side of his neck. Granted, the drugs she had forced into him were intended to slow the rate of his heartbeat, but...

It seemed an unconscionably long time, but Sally was determined to wait. Just the faintest of signs was all she asked... There! So faint, she'd almost missed it, but she held her breath and waited once more. It came again, just as weak, but definitely there, a slow pulse that told her that Tom's heart was still functioning, sending the vital supply of blood coursing around Tom's body, performing the bare minimum of maintenance necessary while he was in the comatose state.

What to do next? This was the one question that seethed in Sally's mind, demanding an immediate answer. Herein lay the weakness of her plans, she suddenly discovered. Everything she had done for Tom prior to her leaving for Leverpole had been based on experience, following a sequence of events she had lived through once before when achieving her own cure from the same mysterious illness. However, she had been unconscious herself at this stage of her recovery, and as she lived alone, had not had a guardian to watch over her.

Now, looking back, it seemed to her that the trip to Leverpole she had insisted was necessary had been a self-indulgent attempt to flee from responsibilities, avoiding the debt of honor she owed Tom for his unquestioning support and assistance when she had needed it most. Suppose he were now to die because she had tarried so long away from his side just when the roles were reversed and *he* needed *her*...

As she staggered clumsily to her feet, a thought struck her. She reeled as she felt a physical stab of pain in her heart. As soon as she caught her breath, she crossed the room in a single stride and flung open the door. "Water! I need lots of hot water or my patient may die! Someone find the medicine supply I left here, and some extra blankets!"

She slammed the door to retain the warmth the peat fire had patiently built without waiting to see the reactions her demands had produced. Her travel bag of plants and herbs arrived almost before she had seated herself once more at Tom's side, and was supplemented further when an older woman knocked politely before entering. She carried a large bag, which she placed on the table before announcing herself.

"I am called Peg, goodwife to Bryn, and this is a collection of all the medicinal plants I have available in my apothecary, some in more plentiful supply than others, but these are what I have, if there are any you may need."

Wordless with gratitude, Sally hugged the newcomer like a long-lost sibling. Not only did she now have access to all the medicinal plants and herbs she could possibly need, apparently, and totally unlooked for, she was going to have the wisdom and experience of another medicine woman to call upon!

"Tell me what you have observed in him in the time I was...not here," Sally said, stumbling a little on the words as she realized that she had no real idea of how long she'd actually been away.

Peg thought for a moment before replying. "The day Rolan took you downstream..." she began, and paused as Sally drew a sharp breath.

"It's nothing," she stammered. "It's just, I'm embarrassed, I never even thought to ask him his name. What did he say when he—"

Peg shook her head. "That was the first day, and only three more have passed since then, mistress Sally. He was to do some trading on Bryn's behalf. He isn't expected back for at least another two or three days. That's why we were so surprised to see you today, and in the company of a traveler, arriving by road!"

Sally stared. "There is much I have to tell, but that will have to wait. Suffice to admit that I...lost track of the passing of days for reasons I will explain later. For the moment, I need to know how long Tom has been lying, hovering between life and death, under the medication I prepared for him."

"The sun has set three times since you left, Sally. This is the mid-morn of the fourth day."

Four days, Sally thought. Of course, she didn't really know how long she had been unconscious herself, with no guardian watching. She reached out and tested his pulse once more—faint, and slower than she would have thought possible, but steady. Considering the warmth of the room, he was colder than she would have liked. It was definitely time to attempt to revive him. Surely the medicine had had time to work its magic by now.

"He is cold to the touch, or was when last I checked early this morning," Peg said, diffidently. "Even though the room is warm, he seemed chilled to me."

"Yes, you're right. We should at least wash him down with warm cloths, try to bring his temperature up in that way. Have you managed to bathe him, or possibly force a few drops of water through his lips?"

"He has been bathed several times a day while he has slept. I knew it would be difficult to get water into him by any other means, if not impossible. I made sure that his skin was moistened to prevent cracks and sores developing. I hope I did the right thing?" Peg seemed in awe of the young-er woman's medical knowledge.

"Since you couldn't get drinks *into* him, it makes sense to moisten his skin. I'm sure some of it must have soaked in," Sally said, hoping she sounded more confident than she felt.

The first pans of water arrived, along with a supply of clean, folded cloths. Peg seized one of these and ripped it neatly into strips. Sally took the first of these and began swabbing Tom's body with warm water, starting from his forehead. The cloth began to take on a tinge of blue from the woad before she reached his knees, prompting her to take a fresh cloth when she started once more from his forehead. Peg had reached as far as Tom's waist by that time, and they worked silently, efficiently, keeping out of each other's way. The woad made it difficult to be certain, but her fingertips told her that his skin seemed to be softer, easier to massage. And was it her imagination, or was there the first sign of Tom's body beginning to warm through? She dared not say anything yet, but sent up a silent prayer to anyone who might be listening that she was not mistaken.

Peg was first to break the silence.

"Sally! Look! His toes!"

Sally had just begun another careful sponging of Tom's rugged features, and looked up just in time to catch the faintest suggestion of a twitch of movement in the toes of the patient's left foot. Her fingertips flew to the side of his neck, seeking for any indication of a pulse. Her heart leapt as she felt it immediately, and somersaulted as she felt the next few beats follow. The tempo and regularity of the reawakening flow of life-giving blood soon steadied and grew stronger. There could be no doubt about it; his vital signs were starting to pick up and return to their normal tempo. Her reaction was automatic, unthinking. She laid her lips upon his and kissed them tenderly, feeling the warmth returning to them, breathing her very soul into his mouth, willing him to come back to her from whatever limbo he had spent almost four days in as a result of her kill-or-cure method of treating his symptoms.

As she emptied her lungs and needed to breathe herself, she felt his chest expand and rise under her left hand. She stiffened in alarm. Was he returning to full consciousness too rapidly? She had no earlier experience to guide her in this. How could she judge the best way of returning to full consciousness?

As she lifted her head and took another deep breath, she felt his chest relax and fall under the lightest of pressure from her hand. She felt the faintest puff of breath against her cheek. It smelled foul, stale, as if it had been trapped stagnant inside his chest for the whole of the time he had been in his drug-induced coma, but for the moment, she didn't care. The signs were encouraging. Tom was strong enough to breathe on his own, without assistance from her or from anyone else. But it surely wouldn't harm him if she took this opportunity to kiss those beautiful blue lips once more.

Completely oblivious to Peg's presence in the room, she filled her lungs once more and sealed her lips around Tom's. Once again, she was aware of his chest rising under her left hand, then falling as she paused to take a new breath herself. The stale stench of air trapped inside a confined space for far too long soon disappeared and she could taste the difference in the cleaner, healthier air pumping out of his reawakening lungs.

It happened as she pulled back to take another breath of

her own. The fingertips of her left hand felt his chest muscles contract a touch stronger than they had until now, and some instinct warned her that Tom was about to cough. Instead of placing her mouth over his once more, she found herself sliding her right hand under his neck to support his head. His eyes flew open and locked with hers for an eternal instant before his head flipped hard to one side and he was wracked by a series of deep, hacking coughs. Sally eased him to a half-upright position as the paroxysm passed, and he rid himself of an impressive quantity of semisolid waste so thick it reminded Sally of a domestic cat disposing of a hairball.

"Rest, Tom! I have prepared a drink to revive you. Can you sit unaided?"

He nodded, signing that he dared not attempt speech yet. Sally was delighted to see that he understood, and strode briskly to a table, the only furniture the room contained other than the bed on which her beloved patient lay.

"I promise this will taste much better than the last draught I forced between your lips, *cariad,*" she said, dropping into a term of endearment common in her own tribe but not used in commonspeak. A startled glance passed between Tom and Peg, but Sally was so preoccupied she barely noticed. All that concerned her was the condition of the draught she had prepared with all the love and devotion she could muster.

She knelt and offered it to him as a servant would to a mighty lord, but he frowned and shook his head.

"You are no serving wench, Sally, but a wise and skilful healer. You must not abase yourself to such as me; I quite forbid it. I will accept your potion, without fear or hesitation, but only when you stand and offer it as a gift between equals."

As he finished speaking, he swung his legs to one side and stood off the bed, swaying very slightly for a moment, then visibly bracing himself and squaring his shoulders to reach his full measure of inches. He stretched out his right hand, accepting the goblet from Sally. With a formal nod of thanks, he raised it and placed it to his lips, draining it without the slightest doubt or hesitation.

"That was indeed a powerful draught, and well sweetened ...with mead?"

Sally nodded.

"Amongst other things, all found in nature's bountiful pantry, for those who know where to look." Tom handed the cup back to Sally and looked slowly around the room. "How long was I...?"

"Peg says it has been almost four whole days. Someone has been watching over you the whole time. Now, please get back on the bed. I need to examine you, to see if the treatment has worked."

Other than checking his eyes for any trace of shadow or lack of focus, there wasn't a lot Sally could do. She had no intention of admitting that, however, nor would she do anything that might erode some of the mystique that enhanced the reputation of every healer.

"How are you feeling?"

Sally was aware how stupid, formal, even trite her question sounded, but it was voiced before she could stop herself. She was so concerned for the first person ever to show her any real affection, she simply had to know.

"If I am to be honest with you, Sally, what I feel most is...hungry!"

Recalling how ravenous she had felt on waking, Sally laughed out loud while Tom sat and bounced on the bed, wheezing with suppressed, almost silent mirth. Once Sally had discovered enough control to explain for a bemused Peg why she had found Tom's statement so funny, the older woman understood the connection and scurried from the room to arrange for the provision of a substantial meal.

As soon as they were alone, Tom hauled himself off the bed. They fell into each other's arms and stood there, swaying in the center of the room, caressing each other, exchanging sweet, tender kisses, vowing never to allow themselves to be parted for so long ever again.

After a few blissful moments of exchanging kisses and endearments, Tom pushed gently and with reluctance out of the embrace. "You called me something as I awoke, a word I have not heard for many years, an ancient language not spoken in these parts."

"*Cariad*? Is that the word?"

"It is! And south of the river the language is sacred to the druids, mystic priests to their people." He gestured with one arm, pointing out over the Mersea. "On a clear day, you can just make out the hills and mountains where they live. I traveled there from time to time, and the word is a term of endearment, if I remember correctly?"

Sally stared. "The druids you speak of have never visited the part of the country where I live—lived," she corrected herself, "but it seems the term has the same meaning in our local dialect. *Cariad* is a term used between...young romantic couples..."

She stumbled to a halt, feeling herself on unfamiliar territory. What did she know of personal relationships, emotional ties with another person? Nothing, she told herself. Her choice of the solitary existence of a healer, constantly at the beck and call of others, had made sure that was not a possibility.

Gentle pressure on her hands made her suddenly aware that Tom's fingers were firmly laced around hers. Without haste, solemnly and sincerely, he kissed the back of her hands without breaking eye contact.

"Perhaps we should join Bryn and his family. My nose tells me that a meal will soon be served," he murmured, sliding his arm around her waist and turning toward the door.

The meal was more than adequate to satisfy the most voracious of appetites, especially one enhanced by four days of involuntary fasting. It was served in the midday sun, on the forecourt, this being the only place a table could be set big enough for all Tom's clan runners to join them in the feast.

As they seated themselves, and the first round of drinks were served, Tom glanced at the assembled guests and frowned. "We appear to be short of two of my people. Where, pray, are Mig and Mag? They should be honored guests here, for it was they who willingly lent their muscles to the shafts of the wagon and sped Sally and myself from our settlement to this farm! Bryn, what has happened? Are they away on an errand? Have they been obliged to return home for some reason? Why have they not joined us?"

At the head of the table, Bryn and Peg exchanged a few quiet words in a rumble so low they could not be overheard. Peg stood and looked directly at Tom. With hands clasped demurely just below her waist, she said, "I must beg your forgiveness, sire, but your marvelous and unexpected revival from what many of us thought a death trance had quite pushed this from my mind. Two of your men were unable to rise from their beds this day. I find all your people so alike, I could not be sure who they were, but they are alike as two peas; are they perchance twins?"

"As it happens, you are correct. Mig and Mag are twin siblings, and generally inseparable in all things. Even when one is ill, the other is generally affected too."

"Tell me of their symptoms!" Sally exclaimed "I need to know, for their illness may be the same one Tom and I suffered recently."

"They both complained that the morning light was too strong and hurt their eyes. Also, they were hungry, but could not face even the thought of food, and even a small amount of tea was more than their stomachs could hold, for they were ill as soon as they tried to drink."

"Then I must beg our host's pardon and withdraw from this feast, for I feel it is vital I visit them immediately before they sicken further," Sally insisted, standing and facing Bryn with her head bowed, awaiting permission to leave.

"You take your responsibilities as healer seriously, that I can see," Bryn said, approvingly. "And it would therefore be both rude and unwise of me to refuse your request. Go, and with my blessing if it will assist you to find a swift and effective cure! Allow me to show you where they sleep. After you have seen them, you may want to move them, perhaps to the room where Tom was treated? If this is a serious illness, and one that may easily be passed from one sufferer to another, then we ought to separate the patients from the rest of the household and our guests."

The visit was brief, and needed no more than a casual glance to confirm that the twin siblings had indeed deteriorated in the few hours that had passed since they had reported sick. Sally was very concerned to see their condition, and Peg confirmed that she was shocked to note the speed at which the infection was gaining control. At once, Sally called for hot water in large quantities and began a careful stocktaking of the herbs and medicinal plants she had on hand. She was worryingly short of most of what she had packed in her gather sack back in Yorkshire, and the specific plants she had used in the concoction she had prepared were almost gone.

"Do you know the names of these three plants? And do you know where I can find a supply of them? For I have almost none left, and I cannot prepare the medicine I used to cure Tom unless I can find more of them."

It was fortunate that the dried plants closely resembled the living flowers they came from, and Peg was able to identify them straight away. Two kitchen girls were sent immediately to gather the plants from a local wood while Sally arranged for the latest victims to be carried into the side building that had been commandeered as an infirmary. She bathed both of them thoroughly when the first pan of hot water was delivered.

"I do not like the speed at which they have both broken out in a fever," she murmured as she finished washing the second brother and straightened up, feeling her bones creak from the continuous bending over. "I remember feeling hot and fevered when I knew I was sickening, but I cannot believe it happened quite so quickly."

"You were not fully aware of your surroundings, sister, if you were as badly affected as these poor souls, and from what you have already told us, you were not in an ideal condition to make a reliable judgement at that time."

Sally had to admit that this was a very astute assessment from Peg, but one of the serving girls chose that moment to appear at the door with a modest amount of all three plants Sally had asked for, and it was possible for her to begin preparing a further batch of the potent brew. Both girls returned several times while Sally was measuring, chopping, and preparing the ingredients, but she barely noticed their comings and goings. She had to get the quantities exactly right, or risk killing her newfound brothers instead of curing them.

She found the repetitive movement of chopping and slicing, together with the concentration required to mix exact measures, calmed her mind and enabled her to perform the tasks without fumbling or faltering. Peg watched in silence, and her appreciation of Sally's self-evident skills and knowledge increased by leaps and bounds.

Soon, Sally was satisfied. Both the cure and the sleep draught were ready for use. She turned to Peg, who had stood patiently on one side, clearly wanting to become involved, but not wishing to push herself in on Sally's methods of treatment.

"Would you mind helping me? I need you to raise the head of both patients while I try to persuade each of them to swallow a concoction, which I have tasted myself, and I can assure you that it tastes just as vile as it smells! It is possible that, even unconscious, one or both of them may try to resist when I attempt to feed it to them."

Peg was a typical farm wife, accustomed to heavy work, but it took all her muscle power to restrain both patients as Sally administered the medicine. However, the sleeping draught was accepted without problems. Sally checked the vital signs of both patients as their breathing slowed and became shallow. She also checked their temperatures as best she could. She was convinced that the thick layer of woad would keep their body temperatures somewhat higher than would have been the case without the insulation of the waxy shell. Finally, she nodded her satisfaction that the slow beat of the pulse in both patients was sufficient to sustain them as the medicines did what they were designed to do.

A sudden knock at the door forestalled any comment from either woman. The door flew open and one of the farm hands ran to Peg, concern written on his face. "Ma'am, Rolan has returned from Leverpole. He says that..." He caught sight of Sally and stalled in mid-sentence.

"Come, Peter! You know our guest, Sally! What is Rolan's message?"

Peter crossed himself surreptitiously, but Sally saw it. "Rolan says he returned without...our guest because he had heard tell she was taken by the press gang when they invaded Tess O'Reilly's tavern. He also said that Tess herself is rumored to be seriously ill, but not as a result of her injuries."

"How so then? She was in full health when last I saw her, though I cannot say if she escaped injury at the hands of the press gang."

"They say she was stiff and sore, and too weak to rise from her bed, and as she has run the tavern on her own since she was widowed, she has never missed a day until now."

Sally looked at the siblings lying in the improvised infirmary, and without any shred of evidence to support it, she felt certain there had to be a connection of some sort. The only connection between Mig and Mag here at Bryn's farm and Tess O'Reilly in Leverpole was her presence at both locations. She felt a jolt of guilt stabbing through her heart as she recalled the earlier connection she had made between her own illness and Tom's. Was it possible that her recovery from the mysterious ailment had not been complete? She knew that the disease, whatever it was, wherever it had come from, had taken a number of lives in her own community before she had been forced to find a cure for herself. What if her body still retained a small amount of the disease, not enough for her to show symptoms or feel the effects, but sufficient for it to infect others as she came into contact with them? She felt physically sick at the thought. As medicine woman and healer, she had taken a solemn oath to help others, cure them of their ills, but it seemed she had somehow become a source of infection for all she met!

There was but one course of action open to her. Swiftly, she stepped away from the patients, distancing herself at the same time as far as possible from any direct contact with Peg and Peter.

"Listen carefully, and do just what I say!" She heard a command tone in her voice, which did not come naturally to her, but she had to use to reinforce the importance of what she had to say. "I have good grounds to believe that I am not as fully free of this deadly malady as I first believed. Anyone who comes in contact with me seems to suffer. First Tom, then the two stalwarts who ferried us here, and now Tess! I must leave once more—alone this time—and make all possible speed back to Leverpole to try and cure Tess before she sickens so far as to be beyond all help!

"I have prepared more medicine than I needed, deliberately so, but now it seems it will barely be enough. Everyone here must be given a small portion as soon as I have left. Rolan, the boatman, must choke down a full dose, and also the traveler, William, who brought me here. They have been close to me far longer. You must also tell William that I have need of his horse to get to Leverpole swiftly, but I will return with his steed, or arrange for another to ride back here with it, as soon as possible. Don't touch me! I must leave at once!"

Stopping only to measure out a portion of the medicine she hoped would be enough to save Tess, she circled the room to avoid getting closer to any of its other occupants.

As Sally opened the door, Peg cried, "Sally! You cannot ride through the night without a cloak to keep you warm. Take mine!"

Sally caught the cloak as it was tossed across the room, and nodded her thanks for the gesture. She fumbled with the buttons until she worked out how they held the cloak around her shoulders, and headed straight for the paddock where she had seen William's horse tethered alongside the caravan. The bridle rope was easy to free from the tethering stake, and she threw herself across the startled horse's broad back with a lusty yell, pointing him toward the last sliver of the sun's disc as it set in the west over Leverpole Bay.

Chapter Seventeen

Sally had never tried riding a horse for an extended journey. Horses were definitely something only rich people could afford, at least in the part of Yorkshire where she had lived, unless you counted the occasional group of travelers. She'd had more contact with these people than most, mainly because of a shared interest in herbs and medicines. She had frequently traded with them for plants not found locally that she needed for common medicines. She found them a friendly and polite people. From her point of view, the fact that they preferred barter to coins was a definite advantage.

Half an hour from Bryn's farm, she was discovering that riding was not as easy as it appeared to be. She bounced around like a sack of stones, even though the horse was ambling along at little more than a fast walk. At this rate, she'd be lucky to arrive in Leverpole by sunset, but unless she could find a way to sit more securely and exercise a greater degree of control over her mount, she felt in great danger of being tossed to the ground while the horse was quite likely to amble onwards, unable to notice the difference the loss of her light frame would make.

At least there was no problem keeping the horse on the road. There was only one road that hugged the banks of the Mersea as it flowed toward the busy port she could see in the distance. She tried to think of the way the few riders she'd seen sat on their mounts, and began to rise and settle in the saddle in time to the horse's natural rhythm. The ride improved immediately as she caught the knack of it. She also remembered vaguely that riders seemed to use their knees as much as the reins they held to control the horse, and experimented with this technique until she found a way of encouraging her mount to a faster gait, which also became much smoother and more comfortable. Walk became trot and she no longer feared arriving in Leverpole after dark. She wasn't inclined to push her luck by asking the horse to extend to a gallop, however. She was certain she'd fall and quite possibly injure herself if she rode at full tilt.

As she trotted through the outskirts of the town, she wondered how difficult it might be to find her way to the tavern approaching from the river side rather than by road. She breathed a great sigh of relief as the road meandered all the way down to the banks of the river and she saw the shell outside the riverside entrance of Tess O'Reilly's tavern.

She managed to haul her borrowed mount to a standstill close to the hitching rail and slung her leg over the horse's neck, intending to slide to the ground...

Where she immediately crumpled to a graceless heap, having failed to realize that the muscles in her legs were dead, lifeless, and unable to support her after riding for so long. More by luck than by judgement, she'd managed to keep hold of the reins, and regained her feet using the horse as a support and counterweight. She stamped around until pins and needles signaled the return of blood circulation in her legs, then nickered a thank you to her mount as she found an apple in her pocket and offered it as a reward.

Sally hadn't gotten used to the idea of planning ahead. In her chosen role as medicine woman in a small village, it hadn't been necessary, and it hadn't been possible over the last few days of unplanned travel and chance meetings with different people. She hitched the bridle to a convenient ring that showed signs of having been purloined from the wharf and remounted in the hostelry walls for the purpose of "mooring" horses rather than boats. She thought about what she was going to say to Tess O'Riley. She had to assume that Rolan was still at the tavern; if he wasn't, she didn't know how she could possibly find him in a town as big as Leverpole.

As she approached the door, it flew open before she could knock. Tess O'Reilly stood there wearing a cleaning apron and holding a polishing cloth.

"I thought I heard someone arr...Sally! Mary have mercy on us, what happened to you, child? Where did you go? I've been so worried...never mind, come in, come in! You look terrible. Take a seat in the kitchen; let me see you!"

Tess practically carried Sally indoors and thrust her onto a convenient chair. Had Sally even tried to answer any of Tess' rapid fire questions, she probably wouldn't have been heard, so she allowed Tess to fuss over her for a few minutes, accepting a glass of something cold and sweet that only served to prove just how thirsty she was after her dusty ride from Bryn's farm. By the time she had recovered sufficiently to respond coherently to Tess' ministrations, the tavern keeper had placed a bowl of warm water scented with roses on the table and some cloths to wipe away the grime of the journey. A plate of oatcakes and a mug of something steaming had appeared from nowhere. Between grateful bites and swallows, Sally explained in a few sentences why she had felt compelled to return to the tavern. She glossed over her capture and escape from the press gang, as there was much in the detail of that part of the story she still didn't understand herself. The expression on Tess' face as she told what little she was prepared to reveal told Sally that she would have to give a fuller explanation at some point, but for the moment, Tess seemed content to listen to what Sally chose to tell.

"Well, when those ruffians charged into my tavern the other night, they caused a lot of damage, but now you've told me who they were 'recruiting' for, I suppose it could have been worse! He took seven or eight of my regulars—steady, paying customers at that—and I don't expect to see any of them again, if they've been pressed to that particular ship and captain. A right blackguard with a fearsome reputation, and no mistake! And yet you escaped."

Tess' pause suggested she was hoping for a few more details, but Sally held her peace. She tried to steer the conversation in the direction she wanted it to go. "Bryn's farmhand, Rolan, who was with me, do you know what happened to him? He didn't return to the farm, at least not before I got there and left again."

Tess nodded. "He was one of the lucky ones. He came back later that evening, said he'd gone outside to 'water the weeds' in the privy just before they burst in, so he wasn't taken. He was a great helping cleaning up the mess they left me, so I didn't charge him for bed and board that night. He was reet stiff and sore the following day, and worse this morning. He couldn't even raise the strength to get out of bed, and I don't know what might be ailing him. Bryn's credit is good with me and throughout Leverpole to my certain knowledge, so there isn't a problem with him staying a few extra nights, but I need to know if you intend to treat him here, or to travel back to Bryn's farm?"

"If he is, as I fear, affected by the same strange malady, it will not be possible to move him. But the messenger who arrived at Bryn's farm this morning, William, said that you had been taken ill yourself, possibly with the same malady. Was that not true?"

"A tavern keeper cannot afford a day's illness, Sally! 'Tis true I woke with a sore head this morning, and feeling as I might if I'd eaten some underdone pork, but I've learned enough medic to cure myself of all the common ailments, and I felt much improved by the middle of the day, so I came down to do battle and make sure my staff weren't drinking all my profits for the week!"

"Hmm." Sally noted this, but made no further comment for the moment. She promised herself she'd make the opportunity to sit in a quiet corner and discover if Tess had used any plants or herbs that she hadn't come across in her own experiences. Whatever she'd used seemed to have worked swiftly and effectively. She had another question that needed answering. "Tell me, has anyone other than yourself been in close contact with him? For I think that is a likely cause of the infection spreading."

Tess shook her head decisively.

"Nay, lass. I took him straight to a private room, which I try to keep vacant as far as I can for Bryn or his family and farm workers. They are frequent visitors."

"Good! Then I must see him at once. The disease sets in with frightful speed!"

Sally rose and picked up her travel bag of medicines and herbs. Tess led her out of the kitchen, calling to an unseen servant to bring hot water to the room, which was at the end of a narrow corridor on the first floor.

The window was open with the shutters drawn. The air in the darkened room was fresh, but there was a faint odor of sickness underlying.

"He complained of the light hurting his eyes. 'Twas his last coherent utterance before he lost consciousness just after dawn this morning," Tess breathed.

"My thanks for that. It gives me an idea how far the disease has progressed. I may yet have time to attempt a cure," Sally replied as she felt for his pulse and checked the feverish temperature of his brow. She started sponging him down using a bowl of water at the side of his bed, and had wiped the sweat from most of his body when the kitchen girl knocked on the door with the hot water Tess had ordered.

"Tell her to place it outside the door and leave. She should not risk coming into the room."

Tess nodded, and went to bring the water herself while Sally started measuring the ingredients for her remedy.

Waking Rolan even partially was not easy, but Sally knew that it would not be possible to get the remedy into him unless he was able to swallow. A gentle throat massage helped, and the sweetness of the soporific she administered afterwards settled him into a restful sleep, which Sally was grateful to see. As his breathing slowed and became more shallow, Tess grew concerned, fearing Bryn's man was about to die, but Sally was quick to reassure her.

"The body heals itself best when it is allowed to rest. In all my patients so far, they reach a state where they hover at death's door for awhile, and their breathing comes close to stopping. The heart slows too, but so far, each of the victims have returned safely. I was the first of them, and look at me now!"

Tess studied Sally and nodded. Sally took the opportunity to do the same, seeking any clue to assess Tess' state of health.

"You do not appear to have taken any harm from treating Rolan, probably because you have washed yourself each time. Am I right?"

Tess smiled. "I try to keep the tavern clean. Why wouldn't I do the same for myself?"

"On this occasion, Tess, your good habits might easily prove to have saved your life. But I'm going to give you a small portion of my special brew anyway, just to be safe...no, don't thank me just yet! It will still taste just as foul, but I don't think I need to insist on you taking the sleeping draught as well. You appear healthy enough. You can still serve your regulars in the tavern this evening, but if you start to feel either feverish or sleepy, you must promise me you'll let another take over your duties tonight."

Chapter Eighteen

Too tense with worry to sleep, Sally kept silent vigil over Rolan through the night, bathing him with warm water, sharing with him every labored breath he took.

By the early morning's light, she could tell his color had improved, and he was breathing easier. Just as she started to ask herself if the treatment had worked, Rolan stirred, murmured something, and tried to lick his lips. Sally slung an arm around his shoulders, raised him slightly, and fed him a small spoonful of fresh water.

"Don't try to speak yet," she cautioned him. "You've been ill—very ill, I believe. But the worst is past. Try to drink, your body needs it. More solid fare can wait awhile."

There was a brisk knock at the door. "Sally, has Rolan awoken? Is it safe to enter?"

"Yes, Tess, he's much improved. Come in, but stand clear of the bed."

Tess was carrying a small platter covered with a clean cloth. "I thought some fresh-baked bread and warm milk might tempt an invalid for his first meal," she murmured. Rolan struggled, and eventually managed to prop himself on one elbow.

"The milk first, I think. He may find chewing bread too difficult as of yet," Sally countered. "I remember how weak I felt when I first woke."

There was a fusillade of frenzied knocking on the door, and a young lad thrust his head into the room. "Tess, the press gang are on the street again; they're heading this way!"

Tess took control immediately. "Sally, they mustn't find you here! You managed to escape their clutches, and they won't forgive *or* forget! Up in the attic—hide!"

Dog had remained silent and unmoving in his corner, totally unresponsive to the alarm and raised voices. Sally frowned. She hadn't expected this of him. She checked in mid-stride and bent to feel his muzzle. It was both dry and cold.

This was not good. She felt his flank, and sensed immediately that his breathing was shallow, his chest muscles stiff, barely moving. Confused sounds from the angry mob grew louder down on the street; soon they would have the door ripped from its hinges. The shouts had become a rhythmic chant, reinforced by the stamp of marching boots.

Was Dog also sickened by something?

There was no time for further investigations or treatment. Sally whirled round to the pot-boy. "Hide him in a closet with a blanket to keep him as warm as possible."

Without waiting to see her command obeyed, she ran across the room, bounced onto a table, and used the momentum to reach the access hatch of the attic directly above. There was barely time for her to slide the hatch into place before the door downstairs splintered and the press gang barged in.

This time, they made no attempt to conceal the weapons they carried—knives, for the most part, and a few who preferred knuckledusters or marlin spikes. Sally lay flat, terrified in the total inky blackness of the crawlspace under the eaves, scarcely daring to breathe.

"So, where's the poxy doxy we took wi' the rest o' the 'volunteers' then?" sneered a sinister voice. Even through the solid joists she was lying on, Sally could hear it wasn't the same thug who'd been the spokesman for the original raiding party, but he sounded just as vicious.

"We found her here. This is the only place the slut'd run to after she escaped!" he continued as he reached out to grab the pot-boy by the ear. "If'n ye don' tell—and that right smart!—young un here's gonna look lopsided th' rest o' his miserable life!"

Before he laid a finger on his intended victim, a blur of black-brown lightning fizzed across the room as Dog burst from his hiding place and clamped almost every tooth in his head around the bully's right arm just below the elbow. He toppled with a shriek of agony, flailing the mangled arm desperately. Dog hung on grimly. His jaws were now all but closed, the right hand in danger of being amputated completely. As the self-appointed leader of the gang screamed and twisted from side to side, Dog became an unintended but very effective weapon, toppling other press gang members like the tumbling skittle pins of a nine-man-morris. Two of them were severely injured by falling on the other's knife. For several seconds, pandemonium reigned.

The tramp of heavy boots on the stairwell heralded the arrival of more bodies as pub patrons surged to the rescue of their much-loved hostess and her guests. Though armed with little more than a heavy beer tankard or a short cudgel, they had the advantage of being on their feet and uninjured, and it was no contest. Within minutes, a dozen press gang ruffians were trussed tightly, then tossed like sacks of poor quality corn-chaff over the banister of the stairwell and stacked in a corner of the snug downstairs.

Sally was more concerned with the continuing battle between Dog and the leader of the press. By now, Dog had every advantage. His victim was bleeding profusely from several deep gashes, his cries reduced to the whimpers of a barely-conscious child. With no thought for her own safety, Sally dropped from the attic to separate the combatants, growling and barking at Dog as she slapped him hard around the jaw and muzzle.

Dog reacted by stiffening, splaying his legs and standing frozen over his victim, silenced by Sally's sharp bark. With a final, none too gentle tap across the nose, Sally wrenched Dog's jaw wide apart, forcing him to let go of the chief Bully's arm, which appeared to have been reduced to little more than crimson pulp. The man's eyes rolled up as he caught sight of the wound—mercifully, he fainted.

"You won't need to tie *that* one up!" Tess snapped with a triumphant smile on her face.

Sally looked at her in disbelief. "How could I even *think* of binding him? Look at his injuries; the poor man is close to death! He needs healing, not further hurting!"

"He was determined to recapture you, and you can be certain you'd have been beaten within an inch of your own death if he'd succeeded!" It was Tess' turn to show her shock and amazement as Sally began cleansing the unconscious patient's arm. "Why trouble yourself with this scum's wounds? He deserves every one of them!"

"Tess, every day I see many with wounds they did not earn, or illnesses they must suffer though they have done nothing wrong. Should I deny them my medical skills and knowledge? Whatever this man may have done in the past, he lies here before me with grievous wounds, and I would not be a true healer if I did not at least try to ease his suffering. Ah, see! The bone itself is unbroken; that's good!" She looked around the room, then turned to Tess. "If I'm going to try to save this man's arm—and possibly his life—I'll need a bed when I'm done. Have you another room where Rolan can lie and rest? I have done all I can think of for him at the moment. All he needs now is sleep while his body fights...whatever ails him," she concluded tamely, feeling vaguely cross with herself for not being able to name or identify the illness.

"I can do that, Sally, but I still think you're wasting your healer talents on a blackguard who doesn't deserve it, and who certainly won't thank you for it!"

"Tess, illness and injury can happen to anyone. If I only offered my poor skills to my close friends, I'd have very few patients," Sally replied firmly. "And if someone can turn the mattress upside-down and replace Rolan's sweaty sheets with fresh linen, I hope that will be enough to ensure that Rolan's malady is not passed to the new patient."

Tess wasn't convinced, but she realized that Sally had made up her mind and wouldn't give in. She opened the door and barked a few orders to the patrons who were still hovering on the landing, mostly to provide muscle if needed. Rolan was by now half-asleep as a fresh dose of painkillers began to take effect. Swiftly and efficiently, he was carried out of the room, and Sally tried to put him out of her mind for the time being while she concentrated on the new challenge unexpectedly laid before her.

Working without haste, she swabbed carefully all around the site of the patient's wound. It seemed that Dog was not satisfying an instinctive blood lust. As far as Sally could tell, he hadn't ripped away or swallowed any of the flesh. Once she had rinsed away the blood from the man's hand, she could see that the hand itself appeared undamaged.

I'm sure I can rebuild this, Sally thought to herself. *After all, the bone is sound.*

She paused. Something resembling a thin, semi-transparent tube had been punctured, and blood was pulsing out of the tear slowly, but with no signs of stopping.

That's not right, she thought to herself. Her detailed knowledge of anatomy and the inner workings of the human body were not extensive, but she knew enough to realize that life and health depended on the blood supply.

She ripped a long, thin strip from a clean cloth, lifted the fragile blood vessel with the tip of her finger and somehow managed to make three turns around the damaged area. She dared not squeeze or put pressure on it, but the flow of blood slowed and appeared to stop. With even greater care, she eased the tiny, clumsy-looking package back into place and gently padded it within the mangled flesh.

"Bring me your finest needle and some thread!"

The muscle attached to the forearm was clearly damaged—a slight tear, granted, but one Sally sensed would not repair itself without some assistance. She was fascinated by the challenge of thinking on her feet, improvising and finding solutions as she went along.

"Now, if I can make such tiny stitches in that muscle tissue, I can surely close off the wound in the same fashion once I've padded the bone and muscle with the rest of the flesh," she told herself. She was most concerned to complete the task before the patient awoke from his swoon. He was far too powerful for her to control if he returned to consciousness while she was still carrying out life-saving emergency surgery.

She looked at the ragged edges of the skin around the wound. It looked as if the final stage of the running repairs she was attempting was going to be the most difficult to accomplish.

"It's sure to rip once more if I start the stitches too close to the wound," she told herself, and started the first stitch a good thumb's width from the wound track. From the corner of her eye, she was aware of Tess and the pot-boy watching her, but there was no place for any distraction from her self-appointed task. A good six inches of forearm had to be sewn together, and the patient was beginning to show signs of regaining consciousness. She simply *had* to complete her task before he did. He was going to be in considerable pain, impossible to restrain!

She refused to allow herself to panic. She tightened each
of the stitches she made in the skin as much as she dared.
She noticed that no blood seeped from the edges of the
wound, and prayed this was a good sign. Was the blood still
reaching past the wound and into the lower arm? She completed a final stitch and tied off the thread with a neat, sturdy
knot any seamstress would have been proud of, then reached
for the patient's right hand and fingers. The skin was pale,
paler that she thought it ought to have been, but there was
definitely some warmth in it. The flow of blood was surely restricted, and might never be as full as nature had intended,
but it seemed that some of life's vital liquid was still reaching
the extremities of the limb.

"He's lost a lot of blood," she murmured, looking at the
mess on the floor.

"Lazy boy! Don't you *dare* let our guest soil her fingers
with that...*person's* vile body fluids! Scrubbing the floor's
your job, as you very well know!" Tess lightly cuffed the potboy and sent him scurrying to take the cloths and the bucket
from Sally.

Sally turned to Tess. "He is not far from awakening, and I
will need your help to hold him down if he does. I still have
to find a way to make sure the arm cannot be moved while
the wound either heals or...fails to heal."

"Hmmmpph! I still say you should have finished the job
yon Dog started, and left him a lame beggar for the remains
of his miserable existence. 'Twould have served some justice
on him!" Tess grumbled. "Still, you show yourself as a true
healer, and the wandering cleric we see from time to time has
told us we should forgive our foes. Tell me what you would
have me do."

"Lift him from the shoulders to a sitting position. I want
to wrap a sheet around him from shoulder to waist, securing
the right arm snug against his chest so he cannot move it. I
will leave his left arm free. That way, once he has started to
recover, he will be able to feed himself." Sally didn't dare
think about the less attractive but far more likely alternative
scenario. What would happen if her latest patient *failed* to
recover?

Tess followed Sally's directions without demur. The patient was transferred to the room's single bed.

"He needs to be swathed, but not too tightly," Sally explained as she unfolded a sheet and passed one end to Tess. She continued. "By winding the coverings over his body and under the bed, he'll be as comfortable as I dare make him, but unable to move around freely. That would without doubt damage his arm, especially in the first few days when the pain will be at its worst. He's going to need extra blankets. He's already too chilled for my liking, and I'll need some myself. I shall keep vigil over his recovery, and once you have left the room, none must enter until I decide it is safe. I am certain there is still a risk that others may be infected by this disease."

"What makes you think you're safe? You were that ill once ..."

Sally recognized the mean voice inside her head and strove to silence it. She refused to believe that she, a dedicated healer, might be a living, walking source of infection for everyone she met.

A terrifying picture formed swiftly in her mind—a snarling mob, faces distorted with hate, casting stones and other missiles from a safe distance, driving her into a bleak, stony isolation with their menacing howl.

"Plague Sally! Plague Sally!"

Chapter Nineteen

Sally sat close to the invalid's bed through the night, attentive to the least movement in her sleeping patient. Three times he'd almost surfaced from the well of pain; each time Sally had coaxed a few vital drops of her most effective pain-killer past his lips in a tea sweetened with chamomile and wild honey to disguise its bitter taste. On each occasion, he'd relaxed back into the healing semi-comatose state she wanted to last as long as possible. Each time, Sally felt the satisfaction of a small but significant victory that could only enhance his chances of survival. He hadn't reached full consciousness yet, and bore no items that might give a clue to his identity, so his name remained unknown.

A low turf fire burned, but by now the room was uncomfortably warm. Sally had sealed the room as efficiently as was possible with cloths jammed against the door and around the single window. With no ventilation, the air in the room had turned stale, almost rancid, and her head was splitting. Reluctantly, because she knew that too much would make her sleepy, she measured out a minimal dose of painkiller for her own use. It worked swiftly on an empty stomach. Within a few minutes, her head was clear, but there was still the vague irritation of a ringing in her ears.

She caught her breath and listened intently for a second. The ringing *wasn't* in her ears; it was faint but rhythmic, and from some distance. With an automatic glance at her patient, she rose and ran to the window.

"Do I dare open it?" she murmured as she tried to decide. Behind her, Dog whined, making her aware that she was back to her strange habit of vocalizing her inner thoughts.

Yes! Trust your feelings; fresh air is good! *Open the window!*

Dog raised his head and uttered a short, positive-sounding yip.

Sally's head started to spin again. Suddenly, she simply *had* to breathe untainted air, feel a cooling breeze caress her brow. Her hands ripped the cloths from around the window, but she felt detached, as if observing another performing the act. Unhasping the window took less than a heartbeat, and suddenly, she was able to drink deeply of the cold, fresh morning air. Small sounds of nature poured into the room along with the sunshine. In the near distance, a church bell tolled, explaining the ringing Sally had thought originated from her heat-fuddled brain.

The clear bright sunshine and the sweet unsullied air revived her senses at once, and gave a fresh, healthy sparkle to the unremarkable plain features of the room. Was it her imagination, or had the patient's color also improved dramatically as soon as the window opened? *It's probably just the sunshine,* she told herself. Oil lamps and the flickering of a turf fire would make anyone look ill by comparison. She stooped to check his vital signs anyway, and was gratified to see that her instincts were once again correct. The patient's breathing was much easier, and there was something approaching an acceptable temperature in his fingers and toes.

There was a discreet knock on the door. "Mistress Sally! Will you break your fast before we leave for church?"

Of course! And the reason for the chiming bells, just too far away to be seen; it was a Sunday, and the faithful were being called to worship.

"If you are kind and leave something outside the door, I will collect it after you depart. I would not place you at risk of infection. And you may offer a thanksgiving from me and from my patient, who has survived the night. I believe he may be over the worst."

"*Deo gratias!*" Even through the closed door, there was no mistaking the sincere and spontaneous joy in Tess' voice.

"You seem to have changed your mind about my patient, Tess. Do you now believe he deserves to be healed?"

"Sally, your wish to heal someone of their injuries is a

lesson for us all. In church today, I will pray that I may find the grace to follow your example."

Sally had a sudden, vivid memory of a scene described in all its gruesome, horrifying detail by the wandering preacher on one of his infrequent visits—a Roman soldier with a cruel spear, piercing the side of a man nailed to a cross, causing the last remaining drops of blood to pour unchecked from his side. She shuddered, grateful that Tess was unable to see her.

"Tess, all I can hope to do as a healer is treat everyone who comes to me in the way I would wish to be treated myself were the roles ever reversed. Please include me in your prayers, as well as my patient."

By the time Tess and her fellow worshippers returned from Sunday Mass, Sally had aired the bedroom thoroughly, sweeping it clean and sweetening the air by scattering a handful of dried lavender over the embers of the turf fire.

"The patient has become restless. He may awaken before long."

After the briefest of courtesy greetings, Sally spared Tess the trouble of asking the question in her eyes, and continued.

"I am thankful you arrived back so soon, as I fear I would not be able to control him if he cannot abide the pains of his injury."

"I have some news for you," Tess replied as she shrugged off her outdoor cloak and stood close to the bed. "The town constable has questioned this rogue's companions, and they agree that he answers to the name Huw...possibly from somewhere north of the wall built by Hadrian."

"One of the few things we have to be grateful the Romans left behind!" commented Sally automatically. Her small community in far-off York had suffered sorely and oft from rape and pillage under the Romans, and folk were slow to forget. On the other hand, the wall built by Hadrian to forestall incursions from the bloodthirsty savages of the north had meant they had one less frontier to defend against possible attacks.

As if on cue, the patient stirred, more strenuously than before, and appeared to be trying to sit. When this proved impossible due to the tight cocoon of blankets, he attempted to roll onto his uninjured side. Discovering this was not possible was enough to rouse him completely. His eyes blazed with fury as he found himself trussed and bound, and in unfamiliar surroundings.

Tess immediately thrust herself forward, reminding Sally of an unlikely combination of a mother hen protecting her brood and a full grown lion puffing out his mane to intimidate a rival.

"Now you just ho'd y'r whist, oor Huw! Ah, yis! I knows y'r name, or did y' think the mis'rable ragtag rabble you had t' fright th' chillun with could keep that a secret?"

Sally noted that Tess had a mocking edge to her voice. She delivered her speech at a speed far in excess of her normal easy pace, and with the same odd accent she hadn't heard Tess use since their first meeting.

Why's she doing that? she wondered. Tess glanced at her sharply, almost as if she'd spoken her thoughts aloud.

"Yon lily-livered gang o' cowards as calls themselves a press gang didn't need much pressin' themselves before they told the constable this sorry piece o' flotsam crawled aboard somewhere in Scotia. I've had the dubious privilege o' dealin' with others from the north afores. That's how they talk up there, an' I want t' be sure he understands me!" She whirled back to confront Huw, hands on hips, bristling with authority. "You owe your miserable life to the healer woman behind me, and you'd be wise to keep that in mind! Now lie back and relax! You've been close to death, and you're still so kitten-weak you'd fall over if I sneezed!"

The fire in Huw's eyes faded and died. He ceased his futile struggle against the restraints that held him and followed Tess' practical advice. She stooped close and tucked the blankets back into place.

"If you ever regain the use of your right arm, it will be due to the skills of the very same 'poxy doxy' you sought when you burst into my tavern last night. For some reason I cannot understand, she defied me and decided to bind your injury instead of cutting the arm off entirely!" She paused, then stood back to allow Sally to explain the finer details.

"The most important thing is to keep your arm as still as possible, for as long as possible, while the flesh knits together. This will take time, but I can treat you with medicines that will help."

"Sleep is one of nature's best remedies," Sally murmured as the patient's eyes closed and his breathing slowed, "but I feel easier treating him now I have learned his name."

"How so?"

"I have treated people with serious injuries on a number of occasions. I have found that talking to them, both when sleeping naturally and as a result of the drugs I administer, they will react sometimes in words, sometimes by movement, and I am certain they are trying to answer me. Usually I know their names, and I'm sure they can hear what is said to them. Hearing your name called must be a crumb of comfort for anyone trapped in a solitary world of pain as the body recovers from its injuries."

"Hmm." Tess clearly had her doubts, but was prepared to accept Sally's word on this. Suddenly, she looked beyond Sally's shoulder to the open window, where an unexpected movement had caught her eye. "We have a visitor, Sally. I must leave you for a moment."

The visitor proved to be the priest who had said the Mass that morning. Tess led him straight to the sick room and introduced him.

"Father Timothy visits as frequently as he can, and always makes time to visit as many of the sick as he can before traveling onwards. Father, this is Sally. She is a stranger to these parts, but I have already seen how skilful she is as a healer. Such were his injuries, this man would surely have died without her treatment."

The priest said nothing, but raised one eyebrow as he gazed from Sally to her patient and back. In a gentle but confident tone, Sally described the extent of the injury and what she hoped the treatment might achieve.

"Perhaps you will allow me to offer a prayer for his well-being?"

Father Timothy's voice was deep and reflective, neutral, with no suggestion of censure, no doubt of her healing abilities. Sally was also certain that he was not mocking her. He seemed rather to be asking for her permission to add something of a spiritual nature to the patient's recovery.

It can't hurt, and he's going to need all the help he can get. Why not?

As these thoughts chased themselves across her mind, Sally nodded.

The grave set of the priest's face was betrayed by the unmistakeable glint of humor in his pale blue eyes as he nodded his thanks, kissed the scarf he wore around his neck, and slipped easily into a Latin litany of prayers for the sick while he signed the Cross over the patient's head.

"Has our town constable discovered more from the other crew members?"

Tess had supplied a simple meal for the priest. The invalid was sleeping peacefully, and they had withdrawn to a table in one corner of the tavern.

Father Timothy continued. "They all gave his name as Huw, though none of them has his letters and could not say how the name might be spelled. Three of them add that he joined the crew from a port in Hibernia about a year ago. They offered this information unasked, and without having a chance to agree on a story, so I judge they speak the truth, or as much of the truth as they understand."

"Huw! Thank you for this confirmation, Father," Sally breathed "That's good to know; it will help me treat my patient." Seeing the quizzical expression on the cleric's face, Sally explained briefly why she valued this seemingly trivial piece of information. "And if I may ask you for a blessing, such as you gave Huw, I know my poor efforts to cure him will succeed" she added shyly.

Father Timothy nodded. "Sally, I understand why you were reluctant to leave your patient this morning to accompany Tess to Mass. Will you allow her to watch over him for a while, and accompany me back to the chapel? 'Tis but a short distance from here."

"The walk and the fresh air will do you good, too. Looking after your patient, you haven't been outside the four walls of your room in the past two days!" Tess added. "And you needn't worry about him. I've nursed many a sick relative, d'ja know, and paying guest, from time to time. Go, go! You deserve a break!"

Sally didn't consider herself especially religious, but she had always made the effort to attend the tiny chapel in her community whenever the traveling priest visited. For her, it was an opportunity to forget her solitary life as a healer and mix with other people for a few hours.

She felt comfortable in the company of Father Timothy, though he had said little thus far. During their brief walk, she swiftly discovered that his tendency to economize with his words encouraged her to voice her inner thoughts. He was an excellent listener, and a calming influence.

"What worries me most, Father, is the amount of blood he lost before I could begin to treat him. He is so weak, I fear he may not have the strength to recover."

Father Timothy paused as they reached the lych gate outside the chapel and leaned on his staff. "That gives me good grounds to choose the prayers I use with special care," he said, sincerely and simply. "Come, I believe you will find in this chapel the peace you need in your own life. Over the years, I have found that is how it works on me whenever I return."

Inside the chapel, he begged Sally to excuse him a moment while he changed robes.

"Sit over here," he suggested, pointing to a bench close to a pair of curtained booths. "At this time of day, the stained window panes are a joy to behold. The sun is in a perfect position in the sky."

The shadowy coolness of the stone-built chapel was a pleasing contrast to the warm, bright late spring morning. Although it was no great distance from Tess O'Brien's tavern, there was a short, steep hill to climb to reach the church dedicated to Our Lady and St. Nicholas. Sally only realized how much the effort had cost her when she felt the perspiration on her brow cooling and running down her cheeks.

The light through the windows dappled and shifted constantly, rippling silently over the furniture. Sally took a deep breath, enjoying the unmistakeable scent left by the incense used during the morning's service. She willed her body to relax and recharge after the stress and tension of caring for a seriously injured patient.

Just as her eyes drooped closed, she became aware of the faintest of not-quite-regular noises, the tiniest of scratchings. There was no pattern or rhythm to them, but they appeared to be a constant, repetitive stream, identical in timbre and quality. Her eyes flew open once more, her natural curiosity aroused. In a church or a chapel, she had no grounds to fear any danger of attack, but her survival instincts demanded she identify the sound at once, and ascertain that it contained no threat.

She held her breath for a few seconds, trying to determine the direction the sound was coming from, though she knew from experience that it was not possible to control her ears directionally, as a cat may.

Slowly, she tilted her head this way and that. There! The sound originated from the eastern corner of the church, ahead of her and half-right. She exhaled slowly, and stared in the direction she'd identified. A fresh-faced, tonsured cleric stood at a lectern, glancing constantly at a book in a pool of natural daylight on his left, then transferring his attention to something Sally couldn't quite see that lay flat before him. Incongruous to Sally, he held a feather in his hand, which produced the skittering, scratchy sound she'd failed to identify as he moved it slowly and carefully across whatever lay before him. After a few seconds, he stopped, dipped the bare, pointed root of the feather into a small bottle of some sort, and looked back at his book.

He's copying something from the book, she told herself, being much more careful than was her usual habit to ensure that she kept her tongue in check and did *not* speak the words aloud.

The youth seemed harmless, and Father Timothy hadn't actually *ordered* her to remain on the seat he'd indicated. She stood, making considerably more noise than was necessary to draw attention to herself.

"Hello, my name is Sally. I am of the Parisii, who live several days' journey to the east. May I look at your...work?" Sally had walked across the chapel as she spoke, and was close to the cleric's elbow by the time she had finished the sentence. She'd gambled on the fact that he was unlikely to refuse if she was all but upon him by the time her words had tumbled into place and he'd had a second to process them. Sally sensed that her ploy had worked exactly as she'd intended.

The cleric nodded. In the circumstances, a refusal would have seemed churlish. Sally moved immediately to stand just behind the cleric's left shoulder and peered to see what he had been concentrating so hard to create.

Sally had never had the chance to learn her letters, but with some careful thought, she could manage a passable likeness of her own name, and recognized what she saw on the lectern as letters, not a picture. The cleric had just begun to inscribe a second line of script. Each letter was uniform in height and weight, with microfine upstrokes and bold, positive downstrokes. The parchment was a spotless creamy white, laid out as the facing double pages of a book. In the top left corner was a beautifully embellished capital letter, adorned with a score or more of minute figures, flowers, and other artwork in a variety of fresh colors. By contrast, every other letter on the page was a solid jet black.

A satisfied smile brightened the scribe's face when he noted her interest. He deposited his stylus carefully in a small bottle and stood back slightly to give her a better view.

"You have an amazing talent!" she breathed, unable to take her eyes off the page, "I've never seen anything so perfect!"

"Stop, please. I am but a poor student still learning my craft. There are many in the monastery far more skilled than me."

"I find that hard to believe. And the detail all around the first letter—I know the letter S because it's part of my name, Sally—such tiny details, and each one perfect! How do you do it?"

The young man laughed, then cut himself off abruptly and crossed himself as the sound bounced merrily around the bare stone walls, reminding him where he was.

"There is no shame in laughing in God's house. It should be a house of joy!"

Father Timothy had re-entered at some point and had obviously heard at least part of the exchange. Sally replayed the conversation mentally, and decided that she hadn't said anything inappropriate. He sounded sincere, not offended, and she was also thankful for that.

"Brother John is too modest for his own good, Sally! His tutor tells me he is the most promising pupil he has had in years. He has an excellent fist, and is highly skilled both with the blending of inks and in selecting and trimming quills. Show her the tools of your trade, brother! I believe Sally the

Healer has more skills, perhaps more than she knows herself."

Brother John nodded, and led Sally to a side table where many bottles—more than two hands; Sally didn't have a name for the number—were lined up in neat rows. One corner was reserved for a heap of feathers, and four or five sharp knives.

He took a feather from the pile and showed it to her.

"I like to use the biggest wing feathers from a goose, if I can. They are strong, and last far longer than those from other birds." Selecting a knife, he made a single, slanted cut across the base of the feather and held it up for Sally to inspect. "You can see that it's hollow, yes? So, I dip it in a pot filled with ink." He suited action to word. "And use it to form the next letter, like this."

With two long strides, he was back at the lectern and bent over the page for a few seconds. When he straightened his back and stepped away, Sally could see the new letter glistening in the sunlight, razor sharp at the edge. Soon it would start to dry, becoming the next in a row of letters that built into words, marching proudly and with perfect military precision across the page.

"I see how the ink flows *from* the pen, but by what magic do you conjure it from the bottle into the feather?"

Neither man of the cloth had expected the question, and both reacted with a loud, genuine peal of laughter. The sound caromed wildly around the chapel, and even the sunlight pouring through the window seemed to flare and dance with merriment.

"Sally, that's an excellent question! And I have to admit, it's one I've never considered before now. Brother John, perhaps we ought to have a few womenfolk around the monastery to pose the sort of questions nobody else thinks to ask."

Sally wasn't quite sure if Father Timothy's words were intended as a compliment or an insult, but she was determined to have the final word. "Your pardon, Father...Brother..." She paused, confused, wondering if the two clerics were expecting her to use their formal titles rather than their names.

The older priest sensed her discomfort at once. "Titles are fine in public places, Sally, but I'm sure John will agree with me, in private they aren't necessary. One of Our Saviour's teachings is that we are *all* equal before God."

"My thanks for that, Fa...your pardon, Timothy! But John, I would not ask unless I really wanted to know! Can you try to explain for me how the ink is drawn into the pen? Over the years I have learned many things that at the time seemed to be of no special value, yet later proved to have some use, affecting the manner in which I choose to treat my patients."

Sally felt a curious frisson of excitement coursing unheralded through her body, making her heart beat much faster than it ought. This had happened to her a number of times in the past, and on each occasion she had made a new discovery about the healing process soon afterwards. Willingly, gladly, she made a conscious effort to open up her mind and her heart to capture and record the least, most insignificant nuance of a passing, casual word or action that might be the catalyst, the inspiration she needed to nurse her known patients back to full health.

And how many more patients d'you think will come to owe you for their life, their health, their very future?

She decided it was time to change the subject, or at least lead the priest and his acolyte away from an area of her personal life she wasn't yet ready to share with anyone else.

"Show me once more how you cut the quill, John. Do you have to cut it at a certain angle?"

Under the watchful eye of the senior cleric, pupil-turned-tutor John received a well-deserved immediate promotion as he explained in simple, patient terms the skills required to cut quill pens in a variety of ways to use for different purposes. Sally was a swift learner, and they only stopped the lesson when they both noticed a distinct drop in the quality of the light from the window. Shadows had lengthened gradually and unnoticed through the afternoon, and the sun had dropped too low in the sky to flood the chapel with the same excellent level of lighting.

"My patients!" Sally was beside herself with regret and a healthy dose of bad conscience.

"Sally, you can be certain Tess would have sent word if there had been any problems that required your presence."

"Father Timothy, you're probably right, but unless you know of another healer who lives close at hand...?"

"There are none I know of, Sally, other than self-styled charlatans and mountebanks whose only interest lies in selling their worthless nostrums. People foolish enough to buy their dubious wares most often die from poisoning!"

"We must return to Tess' tavern all the same. She has her business to run, and no knowledge of which medicines to use, or how, should there be an emergency! Father, grant me the blessing you brought me here to perform. I simply *must* return before it's too late. Something is telling me I am needed now as we speak."

Father Timothy could see Sally was upset and made no protest. Within five minutes, they were on their way, he making the longest stride he could comfortably manage without breaking into an undignified trot or gallop. Sally had to hop and skip to remain at his side, but held herself in check, denying the urge to race at full speed, leaving the old priest to follow at whatever speed suited his needs.

Although he hadn't specifically been invited, Brother John assembled a selection of writing tools into a leather pouch and made his way to Tess' tavern at a leisurely pace.

Chapter Twenty

"So, if the ink won't rise, you just press on the stem...so?"

Huw was continuing to show small signs of improvement, and Tess had persuaded Sally that nightfall was too close for her to begin a journey back to Bryn's farm. Sally had reluctantly accepted this, and now she sat with Brother John at a table littered with the results of her experimenting with different ways of slicing feathers to make quills. John had nodded his approval of most of them, and had allowed her to dip a few in one of his precious ink pots and try forming letters on an ancient scrap of vellum, which had been written on and washed clean many times.

"That's right, Sally, but if the cut you've made is wide enough, the ink should rise into the quill unaided."

"And if the cut is *too* deep, the ink will all flow out too fast, and instead of a letter, all I'll get will be a big stain on the page instead!"

"Unfortunately, that's what happens to every novice. But you'll learn quickly—we all do."

With utmost concentration, Sally brought the tip of a loaded quill to rest lightly on the vellum sheet and began tracing the shape of a letter **S**. It was shaky, but recognizable, and there were no drips or other accidents. She'd held her breath while performing the operation. Now she let it all out in an explosion of excitement and delight.

"I did it! I can write my name!" She joyfully danced several steps, holding the quill upright to avoid spilling any of the precious ink that remained in its stem.

"Well, it's only the first letter, but you know that, of course! It's a good start. Allow me to show you how it can be smoother at the edges, tidier."

With a few assured, confident strokes Brother John smoothed out the shaky outline of Sally's first attempt, filling it out to a bolder, solid **S**.

Sally watched, fascinated to see her shaky first attempt swiftly transformed to a miniature work of art. She picked up a quill that had been cut but not yet used and studied the tip carefully. The spine was plump, and felt comfortable in her hand. She pumped it gently, imagining how the ink would flow through the tip.

And if ink could be drawn into a quill, why not other liquids? She blinked, and almost dropped the quill. A small gasp had escaped her lips. Brother John stopped what he was doing and looked at her sharply, an unspoken question in his eyes.

"Sally? What ails you?"

She tried to gather her wits, and offered him the quill. "Have you ever thought to try filling other liquids in this tool? Water, milk, ale? Because if 'tis possible, it may assist me with my healing work."

Tess scurried to fetch a few glasses of different liquids from the kitchen. Sally used the brief pause to try to explain her idea to the bemused Brother John.

"Huw lost a lot of blood when his arm was torn apart. I have seen injuries of this nature before, but none so severe. He is perilously weak. I have never been asked to treat anyone who has lost so much blood, and I fear he may lack the strength he needs to recover."

When Tess returned, Sally had persuaded John to pack away all his inks to leave the table clear of everything other than the knives and the small mountain of feathers. Sally and John took to cutting the tips of the feathers at different angles, and Tess was conscripted to assist with dipping the quills into pots filled with water, milk, and other household liquids.

Water rose into the quills immediately and without any assistance. Milk took longer, but remained inside the quill better than the water. Other liquids, such as cream, had to be coaxed into the hollow tube of the feather by being pumped.

"This is too thick, too dense to flow *out* of the quill." Sally was forced to admit defeat when the cream could not be forced out of the quills, even through the wider cut nozzles. She thought for a moment, then added, "Still, I don't think blood is as thick and sluggish as this cream. That may help, but we're only using very small amounts here. Huw has lost a lot of blood. How can I possibly get enough blood into him quickly? Do you have any ideas, Brother John? Have you ever wished for a bigger quill, from the feather of some legendary giant of a bird, so you could write a whole book without constantly dipping in an ink pot?"

Even as she spoke, Sally began to giggle. An image flashed across her imagination—a feather of colossal proportions, balanced across the shoulders of a dozen or more scribes, heavy with untold quarts of blood, impaled in the arm of her bed-ridden invalid. It was too comical for words.

Tess was in the process of pouring them all some wine. She looked sharply across the room at Sally's unexpected mirth and frowned. "What's so funny?"

Sally started to explain about the problem of being able to transfer by any means enough blood to give Huw a chance to recover, but stumbled to a stop in mid-sentence as she became aware of what Tess held in her hands.

"Tess, those skins you carry wine in. They *are* completely waterproof, aren't they?"

Tess nodded cautiously. "I'd be a puir businesswoman if'n I 'lowed me profits t' piss on the floor f'r want o' a few stitches in the seams, d'ja know?"

"I'm sure you're a good businesswoman, Tess. And the skins themselves, you wash them every time they're empty, I take it?"

"For sure! That way it won't matter if the next wine I decant into it is different than the one before!"

"Even better! But best of all would be if you can let me have a skin that has never been used. Can you supply me with one?"

Not wishing to waste time, Tess bustled out of the kitchen and returned scant seconds later carrying three wineskins of different sizes. From the expression on her face, Sally could guess that Tess still had no idea of what she was about to attempt. She studied the available skins, selected the middle-size one, and sat tailor-style on the floor next to the table, pulling out her needles and thread.

"For the moment, I'm tightening the neck of the bottle. Later, after I've filled it, I'll sew in a quill-feather and seal the joint as best I can with wax. That should make it possible for me to carry blood, enough to pump back into my patient."

"And where are you going to get the blood you're talking about? That's one drink I certainly *don't* keep in my bar!" Tess sniffed sarcastically.

Sally smiled to herself. She'd anticipated this, and she was ready for it. "Sure, and don't you think I've had cause to tap a patient for blood from time to time? 'Tis a known cure for the choler, headaches, and a number of ailments of the gut! I've bled myself on any number of occasions, Tess, and I know how to do this safely. More important, I know how and when to stop the leaching. I intend to draw the blood I need from my own veins. Few people other than physicians and healers realize that we are blessed with far more blood than our bodies need, and if through some accident or injury, we lose some blood, our bodies can replace it. Losing a large amount of blood, as Huw has, is another matter, something the body may not be able to cope with unaided."

"In that case, you surely can't be thinking of trying to give him all the blood he needs. You just said he'd lost too much, that his life was at risk!"

"Tess, I also told you that our bodies can *replace* blood. I don't need to give him a lot. All he needs is a bit of help, and his body will have a chance to do the rest."

"Oi still t'ink y'r puttin' y'rsel at risk. D'ja know," Tess grumbled, but Sally was determined to have her way.

"I really *do* know what I'm doing. You must trust my healer skills on this," she said, hoping her words sounded a lot more convincing to Tess than they did in her own ears. "It's quite simple, really," she said, picking up one of the knives that boasted a very narrow, needle-sharp blade. "And it doesn't even hurt that much; it's the merest pinprick. Tess, can I ask you to dip a cloth into a glass of gin, or some other spirit, and cleanse the skin on my arm just here?"

She tapped a spot just above her left wrist, where the blue vein ran close to the surface. The unexpected request for assistance caught the landlady unawares and she hastened to follow instructions. By the time she had performed the task, the chance for argument or protest had passed.

Without giving Tess or Brother John the opportunity to stop her, Sally made the smallest of incisions in her flesh and eased the open end of the quill she had cobbled onto the wineskin into the cut. Blood flowed immediately through the transparent feather stem and into the flat, empty bladder.

"Brother John, cup your hands and hold the wine skin. I need you to keep it off the table but below my arm so the blood flows freely."

And that will also stop you *from arguing with me*, she thought. There seemed no fight left in Tess, who sat and gazed at the proceedings, aware that she had somehow allowed herself to contribute by her actions, even if it was against her own natural instincts.

The wineskin began to expand as the life-giving liquid settled inside it. A curious expression flitted over Brother John's face. "Sally, I feel the warmth of the blood heating the palms of my hands! Are you running a fever?"

"No, Brother! What you feel is normal for blood. We don't notice it ourselves because it's all through our body, and thus the same in every corner, from finger to toe, from hair to ankle. We only notice a difference in someone who is suffering from certain diseases when an affected part of the body becomes hotter or colder than the healthy parts. I judge I can tap at least enough blood to fill that skin without feeling any discomfort or loss. Tess, I must ask you once more to act as my nursemaid, as John has his hands full." She grinned, deliberately making light of the situation. "When I judge the skin is close to filled, you must take a cloth and tie it firmly around my arm, above the cut but below my elbow. This will stop the flow of blood, or at the very least slow it enough for me to close the wound and apply a dressing. John, the task I have for you is very important! You must stand and keep the wineskin at body heat by continuing to cradle it in your hands just as you are doing now. I will need a few moments to remove the dressing from Huw's arm and try to find once more the vein that was damaged when Dog..."

She faltered, with the words "attacked him" unspoken on her lips. The culprit lay silent in one corner, and seemed to react to the sound of his name. He raised his head, looking straight at Sally, and thumped his tail twice on the bare wooden floor. Sally wondered if she was imagining things. Had he *really* responded to his name? With a mental shrug and a vague promise to think this through in a quieter moment, she returned to the next stage of the unprecedented experimental treatment she had planned.

With Tess' help, Sally soon detached herself from the hastily assembled combination of quill and wineskin. She then applied a dressing on the site of the cut she'd made above her wrist, staunching the blood.

Sally cleared her head of all other thoughts and turned to give her full detailed healer's attention to her unconscious patient. Whatever the novelty element of everything she had attempted thus far, she had no doubt that the next task she had set for herself was by far the most difficult of them all. She had no personal experience to guide her, and had never heard of anyone even attempting what she was about to do.

Her eyes met John's. He seemed to sense her mood, and smiled. "I am not able to sign the Cross over you just now, but I am sure the Lord in his mercy will understand if I offer what prayers I may without formality," he said.

Sally nodded her acceptance of his reassurances, not trusting herself to speak, and with a sincere plea of her own to whatever form of higher authority might be listening, she began to remove the dressing from Huw's arm. *Please, let him remain asleep, deep in a nerve-deadening dream where he will not feel the pain*, she pleaded.

As she removed the final wrap of cloth, she was relieved to see that the bleeding had not started up again, and the flesh of Huw's arm appeared healthy, without sign of infection. Less than a full day had passed, and the flesh had not yet begun to knit together. This was also as she had hoped. If she'd been forced to make further cuts in healing flesh, she was certain it would have roused the patient, however deeply he might have slumbered.

Gently, without haste, she parted the layers of flesh, searching for the damaged blood tube. The wisp of bloodied cloth she had placed around it now became the signpost she needed, and she breathed a deep sigh of relief when she found it exactly where she expected it to be.

"I have lived alone for so long, I find it helps me to concentrate if I speak my thoughts while I work," she found herself saying. She hadn't planned this, but when neither Tess nor John made any protest she continued, "It will also help me recall what I am about to do if you would listen and try to remember what I say when we have the chance to speak later."

She didn't dare look away. This was the most delicate stage of all.

"Tess, I need your hands once more. I cannot involve John, for obvious reasons. His role in this must wait for a few more moments. Look at the prepared quills on the table. I need you to find one of the narrowest, slimmest amongst them with the finest, sharpest point. Slide it over the quill on the wineskin. John, once it is secure, you must stand opposite me and lower the wineskin so I can slide the point of the quill into Huw's arm."

Sally hoped she sounded much calmer than she was feeling, and was gratified by the positive reaction from her two assistants. The small tear in the vein was barely visible. The transparently thin tube showed a hint of repairing itself more quickly than the more solid mass of flesh around it, but Sally managed to ease the needle point of the quill into it without great difficulty.

"John, you can pass me the wineskin. Your hands have kept it at the correct temperature, but you must be tired by now. I will stand and try to pump blood into the patient. The most important thing remaining is for both of you to watch carefully for any signs of Huw regaining consciousness. If that happens before I can transfer the blood into him and re-dress the wound, I fear he may damage more than just himself when the pain hits."

Sally grew more confident as each small step was achieved. She held the wineskin directly above the reopened wound and began squeezing very gently on the distended walls, unconsciously mimicking the actions of a beating heart. She could see immediately that her action, combined with the immutable laws of gravity, had the desired effect. Blood was visibly flowing down, through the quill feather, entering Huw's vein. There was no sign of any leak. Every precious drop of the life-saving fluid appeared to be reaching its intended goal.

The skin was close to empty before she sensed that the flow of blood was slowing down. Studying the stained walls of the connecting quill confirmed what she felt through her sensitive fingertips, and she thought rapidly about what she ought to do next.

"Huw is going to need more blood," she said, "but first my body must replace what I have drawn from it. I need a meal—a hearty meal—before I attempt to give him more. I think it best to leave the vein in his arm open. Tess, can we find some sort of stand or rack where this wineskin may safely be hung? I will sit by him and make certain the quill is not dislodged, but we can do no more for him until my body replaces the blood I have tapped from it."

John swiftly pieced together a sturdy trifoot stand, using some sturdy canes Tess found in a forgotten corner of the tavern. A filling dish based on liver, onion, and kale soon followed and was quickly dispatched. Sally hadn't realized how hungry she was.

There was a constant stream of would-be visitors for a while, but the only person to gain admittance to the improvised sickroom was Father Timothy. In a few words, Sally described for him what she had done and added, "He needs your prayers, Father. We all do! Will you grant us a blessing?"

"Of course! There is no doubt in my mind that you are doing something good, something special. I haven't seen your patient since this time yesterday, and I have no doubt that he is far healthier now than he was then. I am happy to pray for him and for all of you, and I shall include prayers of thanks for the miracle you have achieved in saving this man's life."

Sally was shocked. She knew little of the Church's teachings, but she knew enough to realize that for a priest to talk so casually of a possible miracle was close to heresy. "You do me too much honor, Father!" she protested.

Father Timothy stopped her with a shake of his head. "I have seen many who have suffered the bite of an animal and suffered many days of agony and pain. I have administered the Last Sacraments to most of them, and those who have survived have not lived long before dying. This is the first time I have seen such an improvement, and in so short a time!"

Sally had no reply, but bowed her head to hide her embarrassment. Father Timothy took this as a tacit request for his blessing, and duly prayed over her for a few moments before moving to the side of the bed to plead for Huw's recovery.

As soon as they had eaten, Sally chased everyone else out of the room.

"The more Huw can rest, the faster his body will repair itself," she asserted, trying to sound as if she had a wealth of experience well beyond her years in such matters. "I will stay and minister to his needs when he eventually wakes, but there is no need for anyone else to watch through the night. If he stirs, he will be too weak to struggle or do more than perhaps sip a little water, but the longer he sleeps, the better. A still room is what he needs most."

"And someone who has the gift of healing close by," Father Timothy added.

Sally nodded, but on this occasion, she was unable to hide her blushes. "Come, leave us in peace," she scolded, rising to her feet and shepherding them all to the door. "I've got a tongue in my head. I can call if I need anyone."

Chapter Twenty-one

Alone with her unconscious patient for the first time, Sally thought long and hard about removing the hollow quill from Huw's arm, or leaving it in place.

"If I remove it, he may lose more blood, and all our efforts will be wasted," she told herself, and settled under a blanket to keep vigil. Also, removing the quill might cause enough pain and discomfort to rouse him, a prospect she did not want to face on her own. She peered more closely at the quill. The traces of blood inside the tube seemed to have stiffened, clinging to the inner surface. It seemed that any further transfers of blood would need a fresh, clean quill, and more than likely another wineskin if what remained in the first one had also stiffened as it cooled and become impossible to pump out, which seemed to be the case.

Mercifully, Huw continued to sleep. His breathing and his color improved degree by stealthy degree, and Sally had time to think carefully about every step she had taken so far, looking for ways she might improve and increase his chances of recovery.

Tess arrived as dawn broke, with Brother John hard on her heels. Between mouthfuls of a warm oatmeal porridge, Sally explained why she would need a fresh wineskin and asked John to prepare a selection of fresh quills, as fine as possible to slide inside the needle still embedded in Huw's arm.

"The effects of the painkillers will be starting to wear by now," she declared, "and he has already slept an unnaturally lengthy time, so there's no time to lose! We must make a start."

Tapping her own blood still had to be the first part of the task. To Sally it felt never-ending, but in reality it took less time than the previous day.

John and Sally both cradled the full wineskin in their hands to keep it warm once it had been set on the stand. Sally had hoped this would help the blood flow more easily by preventing it from cooling and thickening, and she was gratified when she was proved right.

Sally decided this time that she would remove the quill from Huw's arm and close off the wound properly. She had completed the transfer immediately, without sitting, eating, or resting. She felt a little light in the head, and realized that it would be unwise if she were to attempt to draw more blood from her own system for a third time in less than a full day. She studied her patient carefully, making a special note of his deep, unhurried breathing, and decided he would be oblivious to the pinpricks in his flesh, which she would have to make while sewing together the edges of the wound. That had to be done immediately. She had no way of guessing how deep his slumber was, or how close he might already be to a return of full consciousness and inevitable pain.

She studied the needle point of the quill, protruding from the delicate membrane of the vein she had lanced beneath layers of flesh and muscle. Would the bleeding start again as soon as she pulled it out? She rather thought it would.

Yet there was no way she could prevent that by tying it closed. Blood would be unable to flow past any ligature, and she knew from past experience with other patients that this could only lead to total loss of the limb and eventual amputation. She had to find another solution.

On the very edge of her field of vision, she was aware of a minute distraction, and looked away a moment to identify whatever it was that had snagged her attention. As she refocused below the table Huw lay upon, roughly level with her knee, she saw a tiny spider skitter across a fresh-made web in the angle between the top of the table leg and the trestle it supported. *Such beautiful work*, she thought. *Why do flies never learn to avoid its sticky threads?*

And suddenly, she knew she'd found a solution to her problem. Taking a fresh knife from the table, she carefully eased it into one corner of the web and ran the blade slowly around the two edges that attached it to the table top and the upper end of the leg. It curled as it came away, but remained almost entirely unfolded, the most delicate, diaphanous net imaginable.

She had to concentrate so her hands remained steady as she transferred her prize, stretched between the points of two knives, and held it directly over the punctured vein.

"Tess, your hands are more delicate that John's. When I tell you, I want you to grasp the quill by its upper end and tug gently. You'll find it will pull away easily. I'm going to lay this gossamer web across the wound to bind it. Ready? Now!"

She'd deliberately given Tess no time to think, argue, or protest. As a result, Tess had no chance to think about what she was being asked to do, and the final phase of the operation was over almost before it began. All that remained for Sally to take care of was to lay the web as evenly as possible above and below the wound, then slide the vein back as close as she could remember to the position she'd found it padded between layers of flesh. Sewing the skin together to complete the job took longer this time. She had no intention of re-opening the wound, and needed to close it off permanently. The stitches went deeper, and were much closer together.

It seemed fitting, or at very least a positive sign, when Huw stirred and gave a soft whimper just minutes after the three of them had lifted him back into his bed and smoothed the blankets into place.

"You did it, Sally!" Tess cried. "You managed to complete all the painful cutting and sewing before he began to stir! Brother John, surely this is a sign? Tell me I'm right, please?"

Brother John would not commit himself. "I must discuss all we have seen here today with Father Timothy. He knows far more about such things than me."

"But you were here, and witnessed it all. He was *not*!" Tess protested.

"I will relate for him what we have all seen with our own eyes, and ask for guidance. That is the most a simple cleric such as myself can hope to do, bear witness," he repeated, and would not be drawn to promise more.

Sally all but ignored this interchange. Her concern was for the fast-recovering patient. Huw's eyes fluttered uncertainly as he blinked rapidly and seemed to be trying to focus. He made a piteous attempt to roll his head one way, then the other, but even this was too much effort. His tongue appeared, flickering uncertainly around his cracked, chapped, bone-dry lips. That, at least, was something Sally knew she could do to ease his discomfort. She filled a cup and held it before him.

"Water you may have, but slowly. I will feed it to you, a spoonful at a time, and *I* will decide when you've had enough! You've slept two full days, and your body is still weak. You understand?"

He nodded.

"Good. Now, hold still."

Sally patiently fed small sips of water to Huw, supporting him around the shoulders with her free arm. After a while, she laid the spoon aside and eased her patient onto his bed.

"That's enough for now. You won't be comfortable on a wet mattress!"

Huw's eyes closed. He settled once more and escaped into a pain-free slumber, aided by the herbal extract Sally had dripped into each spoonful of water.

"Sally, please tell me, what was the purpose of the spider web I watched you place in Huw's wound? Are you a healer or a witch?" There was some sharpness in Tess' voice which had not been there before.

Sally shook her head. "I learned some things from the previous healer in my village before she passed away, but most of my knowledge has come from observing things in nature, things that are there for all to see, but many fail to notice. I promise you, there is nothing mysterious or magical in what I do. Have you ever looked closely at the spider's web? So delicate, the single strands so thin as to be all but invisible unless the light catches them. You can brush your fingernail against them and not even feel them burst apart, yet they are strong enough to trap a fly, even several flies, and hold the weight of their bodies until the spider comes to feast on them."

"That's true," Tess admitted. "I never thought of that before. But what do you hope to gain?"

"Each strand is far stronger than it appears," Sally explained, "and is also covered in something sticky, which traps the fly. By placing it over the tear in Huw's blood vessel, I hope to close the rift and repair the damage so his blood can flow freely inside the vein. If I had tried to stitch it closed as I did with his skin, the blood could not pass, and I don't have a needle small enough to stitch with anyway. All we can do is wait now, and see if it works."

Sally continued to monitor Huw's life signs throughout the day. His body seemed at ease, his breathing regular, and his lower arm right down to the tips of his fingers remained flaccid and warm. She took this as a positive signal. It seemed the blood was still getting through, keeping the limb alive, showing no sign of infection.

The sun was low in the sky before Huw stirred. This time he woke more abruptly. His eyes were clear, and he seemed far more aware of his surroundings. Sally was at his side in an instant with water. This time, it was not adulterated with medicines; there were questions she needed to ask.

"Huw, my name is Sally. I'm a healer. Don't try to speak just yet, just nod. You understand?"

He nodded.

"Good. Now, try a sip of water."

"You've been injured, quite badly. I gave you medicine to make you sleep. Do you feel any pain?"

He nodded.

"Is it in your arm, your right arm?"

He nodded.

"That was your worst injury. If you wish to answer no to a question, are you able to shake your head from side to side?"

Huw managed this, and was rewarded with more water and some extra support cushions so he could raise his shoulders to a half-sitting position on the bed.

Sally posed a series of simple, rapid fire questions to work out if Huw had any injuries in other parts of his body that she'd overlooked, or needed to treat as a precaution. Her main concern was the ripped and torn tissue in the arm, and she was relieved when a more detailed examination indicated that Huw had no other injuries needing attention.

"Ship. Captain. Crew."

Huw sounded like someone who'd been temporarily struck dumb and was forced to learn to speak all over again. He was determined to make himself understood, but the words sounded as if they were grating against a desert-parched throat, costing him superhuman effort to make himself heard. Sally decided she could allow him water in larger quantities, and offered him a glass instead of spoon feeding him. He took it gratefully in his left hand and emptied it in one long swallow.

"You're short of fluids. You've had little to drink and nothing to eat for almost three days now," she warned him. "But that doesn't mean you can eat and drink at will. Your body will still want to follow its natural functions, and you must tell me if you feel the need to visit the privy. I don't want you soiling the sheets and the mattress."

Huw nodded—Sally assumed it was to show he understood—and signed for more water. She offered him a half glass, which he sipped at but did not empty. He tried to speak once more.

"Must speak... Cap'n, crew..."

"Crew? D'ye mean the scurvy cutthroats who followed ye when yiz barged into me tavern three nights ago?" Tess bellowed. She rose to her feet and marched threateningly across the room, puffing her solid frame to at least twice its normal size as a common hedgehog would, or possibly a cornered, and therefore dangerous, puff-adder.

Huw had to be at least twice Tess' size, but there was no contest. He had no chance of getting his own way.

Tess glared at him, daring him to persist with his argument. "For y'r information, the town constable has 'em under lock an' key, where they'll remain until someone posts bail. How highly does this cap'n o' yourn rate 'em, I wonder? Mayhap they'll rot in the cell or starve there 'less he's ready t' loosen his purse strings!"

"Peace, Tess, I beg you! Huw needs rest if he is to recover!"

"Rest, Sally? Rest, for the leader of the most despicable, ruthless press gang in the Port of Leverpole? How much rest do you think his victims are granted once he delivers them to the ships?" She whirled on the spot and glared at Huw. "And while I'm on th' subject, who was it hired you t' find him a crew?"

"Cap'n Bates."

"What, 'Bully' Bates, the biggest blackguard ever t' sail the seven seas? And he sent you out once more to recapture our Sally when she proved too smart f'r ye and escaped?" Tess dropped a protective arm around Sally's shoulders as she spoke. "Sally, m'dear, you may never know how lucky you were to escape Bully Bates' leaky tub. I swear he loses half his crew every time he makes port anywhere! But I'm a reasonable woman, so this is what I'll do." She began to tick off her fingers. "First, I'll allow you the grace of a few days' bed and vittles until our healer decides you're fit enough to walk—and that's only because y'r in a bed as is already paid for by a reg'lar customer!

"Next, if you wish to speak to y'r cap'n, I'll allow Bully Bates *one* courtesy visit, here in this room, under the terms you rogues call 'parlay.' One visit only, and the town constable will be present as a witness. You must take my word that he will not attempt to arrest anyone, unless of course he witnesses a crime taking place—assault, or another form of violence, for example.

"And last of all, I said room and board was paid for, but I said nothing about the services of the healer who's already saved your miserable neck several times over the last three days. She's too polite for her own good, but I'm bold as brass, and I think that fine gold ring you wear just about covers what you owe her!" Tess stretched out her hand and fixed Huw with a basilisk glare. After two or three long seconds, his resolve crumbled and he growled something Tess interpreted as his agreement. She twisted the ring from his uninjured hand and dropped it into a pocket.

"Tess, I have never taken money or valuables for healing people!" Sally cried.

"Then it's time you made a few changes," Tess responded tartly. "If you don't like the idea of taking money for yourself, you should use it to buy the medicines you'll need to treat the patients in the next village you come to." She turned to Huw to deliver a final withering comment. "Do I have your word? Do you accept the terms I set out for a parlay with your hiremaster?"

Huw realized his options were limited, and nodded wearily.

Sally took pity on him, though perhaps not as much as she might have done if she hadn't heard Tess' lengthy, florid descriptions of Bully Bates, his parents, his crew, and his sexual preferences. She did, however, persuade him to swallow a draught of medicine containing a strong infusion of poppies that swiftly rendered him unconscious, and therefore free from pain.

Chapter Twenty-two

"Tess, I cannot stay another night. I can do no more for Huw until he awakens, and there are other patients who need me more."

"Including a certain rower who brought you here."

Sally flushed bright red with embarrassment. How *could* she have forgotten Rolan?

"Where is he? Is someone watching?"

"Peace, healer! You could not have tended two patients in two different rooms these past two days, and you left clear word for Rolan's treatment. Someone has been with him constantly, bathing him, feeding him sips of water..."

Sally bounced to her feet, all tiredness forgotten. "I must see him at once!"

"Did I not say he has had the best of care, following your instructions as closely as we could?"

Rolan sat in a chair beneath an open window. Birdsong and the delicate aroma of spring flowers drifted into the room, and Rolan seemed in the best of health.

Sally caught the faintest flicker of a smile on Tess' face and rounded on her. "You *knew*!"

"Knew, healer? I could only *know* what I saw with my own eyes. That the herbs and potions you left had the desired effect! All we had to do was bathe him, and change the linen as needed."

"Yet you allowed me to fear for Rolan's recovery." Sally

pouted.

"But I knew, as you said, that your fears were ground-less, that you would see your patient well on the mend."

"And I feel far better than I have for some time, Sally!" Rolan added. He stood and embraced her, and she was in no doubt that he had regained the full strength of his muscled rower arms.

"You'll take a few extra days *proper* rest, with some wholesome food, before you row back to Bryn's farm. As I recall, you were to transport some supplies, so you'll need all your muscles!"

Rolan could only nod his acceptance of this, and Sally had the satisfaction of the final word on the subject.

Tess didn't give her more than a second to relish her verbal victory. She glanced at Sally, with a curious glint in her eye. "What you're *not* saying, and what I'm hearing in the spaces *between* your words, is that at least one of the 'other patients' you're talking about has a claim on your affections the likes of which Huw could never have. I'm right, aren't I?"

Sally blushed and nodded. "It's true, Tom and I depend-ed on each other throughout our journey, and I'm certain I could never have made it here on my own. When I left Bryn's settlement for Leverpole, he was conscious again, but I had little time to check him properly. I have given him the same herbal treatments I gave Huw, and he slept through the first night, as Huw has done. I am sure this is the fastest way for the body to repair itself, but I started his treatment far earli-er, and at this distance, I cannot say how the other patients have fared. I simply need to see how successful the treat-ment has been and what further medicines or treatments may be needed."

"Sally, your feelings for Tom are only natural. Of course you need to return and check on them. I knew you'd treated Tom before you arrived here, but I know very little about medicines and healing. I didn't realize you might have to..."

"See how effective the treatment has been? That is something every healer does, Tess. Trial and error is some-times the only option we have, though hopefully we don't make too many mistakes. Whenever I have the chance, I test herbs and medicines on myself so I have some idea what to expect when I decide to use it on a patient."

"Bryn's settlement isn't far. There is enough light left in

the day, if you know how to get there?"

"I was lent a horse. Surely he can find the way back, and if need be, I'm sure I..." Sally bit her tongue. Tess cocked her head to one side, waiting for the end of the sentence. "I'm sure I will remember where to turn," Sally mumbled. She wasn't sure how Tess might react if she even hinted at her apparent ability to understand and even communicate with animals.

Tess was clearly not convinced. "Why do I feel that's not what you were about to say, Sally? I sense that you are not capable of telling a lie, but you aren't telling me the whole of the truth! There should be no secrets between us. You can trust me."

In a way it was a relief for Sally to tell the older woman of the curious song duel with an unidentified bird at the beginning of her journey, and the understanding that was steadily developing with Dog.

"There are many tales told around the hearth fires on long winter nights, tales in which animals have the power of speech," Tess mused. "All our children seem to love them. One thing I have learned in my years of running a tavern is how to keep my mouth shut. And I have also heard many stories in that time, some far stranger that yours. The horse yon tinkerman William lent you has been fed and rested, and you are right to think that he has the wit to find his way to Bryn's farm. William is a frequent visitor to these parts. Have you prepared more medicine if Huw needs it in your absence?"

"Yes, I have thought of that. But are you sure you can spare the time?"

"I have others who can look after the tavern if I have to slip out from time to time, and I wouldn't trust anyone else to nurse him. In the beginning, I may have thought you far too kind to insist on treating him, considering the rogue he is, but you can be certain I will not allow your patient to suffer."

"Thank you, Tess. I'll show you the preparations, and the dosage, but I really must leave as soon as possible. I grow more uneasy for Tom and the others with every hour that passes."

"Then you must whisper words in the horse's ear that will set a spur in his flank and a spark beneath his hoof!"

Sally leaned flat on the horse's neck and murmured continuous soothing sounds of encouragement. Her mount responded by laying back his ears. There was an unmistakeable gleam of understanding in his eye as he raced along. He was an easy ride. Sally hadn't ridden more than once or twice in her life, but she felt secure and in no danger of falling. They moved so smoothly she was almost convinced they were flying, barely touching the ground.

"*Run, run! Fun, fun!*"

This time, Sally realized that the voice drumming rhythmically inside her head had to be coming from the horse; there was no other possibility. Somehow, this didn't surprise her, nor was she alarmed. Why should she be? The horse was bigger than Dog or a tiny bird. He must have a bigger brain...

Tears blurred her vision, caused by the buffeting wind of passage. Just as she wondered if she was going to miss the turn, she felt a new emotion, not words this time, but a warm, exhilarating feeling of *belonging*. With a triumphant nicker, he eased fractionally from their headlong sprint, angling slightly to the right and arrowing along a well-beaten track Sally barely had time to recognize before he slowed to a shuddering halt in the forecourt of Bryn's farmhouse. Alerted by the thunder of hooves, a dozen or more people spilled out of several doors to greet them.

Sally bounced off her mount and hit the ground running. She headed straight for Bryn, who caught her in his arms.

"How is Tom? I must see him straight away!"

"He seems fully recovered, Sally. As for Mig and Mag, the fever rose in both of them for awhile, as happened with Tom, but they sleep untroubled. I was with them when you arrived."

Sally pushed her way out of Bryn's embrace and scurried off toward the separate building that had been converted to a temporary sickroom.

A young farm girl was sitting as nurse to two tiny, delicate frames lying in beds designed for much larger occupants. She looked up and smiled as Sally entered. "Healer! Your herbs seem to be working. These two have slept for much of the time, just as Tom did. The fever has also broken. They breathe more easily. It seems the treatment you decided upon is working."

"You've saved me several minutes by telling me exactly what I needed to ask. You have the instincts every healer needs. I'll need warm water, not too hot, mind, and some clean cloths."

She was already feeling for a pulse in the final two patients. She was relieved to note that it was slow, but strong and steady. The woad made it impossible for her to judge the state of their health by looking at the skin color, but the texture of their skin gave her no cause for concern. Her bag of herbs and preparations was where she had left it on a side table. By the time the farm girl returned with the first ewer of warm water, she had picked out what she needed to put together a fresh potion.

"Can I ask you to help me prepare a medicine? I meant it when I said you have the instincts needed to be an excellent healer."

The young girl somehow managed to look shocked, embarrassed, and pleased, all at once.

"That would be an honor, ma'am!"

"Nay, I'm not *that* much older than you! My name's Sally, and I'm happy with that. What do I call you?"

"I was baptized Clare. My father is Bryn's chief farrier."

"A fine name for a healer! Did you know that the saint of that name devoted her whole life to caring for the sick?" Sally said warmly. She liked this earnest young girl already. "Now, this is what I need you to do..."

Sally's long day became an even longer night as she and her assistant kept a constant, watchful eye on Mig and Mag. As dawn broke, they both stirred, stretched, and opened their eyes within seconds of each other, as if waking from a single night of refreshing, natural sleep. Sally found herself wondering if there was a special bond between twins, or how they might somehow share feelings, pain, suffering more than other siblings not born at the same time. *This is no time for such strange ideas*, she scolded herself. *You have more practical matters to think about!*

She stood over them and tried to appear older and wiser, a healer who knew all the answers, or at least pretended to. Two pair of impossibly blue childlike eyes sparkled with bare-

ly contained mischief, following her every move, and she realized that she wasn't going to be able to fool them.

"Right, you two. You both seem to be past the worst of
your illness, but I can't tell you apart. I need to know who's
who, and please don't try to trick me. I may need to give you
slightly different medicines at some point."

A swift glance passed between the two patients, and a
nod was performed in perfect unison. The figure in the bed
on her left spoke.

"That's fair, Sally. Know then that I am Mig, older by
some five minutes than my brother Mag."

"But not necessarily any wiser than me because of that!"
the other interrupted as they both collapsed in unbridled
laughter. Sally seized this opportunity to establish some pre-
tense at imposing her authority, and tied a bright yellow ribbon securely above Mig's left elbow.

"And if I ever have cause to think you may have switched
this ribbon, I'll mix a posset of herbs that tastes so vile, you'll
regret it minutes after I pour it down your necks—and yes,
you'll *both* get the same dose!"

"More medicine?" Mag protested. "But you just said we
were cured!"

"No, what I said was you appear to be *over the worst,*"
Sally corrected him, with a steely, unpitying look in her eye.
"I may still have grounds to continue treating you with further potions until I'm sure you're fully fit once more! Whatever it was that reduced you to weak, helpless kittens these
last three days was a malady I have not treated until recently. I need to be certain it has run its course, lest you infect
others."

There was a quiet knock on the door, and Clare's voice
trilled. "May I enter, Sally? I have eaten in the kitchen. Bryn
and his family are waiting for you before the evening meal is
served for all. I'm ready to watch over your patients, if you
wish."

Sally realized that she hadn't eaten all day, and only
sparingly for several days. Suddenly, she was ravenous. She
thanked Clare profoundly and sincerely, and showed her the
simple infusions she had prepared to ward off headaches and
other ailments that often appeared while a patient was recovering.

"I'll return as soon as I may," she promised before scurrying off, "but not before I'm satisfied that Tom is fully re-covered," she whispered to herself once the door was closed behind her.

The meal inevitably turned into a feast, a celebration and a thanksgiving to mark Sally's early return, the successful treatment of three people, and as Bryn's wife, Peg, put it, "simply because we like to have a reason to feast!" Apart from one or two occasions when the whole of her village had gathered for a communal meal on a feast day, such as Christmas, Sally had never sat at table with so many people before. The number was greater than all her fingers and all her toes reckoned together. She dared not even try to give the number a name.

Tom had made sure there was a vacant stool for her at his side, and she was glad of his thoughtfulness and his close attention throughout the meal. As the final dishes were cleared away and fresh new wine was poured, he caught her hand and squeezed it gently. Sally was both flattered and flustered, but shook her head very slightly and disengaged her fingers.

Tom's bushy eyebrows shot upwards like startled cater-pillars. "What's wrong, Sally? Have I offended you? 'Twas not my intent!"

"No, Tom! Remember, I named you *cariad*—dearest, loved one—in what might have been an unguarded moment, but it was sincerely meant. Now my healer training has me thinking that you, and everyone else who has fallen victim to this strange illness, has been physically close to me, and I begin to think that I may have unwittingly infected each of you with a disease that near killed me before I left my home."

Quietly, and hopefully without alarming others around them, Sally explained why she suspected this might be so. As she finished, and while Tom was silently digesting all she had told him, an idea came to her.

A lavabo cruet was close at hand, three-quarters filled with fresh water to rinse fingers between courses. She pulled it toward them, but before using it, she rooted in the pouch on her belt until she found a grey-green powder that she measured and poured, mixing it with the point of a knife until it dissolved. She washed her hands, but made no attempt to dry them on a cloth, then indicated that she expected Tom to copy her actions.

Tom took the hint and followed the tacit instructions, but the expression on his face clearly stated a total lack of understanding as to why he was being asked to perform this ritual. Once he had shaken off a few droplets of excess moisture, Sally reached out and caught his hands in hers.

"Now we have both washed, I feel we can touch without the possibility of passing this illness back and forth like children playing toss ball. Tom, my dearest, I have been aching to hold you, but I would never risk making you ill again."

The cheers and thunderous applause that erupted all around made Sally aware that her declaration, intended for Tom's ears alone, had been witnessed by everyone present. It was too late now. The words could not be recalled, even if she had wanted to, which she didn't. She rose, and spread her arms to plead for order.

"Tom and I both thank you for your goodwill, but there is another matter I would mention, something that is for the good of us all." She paused as a murmur rippled around the room and was stilled. When she sensed she had everyone's undivided attention, she continued. "Those of you who saw first me, then Tom dipping our hands in a bowl of water may have thought it was some strange ceremony, unknown in these parts, but that is not so. What we were doing, and what I am asking you *all* to do as well, was a simple act of washing, cleansing our hands in a preparation of soapweed, to avoid the possibility of passing this malady from one to the other. Though I cannot be certain, I believe it may be spread by touch."

Startled cries led to shouted questions from all sides at once, and Sally felt overwhelmed until Bryn strode forward and struck the tabletop with a quarterstaff until order was restored.

"That's better!" he growled. "Now, listen to what the healer says! If she thinks we should wash more often, for whatever reason, I for one would agree with her. Some of you seem to think that a bath at Christmas, whether you need it or not, is enough. Well, I don't agree!" The lavabo was barely big enough for one of his spade-like hands at a time, but he managed to wash them both in a public display of his support for Sally. As he finished, he turned to address her. "Have you more of this soapweed you speak of? Enough to tip into a few more bowls of water?"

Sally didn't need to check her pouches; she knew she had plenty, and she was already reaching for it as some of the kitchen girls ran out with extra water bowls. Bryn sent orders for everyone in the community to perform the same ablutions ritual, down to the last shepherd boy on watch in the farthest field of the estate. Amazingly, everyone was accounted for in under two hours.

"It's important, everyone must take care to wash frequently until we can be sure this illness is no longer amongst us," Sally told the assembled families before they returned to their daily tasks. "And especially when preparing food or eating. The elderly, the infirm, and young children may need someone to assist them. Soapweed is plentiful, and needs only to be pounded between two stones to release the sap."

"Will you be leaving us again so soon?" Bryn asked, a worried tone in his voice. "We would much rather you remain amongst us, but it sounds as if..."

"I have no wish to leave you, especially not Tom, but I have begun treating two other patients, and I must see how they are responding. One has suffered a grievous wound, and might not survive his injuries. As a healer, I have little choice. I must return to Ma Reilly's Tavern, if only for a short while."

"Then I shall travel with you," Tom growled. "You know not how lucky you were to escape the clutches of the brigands and cutthroats who haunt the harbor in Leverpole! I have traded there a few times, and you *need* protection!"

"And don't think you're leaving *us* behind either!" howled Mig.

Not to be outshone, Mag added, "You'll need a wagon for your poisons and potions, and you won't have to stable two horses if we pull it."

"'Tis but a short step from here!" There was a plaintive, almost desperate note in Mig's final plea. Sally could not help but smile. They reminded her strongly of small children begging for a treat. Mig and Mag took this as her consent and rushed away, presumably to gather a few items they considered necessary.

"Take the help and support so freely given, Sally, and also my blessing," said Bryn. "Don't be fooled by the stature of those two. They are Brigantii. Everybody knows the tribe's reputation! They'll fight like cornered bears when they have to, and I've not seen them bested yet when they work as a pair. I have my contacts in the town. Tess knows who they are, and I will be sent news of everything. Now, collect what herbs and medicines you need. Mig and Mag are loading the wagon already."

"Along of all these medicines, herbs, and other remedies, have you no personal possessions you wish to pack? We cannot be sure how long we may remain in Leverpole." The question was calmly asked, but there was an edge of concern in Tom's voice.

Sally shook her head briskly. "When we first met, I was carrying everything I wished to keep from my earlier life, which I now realize had been dull and tedious up to that point. But if I could ask for something, it would be a change of clothing. Look at the stains on this garb! Blood, plant juices, powders, potions, and smoke. Many of them will never wash away, and I would not blame any patient who thought me a slattern who had no care for her own appearance! How can I persuade others how important it is to wash frequently when I look as I do?"

"Is that all? Sally, that's easily sorted!" cried Peg. She disappeared into the farmhouse, emerging less than a minute later with an armful of clean, neatly folded feminine garments. "I'm sure we can find something in your size," she said. "And I agree, what you wear at this moment is probably only fit for burning! Come, use the sweat-house to remove the worst layer of grime and I will assist you with dressing afterwards."

Peg led her into a small, low, round building and immediately began to strip her clothing.

"Be easy, Sally. We have an arrangement. The men all know that this night each week only the women on the farm are allowed to use the sweat-house. Hurry now and toss that cloak aside... Sally? Are you listening?"

Sally hadn't been prepared for the heat in the enclosed space, and was finding it difficult to breathe. She felt dizzy and all but collapsed onto a low bench that ran along three quarters of the wall, leaving a gap at the entry door.

"I'm fine, Peg. I just need a moment to...adjust to...this." She waved her hand vaguely at everything in general and nothing in particular. "In Leverpole, I visited another sweat-house," she said once she could breathe. She had to breathe carefully and not too deeply. She felt each slow intake of breath every inch of the way along her windpipe and into her lungs. There were wispy clouds of moisture hanging in the air, but she didn't think they were lubricating her throat. If anything, quite the reverse. The inside of her throat tickled, as if wiped completely dry of any and all saliva, but it was a pleasant, soothing heat. Soon she felt beads of perspiration forming on her brow and her shoulders, between her breasts, all over her body.

Peg, now totally naked, was at her side. "Was that your first steam-house, Sally? In that case, we'll not stay too long, but long enough for you to scrub yourself properly clean, and a few minutes longer to enjoy the warmth and the pleasure of *not* working every minute of the day."

Peg stood and padded across the room. A cairn of stones stood neatly in the corner. Peg stooped and filled a ladle with water. *Why is she doing that?* she wondered. *The room is so warm, why does she want to splash cold water on the stones?*

Hissing like a nest of evil, venom-fanged vipers, a giant cloud of steam formed over the rocks and Sally felt the temperature of the air around her increase so swiftly it literally took her breath away for a few brief moments. *The water doesn't cool the stones,* she thought. She remembered the same totally unexpected heating effect in the steam-room in Leverpole, but she couldn't think coherently. *It actually heats them!* Her brain was spinning from a combination of her breathing problems and this new conundrum.

Peg saw the expression on her face and smiled gently. There was no trace of tease or mockery as she explained, "Many feel the same way the first time they use a steam-house. It's one of the few good things the Roman invaders left behind when they ran home with their tails between their legs. The Viking invaders who came later also knew something of how a steam-house works. Me, now, I know nothing of how it works, but I can light and tend a fire to produce the steam, and I know enough to make it as hot or as cool as may be deemed comfortable by the amount of water I splash on the heated stones. But please don't ask me *how* the cold water draws so much heat from the stones, because I don't know. Sometimes I'm convinced that there really *is* magic in the world. Real, practical magic such as this, perhaps?"

A sudden thought struck Sally. She turned to Peg with an impish grin and said, "If we're going to sit here and relax for a while, would you like to try something? I have something in my gather sack that I think will please you." She took a pinch of powder from a pouch, crumbled it to a fine dust between her fingers, and stirred it into a water scoop. She handed it to Peg. "It's from the lavender plant. I use it to make a patient's bedroom smell fresh and healthy. It seems to speed up their recovery."

Half an hour later, skin glowing an even pink from hairline to toenails, Sally and Peg reluctantly left the steam room when it became noticeably cooler. Peg led Sally through a cooling pool "to close up the skin, and stop the sweat oozing," she explained. Clean, rough towels removed the last of the moisture, and Peg sorted through the clothing she had brought for Sally to try on.

"You have a good eye for size. Even the boots are an excellent fit!" Sally exclaimed when she had made her choice. She was almost unrecognizable, clad in a pale yellow tunic and brown leather trews with a drawstring around the waist. The boots, which had particularly pleased her, had each been fashioned from a single piece of leather and supported her ankles, stitched together by a true craftsman. They also had a slight heel, which added about an inch to her height.

"You should choose at least one more garment, Sally. Perhaps a long, loose gown of some sort to protect your clothes while you treat patients?"

"Thank you, Peg! That would be very useful, if I may."

"I think you should take an extra one. That way you'll have something to wear while the other is being washed."

"You're too kind."

"Nonsense! Your skills as a healer are very important. You need some suitable clothing!"

Peg would hear no further argument or protest, and Sally had a fully packed bag of more clothes than she had ever owned at any one time in all her nineteen summers when she joined Mig and Mag, standing relaxed but clearly impatient to move off next to their wagon. Once her personal luggage was stowed, there was nothing to prevent them moving off with plenty of light left in the day. Mig was sure they could make the journey in two hours. Mag disagreed, claiming it could be done in half the time "as long as my brother pulls his weight." This gave rise to a spirited discussion, and the comical sight of the siblings screaming insults at each other as they snatched at the towbar and raced away.

"How can they spare the breath to scream at each other like that, and still have the energy to haul this load?" Sally gasped, clinging to Tom for fear of being thrown before the rough farm track met the more even road that would take them to Leverpole.

Tom laughed out loud.

"I've known those two for many years. They've never been any different, and the banter only seems to spur them on to greater efforts. Relax, Sally, we are in truth safe sitting here."

He placed his left arm around her waist and persuaded her to loosen her death grip on his shoulders. His confidence flowed into her, and despite her initial concerns, her trust in Tom overcame her fears, and she even managed to doze in his arms once the wagon rumbled onto the smoother surface of the well traveled road, which imitated the curves and bends of the Mersea as it flowed toward Leverpole. The curses and insults became quieter and less frequent, and eventually petered out as the brothers settled in the traces and concentrated on proving that their claims about the journey time was no idle boast.

Tess was sweeping the tavern forecourt as Mig and Mag argued their way to a standstill and shrugged their way out of the shackles and traces. The journey had taken roughly one and a half hours, and neither brother was prepared to admit that they were in fact equally right—or equally wrong—in their respective estimations.

Tess paused and stared at the diminutive woad-daubed figures who seemed to be on the point of coming to blows. She switched her grip on the broom, brandishing it like a quarterstaff, equally effective in attack or defense, and strode toward them. Sally hopped out of the wagon and placed herself between the advancing Tess and the sparring siblings, absent-mindedly slapping each of them on the head as she passed to bring them into line.

"You can't imagine how relieved I am to be back, Tess. Allow me to present Mig and Mag, who are as loyal to me as they are to each other. Don't be fooled by their war of words. For them, this is a perfectly normal conversation, and I've yet to see them come to blows."

Tess seemed unable to take her eyes off the twins, who were now unloading the wagon smoothly, efficiently, and in apparent harmony.

"You'd better come inside. You can have the room next to Bryn's reserved room, the one where you're treating Huw." Tess spat the name out as if it left a vile taste in her mouth. "As for your two helpers, I—"

"Three!" Tom poked his head out from under the tented cover, where he'd been pushing the luggage toward the twins.

Sally saw the confused expression on Tess' face and burst into laughter. "Tess, I assure you I have *not* acquired an instant family in the few days since I left your hospitality. This is my close friend, Tom, who guided me here safely through the mountains that separate my birthplace from this region. He is of the same Brigantii tribe as Mig and Mag, and underneath the single layer of woad they prefer to wear rather than several layers of clothing, their skin is as fair as yours and mine."

"My thanks for that, Sally. For a moment I thought that legends walked out of the storyteller's yarns and lived amongst us! I have rooms enough for all, at the moment. Come, I'll show you."

Mig and Mag politely declined the first room they were offered, and asked for a ground floor room overlooking the yard where they had left the wagon. "We have little in the way of personal luggage, other than the tools of our trades," Mig said.

"So the wagon is really the one thing we wish to keep a watchful eye on!" Mag said, completing his brother's chain of thought. Sally had become accustomed to this habit by now, but Tess hadn't been expecting it and it threw her off her stride for a moment.

"You'll get used to sharing conversations with the two of them, I promise." Sally laughed as she saw the expression on Tess' face.

"We'll see." There was a guarded note in Tess' voice, and as Sally glanced at her sharply, she changed the subject abruptly. "Do I guess you're wanting to check on your patient before the evening meal is served?"

"Huw's welfare was my main reason for returning as

swiftly as I could." Sally nodded. "Has he been conscious or in pain? How—"

Tess tutted and shook her head. "That I cannot answer, Sally. I lack your healer knowledge and skills. He has been conscious most of the day, I believe, and someone has been at his side constantly since you left. He claims to be pain-free, but how anyone other than me understands his thick speech is a mystery."

"Then I must see him now." Sally rose from her stool, and laid a restraining hand on Tom's arm when he made to follow. "Tom, dear heart, I must first check Rolan and ensure his illness is no longer a danger to others. I could never for-give myself if you were to suffer a repeat dose due to me not insisting you remain at a safe distance. But if you promise to remain in the passage outside the sick room, I could proba-bly allow that."

Tom was clearly uneasy about the idea of Sally examin-ing a powerful sailor with an uncertain temper and a reputa-tion for violence, but he could see the logic of her argument and nodded his reluctant acceptance. Mig and Mag had start-ed another round of interminable bickering as they left the kitchen and headed for their room. This time, the language was one Sally didn't recognize: she assumed it was most likely their native tongue.

Outside the temporary sickbay, Tom stopped and seemed to flow bonelessly to an amorphous blue mass that solidified to resemble a rock against the wall, close to the door. A quarterstaff was slanted roughly where his knees ought to be. The butt end touched the wall, a few inches over the skirting. It was angled upwards and across the passage. No-body was going to pass the silent sentry unnoticed. Without even trying, Tom had made himself invisible, resembling something between a piece of furniture and an odd sculpture decorating the hallway.

Sally entered the room and smiled at Tess, who had heard her approaching along the bare wood planks of the corridor.

"How's he doing?"

"Much improved, healer. But why don't you ask him yourself. He was conscious just a few minutes ago, asking for a drink."

Huw's eyes opened. He raised his uninjured arm in greeting.

"The water is welcome, healer. How long before you'll allow something stronger?"

"You'll live longer without the demon drink," Sally retorted.

"No, I won't, healer—it will just *seem* longer!" Huw grunted with a wry grin, indicating he'd understood and accepted Sally's attempt at humor. Sally breathed a sigh of relief. Anyone who could make even a feeble joke was likely to be relatively pain free and on the way to recovery.

"I need to remove the dressing and look at the wound. This may hurt."

Sally worked swiftly and as gently as she could. The final wrap of bandage was stuck to the skin by a mixture of dried blood and other discharge from the wound, but she had expected this and managed to sponge it away with warm water. Huw flinched once or twice, but remained stoically silent.

The flesh around the wound was slightly puffy, but the color and the temperature of the skin was, as far as she could judge, normal and healthy.

"Can you flex your fingers?"

Huw hesitated, then furrowed his brow as if concentrating on a difficult task. The fingers of his right hand quivered and bent very slightly into a claw. A fleeting grimace of pain crossed his face, and a moment later, his whole body relaxed and he sank into the thin mattress, exhausted.

"You managed it! Well done!" Sally enthused.

Huw opened one eye and scowled. "Don't mock! That took all my strength. How can I ever work again?"

"Would you rather I had cut it off completely? And there are exercises; you can learn to use that arm once more if you work on it."

"Huh! What makes you think he knows what the word work means?" Tess sniffed. "In all the years I've run this tavern, I've never known him do a proper day's work yet!"

"Well it's time he learned. He won't be able to carry on as raw muscle in the press gang!" Sally responded.

Huw's eyes widened. This was clearly something he hadn't yet had time to think about. He turned his head and gave his full attention to the running repairs Sally had made to his arm.

"Are you still in pain?"

"Not as much as I'd expected, and I allow, you've made a neat job of this."

"Thank you."

Huw stared at Sally, as if trying hard to hear if there was a trace of sarcasm or insincerity in her voice. She stared right back at him, and he was first to blink. He changed the subject.

"How did you get that wolf to—"

"Not a wolf. He's a dog—a big one, with no apparent owner, but a dog nonetheless. As for how I got him to let go, why, I simply asked him to."

"*Asked?*"

This was in perfect unison from both Huw and Tess. Confused, Sally looked from one to the other, startled by the disbelief in both their voices.

"Asked...told...does it really matter? I couldn't begin treating your arm until he let go of it, could I?"

"Matter? Of *course* it matters!" Tess cried. "You just said yourself this dog's wild and doesn't appear to have a master or any other owner. So what spell did you cast to command this brute?"

Sally gazed at Tess. For once, there was a hint of sadness, almost reproach, in her normally cheerful, happy eyes."I'm no witch, Tess, whatever you may think. I really thought you, of all people, had understood that

"So, how *did* you manage to control the dog?" Though still in pain, and obviously surly at being under any sort of obligation to anyone, Huw managed to rephrase Tess' question.

"How do you ask anyone a question?" Sally was genuinely puzzled. "You simply find the right words, and remember to say 'please' when you ask for a favor. What's so hard about that?"

"The right *words*, Sally? When you're dealing with a *dog*? Think about what you're saying!"

Sally cocked her head to one side, an unconscious action she often performed when thinking hard about something or other. Unnoticed in the corner of the room, Dog copied her.

"I...didn't have to think about it, and there wasn't time to spare anyway!" Sally said, thinking back to the chaotic scene as she forced Dog to open his jaws. "I just told Dog to let go...like this..." She produced a short, impatient-sounding noise from her throat. Dog looked up and responded with a completely different sound, which sounded like a very young puppy being told off by his mother. "No, it's alright," Sally's gaze flicked to Dog as she whispered these words, clearly intended to calm and reassure him. She turned to concentrate on Tess and Huw once more. "I can't tell you the how or the why of it, but Dog and I understand each other perfectly well. Be grateful for that, Huw, because I haven't the strength I'd have needed to force open his jaws if he'd decided not to cooperate, and I don't doubt he'd have had your arm off in just a few more seconds."

Tess had been observing Dog throughout Sally's explanation. Now, she nodded thoughtfully. "I'm watching the mutt as you speak, and something tells me that—unlikely as it may seem—what you're telling us is the truth. Now, I remember as a child being told of people who claimed they communicated with a variety of animals, and also the fable that all animals are granted the power of speech for an hour on Christmas Eve. Sally, you have a rare gift. It is one you should treasure. I can see no harm in it, but you need to be careful who learns of it. It could easily frighten some, and set others against you!"

"There are also those who would see your gift as God-given."

Sally and Tess whirled at the sound of Father Timothy's voice. He had arrived unnoticed, and overheard at least part of Sally's explanation. Tess dropped to her knees. After a moment's hesitation, Sally went to copy her, and even Huw attempted to raise himself from the bed. The elderly priest tutted, shook his head gently, and signaled that they should all remain as they felt most comfortable.

"Tess is right in this, Sally. Your gift is one that is rarely given, but it *is* a gift, not a curse, and certainly not to be feared as something unnatural, the supposed power of a witch or other person claiming to have a mastery of magic. Have neither of you heard of Francis of Assisi? No? Then I will tell you. Although he came from a noble Italian family, he chose to live most of his life as a poor monk, and there are many stories of him communicating with all manner of animals, using them to demonstrate God's goodness for all who would listen."

"That's well and good, Father, but it doesn't seem to

lessen my pain," Huw interrupted.

Father Timothy sighed. "That's not how these things work," he began patiently, but Sally was already in motion.

"You must rely on *me* and what healing skills I can offer for that, Huw! Your pardon, Father, but there are practical things I can do to help Huw's recovery without any assistance from...above!"

She rearranged his pillows and sheets, checked the dressing on his wounded arm for any signs of bleeding, and coaxed him to swallow more medication. After a few minutes, Huw closed his eyes and drifted off. They withdrew to an adjoining room, leaving the door open. Dog made to follow, but Sally fixed him with a stare and a low rumble of throat growl. Dog stared back at her, then curled obediently into a ball at the end of the bed, alert and watchful.

"What was that?"

Sally looked nonplussed. "I simply told him to watch," she said. "Was that wrong of me?"

"Not wrong, Sally, not by any means! Unlikely, perhaps, and if I had not seen your...relationship with Dog already, I would not have believed it possible," Father Timothy said. "I don't think you realize just how unusual your talent is! Have you ever talked to other creatures?"

Reluctantly at first, then with growing confidence, Sally related briefly her singing contest with the unseen bird early in her journey, her unexpected but most useful connection with the borrowed mount as she rode back to Bryn's farm, and the way in which she had managed to calm William's panicking horse. By the time she finished, she was beginning to appreciate the rarity of her talent for understanding animals that had not been granted the human gift of speech.

"I still don't understand. Why did you return to Leverpole once you had reached Bryn's farm and made sure that your friend was recovering?" Tess wanted to know.

"Why?" Sally seemed genuinely puzzled. "Because I *also* had two patients here, or had you forgotten that?" She pointed to Huw where he lay uncomfortably.

"Yes, and of them, one's an ingrate who'd as soon slit your throat for a few coppers as thank ye f'r saving his arm and more'n' likely his miserable life!"

"Be that as it may, Tess, he's a patient, and I am bound by the healer's code to provide care for any and all who need or ask for it."

Father Timothy stirred. "In that case, I may be the bearer of some news that will be of interest, and may even supply an answer to this problem. A fast trader ship arrived at Birkenhead Priory at dawn. She carried very little in her holds. Her main purpose was to bring news from the High King, Cormac Rú. It seems there has been an outbreak of a disease throughout the Kingdom of Tara, the largest of Erin's Seven Kingdoms. It spreads quickly, and the herbs, potions, and tinctures they have tried have failed. None of his physicians can find a cure. Cormac is distantly related to Lord Sefton, and appeals through him for what assistance we can provide. Sally, I know that you have neither family connections to Leverpole, nor any other reason to offer your healer skills on our behalf, and to a total stranger."

"But I am a healer! What skills I may have, I have always used to help others in need. You yourself have already pointed out that I helped this patient, Huw, in the same way I helped my friends. Most of those I have treated over the years have been people I know only slightly, and sometimes not at all. We of the Parisii have a saying—'there are no strangers, just friends you have yet to meet.' There is only one thing I will ask, which is for my friend Tom to accompany me on the journey. I have learned much from him since we met. He has protected me and helped me many times along the way. I may also need his skill with languages. He has traveled much more than I have; explaining medicines and other treatments to the king of another country may not be easy!"

"And what of me?" protested Huw. "If you take ship to Eire, who has the skills and the knowledge to complete my treatment?"

"I cannot leave at once. There are things that need to be attended to," Sally assured him. "And I would not make Tom's decisions for him. He must be asked if he is prepared to follow me over the seas. But if he does, which I hope he will, then I will leave a supply of potions Tess or one of her servant girls can give you while we are away. You are out of danger now, that much I can tell from your eyes and the fact that you no longer burn with fever. What you need more than anything else is rest, and I'm certain Tess will provide that."

Tess gave Huw a long, hard stare, then nodded silently and with some reluctance.

"And I'm sure Bryn will continue to let this room from you, especially if you tell him I have requested it for a patient," Sally murmured. This seemed to dispel any reservations Tess still held. She nodded again, this time more positively.

"I wish to travel with you," Father Timothy said with an air of authority. "My language skills are at least as good as any traveler's, and I have a feeling that I may have other skills to offer. Brother John can perform most of my duties in this parish, and I will arrange for another priest to visit from time to time. Tess, do you know if Bryn has his letters? It would help if I can write a short note to him."

Tess confirmed that Bryn could read and write, and Father Timothy's note was despatched by a messenger who returned Bryn's mount at the same time. Sally made a careful examination of Huw's arm, not knowing how long it might be before she had the opportunity to look at it again, and redressed it with an extra thick layer of salve over the wound. She completed the dressing with a sturdy length of willow bark, which she hoped would keep the wound covered for at least fourteen days. It pleased her to see that there was no trace of infection in the flesh, which was healing swiftly.

As expected, Tom was more than happy to agree to any course of action that kept him close to Sally's side.

"I have dealt with some from across the waters before," he said eagerly. "Their language is very close to that used by many of the tribes in Cymru not that very far from here. I feel sure we can understand each other, with a little effort on both parts!" He pointed to the purple hills shrouded in cloud on the southern horizon.

Drained by the treatments and the discussions of the day, Huw had fallen asleep. Tess sent for a kitchen girl to sit at his bedside through the night, and the rest of the party withdrew to take what rest they could.

Chapter Twenty-three

It had been a long, arduous day, but Sally felt fully charged, alert, and certainly not ready for sleep. To calm herself, she unpacked, inspected, and repacked her stock of herbs and medicines, wondering if she would be able to replenish her supplies from the plants available in Erin. She wondered, what would the climate be like? Would she be able to find the plants and herbs she depended on for her cures?

As she fastened the strap on her satchel, the candle on the table flickered in response to an errant draft from the window. She crossed the room to close the curtain, and paused. The moon rode high in a cloudless sky, but despite the lateness of the hour, someone was abroad. An untidy glimmer of torches could be seen along the coast road, hugging the banks of the river. She counted more than two hands of flames. They were perhaps half a mile distant, approaching at a walking speed.

She was interrupted in her musings by a brisk knock on the bedroom door. Tom entered without waiting for a response, his face lined with concern. "You haven't retired, good! We need to leave at once. There's a crowd heading this way. It may be the press gang again, or it could be something worse!"

Sally didn't bother trying to ram her feet into her boots. She seized them, rolled them inside two full length robes, and scrambled out of the bedroom door, following Tom downstairs. They exited by the kitchen door and sped across the garden, crashing into the comparative safety of the woodlands. The voices of the approaching crowd were close enough to be heard, snatches of song underlying a rumble of angry shouting.

"Follow me! We have to get to the harbor and find the ship that waits to take us to Eire, and the high king's court!"

"What of Father Timothy?" Sally asked as she battled her way through thin, whiplike branches that flayed mercilessly against her skin. "Does he know?"

"'Twas him who alerted me that a mob was on their way to Tess' tavern. He left his few possessions on board, intending to return on the morning tide. He should be there ahead of us, along with Mig and Mag. He promised to alert the captain to be ready to sail as soon as we arrive. Stay close! We can make better speed now. Here's the track that will take us straight to the harbour."

Sally thrust a final branch to one side, ignoring the vicious recoil slash against her legs, and turned left to follow Tom along a well-trodden path, too broad and even to be an animal track. She held her breath for a moment and listened carefully, but there was no sound of pursuit.

Tom looked over his shoulder. The whites of his eyes caught the moon's rays, blazing in stark contrast to his woad-darkened skin. "Come! We've stayed ahead of the mob so far, but we'll not be safe until we're on board!"

"Are you so sure they're after us? What possible reason could they have?"

"Sally, when just one superstitious fool whispers the word 'witch,' it's enough to cause every idiot who hears it to seize a knife, a cudgel, and a blazing torch and form a hunting party. They cannot understand *how* you heal others, therefore you *must* be...no, I will not sully my lips a second time with the word. Come, we must make our way to the harbor as quickly as possible!"

They sped along the track. The moon above made it easy for them to avoid the occasional trailing vine across the path, but Sally felt exposed. All her senses were on full alert. Every second, she expected to hear a *view-halloo* from the vengeful pack on their heels.

As they rounded a bend, she felt a breeze caress her cheeks and caught the familiar scent of the sea. The tangle of trees on the right petered away to some stunted shrubs insecurely rooted in the gritty mix of soil and sand. Suddenly, they were running close to the river itself. A ship was silhouetted against the skyline with over half its sails unfurled, clearly intending to depart at short notice.

"Yes, that's ours!"

Sally wasn't certain if Tom had said this aloud, or if she'd heard it by some less traditional non-verbal form of communication. There wasn't time to argue or be distracted by this. She concentrated all her efforts into covering the remaining few hundred paces as fast as she could.

Someone was standing on the quay, swinging a lantern on a short pole, clearly expecting their arrival. At the edge of her field of vision, she could just make out a crouched figure close to the prow of the ship. After another three or four long, loping strides, she realized the amorphous lump was loosening a cable, allowing the nose of the ship to inch away from the wharf. She redoubled her efforts, grateful that she had a bare minimum of baggage to carry. Her precious supply of medicinal plants were all that really mattered, and they weighed almost nothing.

The seaman charged with releasing the forr'ard cable had completed his task as they reached the ship and stood bracing the ship's urgent tug to float away with the tide and current, keeping the access plank securely balanced between the pier and the ship's taffrail. With a smile and a silent nod of thanks, Sally rushed past him and flew up the gangplank, closely followed by Tom. The sailor who had released the prow cable followed a heartbeat behind them with the narrow footbridge tucked under his arm. Sally looked up just in time to see another seaman swing onto the ship's stern, presumably after completing a similar operation at the far end of the ship. A series of complicated whistles caused three large sails to be deployed with a promptness and efficiency that can only come from years of practice. They each filled at once, catching every available cherub's breath of wind, and the ship leapt away from the quayside. Within seconds, they were out of range of any possible stone or arrow, picking up an extra impetus from the strong river current in midstream, reaching the open sea unchallenged.

The last traces of land on either side of the river Maere receded to become wisps of memory. Ahead, the palest glimmer of grey false dawn began to show at the point where sky and sea met. Another hour, and the welcome glorious spectacle of the true beginning of a new day would manifest itself on the eastern horizon.

Sally decided it was probably good manners, as well as common sense, to wait where they were until their captain either sent an escort to lead them to his cabin. A familiar smell and a short *hrrrrrrrummmmmmph* between her feet reminded her of the one member of the party she'd forgotten about since leaving Tess O'Reilley's tavern.

Sally took his head between her hands. "I really, *really* hope you won't live to regret throwing your lot in with mine," she whispered in his ear.

Dog looked up and appeared to be giving Sally's statement some thought. Then, with what would in a human be considered a "who gives a damn" shrug, he turned and padded off to curl up inside the newly-coiled starboard prow mooring cable, where he appeared to collapse into an instant deep and dreamless slumber.

As the watchtower on Hilbre Island winked past the port quarter, the ship rolled slightly as she reached the open waters of the sea. Every stitch of sail was piled on to take advantage of the freshening wind and she was instantly transformed. No longer did she resemble a stately *grande dame* raising the hem of her skirt to negotiate the shallow waters of a placid river. As her sails spread, she visibly lifted her hull by several inches, hissing through the waves, skimming over them as lightly as a sea eagle preparing to take flight. High in the rigging, the watchman raised a horn to his lips and sounded a challenge as the sun showed on the distant horizon. The helmsman nodded acceptance of the captain's orders, and settled at the tiller to hold the ship on a steady westerly course.

About the Author

Born in the Year of the Tiger, Paul's natural curiosity combined with the deep-seated feline need to roam has meant that over the years he's never been able to call any one place home. His wanderlust has led him from one town to another, and even from one country to another.

He has always followed his instincts without question or complaint, and in true cat fashion it seems he has always landed on his feet.

"I can't remember a time when I didn't write – my father claims to possess a story I wrote when I was six, which filled 4 standard school exercise books! What I do remember from that time was being told off for doing the Liverpool Echo crossword before he got home from work! Perhaps it was the catalyst of breathing the same air as Hans Christian Andersen. While I was living in Denmark, I allowed myself to be persuaded to write for a purpose instead of purely for my own amusement."

Paul recently released the first volume of a planned Trilogy, Mystery/Romance set in Ireland, "The Chapel of Her Dreams" [also with Whimsical Publications, under the name Paul Freeman]. Other works currently seeking an outlet include a couple of plays and a WWII sub-hunt thriller ... and a Rock Musical intended for children.